Nexus has been fort_____ _____ ____ _s to attract what can only be des_____ ___ _____ most perverse, most imaginative and mo_____ _____ riters working in the genre today. They're the crea____ ___ e crop – and they always deliver the goods. This is their showcase.

This collection is slightly different from previous books in the *New Erotica* series. While they featured only extracts from existing Nexus books, this collection features four previously unpublished stories – from Maria del Rey, Penny Birch, Aishling Morgan and Jennifer Jane Pope. I think it's our strongest collection so far, and hope you agree.

Happy reading.

CONTENTS

INTRODUCTION

The Nexus imprint is the largest collection of erotic fiction published in Britain. The list is as diverse as it is cutting edge, boasting a wide variety of themes, fetishes, locations and sexual interests, while ensuring that only the most arousing stories are published.

With the *New Erotica* series, we hope to give the reader a taste of the variety of the imprint – from Aishling Morgan's fantastical world of priapic beasts and warrior women to Yolanda Celbridge's Sadean stylings. Virtually every erotic activity is celebrated – from bondage to watersports via depilation and orgies – in explicit detail.

We publish two new titles every month, to add to our extensive backlist, so if you're unsure which to choose, then this collection is a good place to start. We hope you enjoy it as much as we enjoyed putting it – and all the other Nexus titles – together.

It's always worth checking out what's new on our erotica website: *www.nexus-books.co.uk* You can order books from there, too, so there's no need to miss out on our great offers.

Have fun!

THE YOUNG WIFE

Stephanie Calvin

Stephanie Calvin's first novel for Nexus, *Disciples of Shame*, has a cast of characters who push the boundaries of erotic role-playing, who allow the most perverse impulses free rein, and for whom there are no limits.

The following extract is taken from Stephanie's second Nexus novel, *The Young Wife*. The naïve and virginal Jessica has married Leo, an experienced older man, and immediately regrets the match. Here her friend Anne takes steps to comfort her.

'**Y**ou are not the only person in the world who hides from things, you know? When I was a schoolgirl, I used to hide my true feelings from myself, just as you have done. I had a terrible crush on one of my teachers: only in my case, the teacher was a woman.'

I looked up, and Anne gave my hand a squeeze before continuing. 'Her name was Miss Rackham. Elizabeth was her first name, but we never called her that. It wasn't allowed. She taught English literature. Poetry, and classics mostly, but occasionally she would read passages to us from more modern books. She would encourage us to try out books other than the ones that were on the syllabus, and I remember her especially reading out an extract from a book about lesbians. I didn't know at the time that it was about that, but I had told her how much I liked it, and she encouraged me by lending me the book.'

Anne looked at me strangely for a moment before continuing and, when she did, her eyes could not meet mine, being drawn to the ceiling, and the pastel walls of her kitchen.

'When I realised halfway through the book what it was about, it set me thinking that she had given it to me through more than just a teacher's normal interest in a pupil, for I knew she might get in trouble if I told my parents what she had given me. From then on, things changed for me. Instead of denying how I felt about her, I used to fantasise that we were lovers, and that she would be secretly thinking about kissing me when she spoke to

5

me. I didn't know then what lesbians do in bed, but I had picked up enough from the book to have an idea, and it excited me to think about me and Elizabeth. I loved to say her name to myself; you know what it's like. I had all sorts of daydreams about me and her. Like her and me together in my bed, or being alone in secluded places, talking and kissing.'

She stopped, and looked at me again, but smiling a little ruefully at the folly of her teenage yearnings.

'Ever feel like that about anyone?' she asked, and I was embarrassed when I let out how I had felt about Leo.

'It was different for me,' she continued. 'I never quite found the guts to tell her how I felt about her until almost the last day of my last term. I was seventeen, and totally in love with her. I knew I had to tell her how I felt before I left. I told myself that once we were no longer teacher and pupil, it would be all right, and that it was that relationship that had held her back from telling me how she felt. It's funny how the mind plays tricks when you are in love for the first time, isn't it?'

I wasn't even sure that Anne was addressing me, because she was staring off into space, as if seeing another time, but I nodded, and murmured a soft agreement, until she continued speaking again.

'I knew that on Wednesday and Friday evenings, she used the gym to practise aerobics, and that she didn't like to be disturbed. Though I felt sure that was only a rule for other girls, and that she wouldn't mind if I came. Especially when she heard what it was I had to tell her. So that was how the oddest evening of my younger life started.'

She turned to me again, and stared intently into my eyes. I remember thinking how attractive she was. How serious, and intense. She spoke, in a low, throaty whisper, and explained, 'What I am going to tell you now, I have never told anyone else, ever. I dream about it all the time, just like that dream of yours. Do you understand?'

My voice caught as I answered her, and I knew I was beginning to be affected by the intimacy of our posture, and the things we were discussing.

6

She began to tell her story.

'When school finished that last Wednesday before we broke up for summer, I hung around in a café by the school after home-time, and went back when I thought she would have changed and begun her routine.

'I wanted to see her in her gym clothes, I think. I wanted to see what her body was like. I knew she was slim, because she used to wear tight navy skirts and neat white blouses, but I wanted to see her in something that showed her thighs and breasts more clearly. She was quite muscular, in that way that tennis players are. You could tell that by the way she moved, but I wanted to see her in something more revealing. Her hair was cut in the sort of flicked-back bob that was common then, and her skin was a perfectly flawless, golden type. You know, like a Californian surfer type?'

I nodded, and she continued.

'I was a little bit unsure about myself,' she said, 'as far as my personality went, but I knew she would like my body, and I was sure I would like hers. I had convinced myself she was a lesbian, all because of some silly book.

'When I got to the door of the gym, I hesitated, to pluck up courage, and then I pushed the door open, and stepped in. She wasn't there, but I could see her bag by the wall-bars, and I knew she was around somewhere, so I looked for her. There were only two rooms connected to the gym: one to the store room and one to the changing rooms. There were no boys at the school, but we had a male changing room leading off down a corridor from the female one. We used to keep all the big gym equipment in it, like the vaulting horse, and the rubber mats, so I didn't think I would find her there. The store was locked when I tried it, and that made me sure that she was still changing. I felt a shiver of excitement at the thought that she might be naked in there, on her own, so I walked as quietly as I could to the door, and opened it quickly, hoping to surprise her. I slipped around the rows of cubicles, but there was no one there.'

She stopped, and I could see we were coming to something difficult for her to tell me. It was my turn to encourage Anne, and I rubbed the back of the hand I held, in a way that a lover would. The truth is, I was getting a bit turned on by the things she was telling me, and I wanted her to know it.

'Go on, Anne,' I said. 'It's all right. You can tell me.'

She cleared her throat and smiled at me, in a way that let me know she understood what the story was doing to me, before she said, 'If I had left then, things might have been different, but I didn't because I could smell her scent in the air of the tiled room. It wasn't very light in there, as only one row of fluorescents had been switched on, and I was content to just stand in the dimness and smell her perfume. I was hopelessly infatuated with her. I had stood there for perhaps five minutes when I became aware of noises coming from the other room, and my heart gave a jump of joy, for I immediately thought that she was in there, moving the equipment around for some reason. I was imagining myself surprising her, and offering to help, so I crept up to the door, which was slightly ajar, and pushed it open, really quietly. The room was lit up, more brightly than the hall that joined it to the other changing room, and it took my eyes a second to adjust.

'First I saw the jumble of green mats that spilled away from the walls, and the vaulting horse that someone had stood in the centre of them. Then I saw the two people moving around by the end of the horse nearest to me, and all the breath went out of me.

'They were too involved in what they were doing to notice me, and I had the chance to step back further into the hallway even before I could see clearly what they were up to.

'Miss Rackham was on her knees on the mats, with her bottom sticking up and pointing towards me. One of her hands was gripping a leg of the vaulting horse; the other one I couldn't see. She was completely naked from the waist up and, though I couldn't see her breasts, my mind was stunned by the sight of her, like that.' She paused, to see if what she had said was affecting me, and then continued, while looking deep into my eyes.

8

'Second after second, my mind made sense of what I was seeing, and I realised that all she had on was a pair of black, lacy knickers, and leather, knee-high boots. I couldn't believe it. My eyes must have moved over her a dozen times. She had a lovely body.

'Her waist was so small that her hips looked broad but, really, she had quite a small bottom. It was just her pose that made it look bigger. Her bottom was all open, and her knickers were pulled up into the crack. I couldn't take my eyes off it.

'Then the bobbing of her head, and the noises she was making, made me look away from her behind, and I felt sick. Some guy was standing there with his cock in her mouth, and I could tell by the way she was acting that she was loving it. I wanted to run away, but I couldn't, and I had to look, over and over again, at what she was doing. This guy must have been at least forty, and she was only in her early twenties, but she was sucking his fucking cock like he was beautiful, or something. I couldn't believe she would do that with a man. Especially one who looked old enough to be her father.

'His cock was this enormous, red-looking thing, and he was sliding it in and out of her mouth, right up to the hilt. I could hear her sucking and nearly gagging on it, and his voice saying horrible things to her.'

I thought Anne was going to stop there and, I confess, I didn't want her to. The story was making me feel really sexy, and I wanted to know what happened next.

'What was he saying? What kind of things, Anne?' I asked her.

She looked at me, and she knew what I was feeling. I could see she was amused at my reaction, even though what she had seen was obviously painful to her at the time. She must have decided something then, because when her story continued she made it more detailed, and exciting, than she had before.

'Oh, the usual,' she said airily, 'you know: "Suck it, you dirty bitch. Suck my big cock." That kind of thing. And Elizabeth did. I could see she was having trouble getting it into her throat, but he just kept shoving it into her mouth. I think he enjoyed seeing her struggle to get it all in. Her hair was short, too, so I could see everything. Her throat was stretched out, and her mouth was straining round the bastard's penis. Really stretched.

'Her chin was wet with spit, and her lipstick was all smeared over her cheek. I think he had been taking it out and rubbing it over her face, making her lick it. He kept saying, "Pretty little schoolteacher likes to suck a cock. A nice big one, isn't it? You are the best little cocksucker, Miss. Is this what you teach the girls, hm?"

'She just kept groaning, and sucking his cock even harder, as if she was really enjoying what he was saying, and I hated her for it, so that after a while, some perverse part of me started to enjoy watching her doing it. After what seemed like ages, he pulled it completely out, and I was amazed, and a bit sickened, at the size of it. It pumped up and down in front of him, like a red club, and he twisted his hips to slap her face with it. She was sticking her tongue out and groaning, and he laughed at her. My beautiful Elizabeth, trying to suck some old guy's cock, while he made fun of her. I couldn't understand it.

'Then he started to tell her what he was going to do next, and I nearly fainted with the horrible thought of it. He told her to rub some spit in her arse, as he was going to fuck her there. I couldn't believe she would do it, but she did. Her free hand came up to her mouth, and she stuck three of her fingers in. She was acting like an animal, squirming and wriggling her backside. She didn't even wait to pull her knickers down, but just shoved her fingers under the bit that was covering her arsehole and started rubbing around under the cloth. All the while she was staring up at him, like he was some sort of god, and he just smiled at her, and rubbed his cock in her face, saying, "Does Miss want it up her arse? Does the sweet little schoolteacher like to have her arse fucked?"'

The words Anne was using were shocking and exciting to me, all at the same time. My sex was tingling, and for the first time in my life, I decided I was going to go with

10

the feelings coursing through me. I wanted to rub myself, as Anne told me that marvellous story, and the thought was accepted by me as soon as it came into my mind. While I squirmed in my seat, Anne continued.

'She seemed a bit frightened, but she still kept rubbing at herself, and I began to want to see it happen. I could feel my own bottom going heavy, and my sex was throbbing. I squeezed my legs together, and tightened all the muscles between my thighs to stop the feeling, but that only made it worse. I had understood by that time why she only used one hand, because I had seen the handcuff shining at her wrist. That made it all more terrible, and even more sexy. Even as I noticed it, the guy reached for the other cuff and unlocked it; then he forced Elizabeth's hand behind her back and snapped it shut again. She was forced to balance on her knees, and hold her back bowed upwards to keep her face off the mats, but he didn't want her like that. He walked casually behind her, and pulled her knickers over her hips. They were very tight, and he had to wriggle them down until they were stretched over her thighs. I strained to see her cunt, and wasn't disappointed, as he forced her head down and it bulged out towards me. She had a plump little thing with puffy lips, and I guessed that she had shaved some of the hair off them, because they were smooth and bare from behind, though a little bit of fuzz was peeping through from the front. He wasn't interested in it much, though I could have stared at it for ever, and I ached to rub it, just like I ached to rub my own.'

We were both getting more than a little bit excited by the story, I could tell. Anne's eyes were slitted, and she squirmed a little as she spoke, while my sex felt like it had melted. I was so excited by the way Anne was speaking, that I couldn't stop myself any longer. Making sure Anne saw what I was doing, I kept hold of her hand with one of mine, and the other crept under the table to rub at the bulging of my own slit.

'This is such a horny story, Anne. Don't stop, please,' I whispered, and watched as her own free hand dipped under the board out of sight. We both started to rub ourselves in time, as Anne began to speak again, and her voice cracked a little when she resumed.

'Like I said, I could tell she was a bit scared of what he was going to do, but I didn't care any more. I wanted him to do it to her. To punish her for not wanting me, and I wanted to see her arse opened, by this bastard who had made her suck his big, hot cock. Her face was turned towards me, and pressed against the mat, so I could see the apprehension growing when he gripped her tight little cheeks and pulled them apart. He grunted in some sort of approval at the sight of her little hole. I could see why. Her arse was so shoved up at him that, when he spread the cheeks, I could see everything too. Her anus was stretched by his fingers, but it still bulged out a little bit, and it glistened where her spit had gathered in the crinkling around it. He slapped her, hard, on one of her cheeks, and she cried out, into the rough fabric of the mat.

'So he did it again, and I was glad, because she cried out even louder that time. Then he started to hiss filth at her, while she squirmed her open arse, the slutty bitch.

' "Look at you, you dirty bitch. You love this. You want me to fuck your little arsehole, don't you?" he sneered, and she groaned a shaky yes into the mat. He kept it up, while his hands cruelly spread her cheeks so wide, that she started to beg him to put an end to it, and fuck her, fuck her, fuck her.

'But he hadn't finished humiliating her yet, and he stepped back from behind her, with his hairy buttocks turned towards me. I was fascinated by them, even though they repulsed me too.

'He bent away from her, and I caught a flash of her sweet cunt shining with excitement. I remember thinking what a slut she was, our prim and proper Miss, and I wished that it was me who was going to fuck her.

'The man had picked up a piece of rounded wood, and I recognised it as a rounders bat. I thought he was going to stick it up her bottom, and the thought made me queasy, in a sexy sort of way. Instead, he rolled the thick end around the lips of her cunt, and she shifted her thighs to open herself for it.

'I wanted to wank myself by then, so I quickly lifted up the pleated front of my skirt, and shoved my hand down the front of my knickers. My cunt was soaking, and my fingers slid easily between the lips. I began to stroke myself, in time to the movement of the bat, and my stomach gave a lurch when he rolled his wrist and slid the end into my pretty teacher's pouting cunt. The groan she made stifled the sound of mine, and they carried on, oblivious to me. I was so turned on that I wouldn't have cared if they had seen me anyway. I watched in amazement as the thick wooden peg slid into her, and she arched her back to it. I could clearly see how stretched she was by the way her arsehole bulged at each outward stroke of the bat. I grew impatient to see him fuck her there. I wanted to see him open the bitch's arse while I watched, and if he didn't do it soon I was going to come without it happening to her.

'He grunted again in approval, then slid the object rudely out of her. Her wet slit gaped, but he wasted no time on it. I saw him place the thick head of his cock at her bum, then press it hard against the opening by the pressure of a thumb behind his rosy knob. She squealed in alarm, trying to draw away from it, but he just gripped her more firmly and thrust with his hairy buttocks. His cock was so long that I could see the head disappearing into the crinkled ring, and heard her grunt of surprise when the first few inches slipped in.

'God, how he fucked her. He was pitiless, and I delighted in what he was doing to her. Her arse was stretched wide by the reddened shaft, and she could do nothing but hold her hips rigid, while he slid it in and out of her arse. I watched her grimaces turn to slack-lipped ecstasy as the movement in her arse must have given her more intense pleasure. She came hard after only minutes of this rough bottom-fucking, and he slid straight out of her when his own turn came. I was close to the edge all through her buggering, but the sight of her open arsehole, and the jets of creamy sperm he spurted into the dark opening, sent me spinning.'

Anne and I were straining at our cunts while she spoke with ever more urgency and, even as this image was unfolding in my mind, the pent-up frustration boiled out in an orgasm of such unexpectedness and sheer beautiful pleasure that I actually howled with release. I rubbed furiously at my clit, and could say nothing but pant my approval as Anne struggled to a finish clearly as intense as mine. Her eyes were slitted shut, and she gasped out more short obscenities as vile as they were wonderful. It was the most extraordinary thing I had ever seen. Less than a foot away from me, a grown woman was masturbating to a climax in her kitchen, while I watched her do it. It was amazing.

Her shoulders shook, and her neat head nodded slowly forward in sharp jerks, until, with a groan from her pursed mouth, her forehead met the granite worktop in a gently pressured halt. I let her get her breath, and she eventually straightened up, only to bend again, convulsed with the same laughter that shook me. In between sobs of hysterical mirth, I asked her if it was true, which seemed to strike her as even funnier, and it was some time before she sobered enough to answer me.

'Oh, yes,' she replied, 'it's true, though I may have exaggerated the bit about the rounders bat. He didn't actually put it in. He just rolled it around her lips for a bit. Everything else was exactly how it happened, even the bit about what I did.'

'And did they see you?' I asked, and she swiftly replied.

'No, I buggered off while they were still recovering. Then I ran to the woods near the school and cried for hours.'

I felt sorry for her, though she didn't look that upset at that moment. I suppose I was sympathising with the girl she had been. A girl who had deceived herself as much as I had. I felt compelled to ask, 'Did anything ever come of it, then?'

She mused for a bit before replying, and I became aware that we were still holding hands at the same moment she did. We just looked at each other with a question in both of our gazes. She squeezed my hand a little, then said, 'Not with her, sadly, but I still have dreams about that evening. Much the same as you, really. I hated the thought of that man doing things like that to her, and I hated even more the thought that she wanted to do them. The worst part of it is that, in my dreams, I am her.'

I was bemused.

'But I thought you weren't interested in men?' I asked her, and she smiled knowingly, then explained to me the strangeness of her mind.

'I'm not,' she told me, 'interested in men in my conscious life, but there is a part of me that loves the idea of being forced to do what most women love to do. It makes it seem all right. Do you see?'

The truth was that I did see. If you are forced to do it, or if you can't help yourself, it makes it seem OK. When you are full of lust, you don't care what you do: just like when you are really hungry you will eat anything. The more wicked or perverse a thing is, the deeper you have to go to unlock it. I understand all this, with the benefit of hindsight, but at that time I was more innocent of the tricks a person's mind can play.

The kinkiness of what we had just done hit me then, and I stared at Anne in shocked surprise.

'I can't believe we just did that, Anne,' I gasped, and she squeezed my hand, before replying.

'I promised myself that I wouldn't try to seduce you, Jessica. Please don't think that's what is happening. You don't, do you?' she continued.

I sat in silence, while I gathered the courage to whisper to her, 'You can, if you want to. I don't mind.'

I squeezed my thighs together, to still their trembling, and felt the sharp throb of excitement in my lower tummy lurch upwards, into my chest. Anne stared and stared, her eyes darkening as the pupils dilated, until I found my own eyes misting at the edges of their focus, as I tried to read the thoughts that whirred behind those black mirrors.

15

'Do you want to come to my room?' she asked, and the question split the silence like the cracking of a whip.

I felt my insides soar with sick delight as I answered, 'Yes', and we rose unsteadily, circling round the table towards each other, like tigers entering a jungle clearing. The last steps before I touched her felt like they were drawn out in time, and I watched my own hand, like a stranger's, drift trembling to her chest. The first contact set off little rockets of activity in the back of my skull, like sharp, cold water from a shower. I couldn't think, and the actions of my body were instinctive and immediate. My free hand curled around her waist, and drifted up, under the edge of her jumper, along the warm, taut skin of her side. My fingers grazed the straps of her bra, and came to rest in the unfamiliar hollows of her back; my hand fluttered nervously against the ropy sinews of her lower spine, as I tilted my head for the touching of her lips. Her dark head moved in a blur to my throat, and the shock of her naked tongue against the delicate skin of my neck made me gasp. She licked urgently upwards to the edge of my jaw, then swooped her soft mouth over mine to gather up my expelled breath. Our lips rolled softly together, in the lightest of touches, until her quick and clever tongue slipped out between the rolling, coral-pink swell of her soft lips, and darted into my mouth. Surprise after surprise, but I went with the feelings that her probings had produced, and coiled my tongue around hers, in a clumsy dance of sudden heat and tingling. Her cheeks were cold, and the soft skin thrilled me where it brushed against my own. I started to roll her jumper up, and was surprised when she grasped my hands in hers, stopping me.

'Not here,' she said, and drew me with her as she walked towards the stairs. 'We must go to my room.'

I made no protest, being content to let her lead me up the stairs, while I studied the lazy swinging of her hips and shoulders. Her bare feet whispered against the boards, making soft counterpoints to the swishing of her calico trousers. The trousers bunched in little puffs around the

16

broad belt that held them up, but they were drawn up tight around the swell of her bottom, and the seam was buried deep between the tight cheeks. The rolled-up ends exposed the tanned flesh of her lower calves, with the flexing of the large tendon at her heels drawing my eyes to its ropy strength. The shadow of her slim legs showed in a patchy outline through the gauzy fabric, and I, unable to resist, stroked the firm curve of her hip.

She paused to let me stroke her hips and lay my head against her lower back, and for a moment we stood awkwardly on the steps while I panted, in hushed excitement, against her spine. Then she resumed the stately upward progress, until we stood before the threshold of her room. She let my hand go, and turned, so that I could pass before her into the curtained dimness within. I stepped hesitantly past her, and stood with my back to the door, listening to it shut over the sound of my own harsh breathing. I felt her move behind me, and my mind gathered stray impressions, while her hands busied themselves at the fastenings of my dress. It slipped away from me, to the floor, letting the slight chill of morning air from the open window cool my bare skin. I was wearing only the plainest of underwear, and suddenly I was ashamed of the plain whiteness of my bra and panties. I wished I could be dressed for sacrifice.

Quick fingers snapped the catch of my bra, and my breasts were pushed forward, free, while the warm breath of Anne tickled on the short hairs of my neck. I shuddered, and the rosy tips of my tits swayed in gentle time to my quivering frame. Anne's cold fingers slipped around my ribs and clutched in greediness at the swollen tips. She pinched both stems with hard fingertips, while the bra gathered in the crooks of my updrawn elbows. I gasped, and pushed my buttocks back at her to steady myself, until I felt the roughness of her trousers rubbing, and the tine of her belt scratching at my lower spine. She released me, for a moment, and I heard the whisper of her jumper sliding over her hair, then the first shocking contact of her stiff, bare nipples against my back. Her

17

perfume rose in waves around me, and I swayed in a near faint when she popped the clasp of her belt open. The trousers hissed over her skin, and she flicked them, with a foot, across the polished bedroom floor. They struck against the skirting board, and the movement drew the attention of my overheated mind. As I turned my head to look, she stopped the movement with a gentle hand and whispered, in the gentlest of sighs, 'Don't. Not yet! I want to play with you like this.'

I stood, stiff-limbed, while ripples of goose bumps ran over my naked flanks, and felt the play of Anne's warm breath on my back. The first light tickle of her fingers at the swelling of my hips almost passed by unnoticed, such was the fevered state of my mind. There was too much sensation. Too much that was new. The unfamiliar room, the presence of another woman, naked at my back, the vulnerability of my circumstance.

Anne's warm hands slid over the tense muscles of my hips, and met over the flat plain of my lower belly, just above the waistband of my knickers. She pushed the tips of her fingers, like blunt knives, between my skin and the tight hem. The sheets of muscle at the side of my bellybutton fluttered at the contact of the soft pads, and I caught my breath when they slipped, ever lower, to stroke and scrape at the flattened tangle of my pubic hair. Anne was leaning heavily into my shoulders, and I felt the hair above my ear float away from her whispered words.

'What are you hiding in here, Jessica?' she asked, and I could not frame a reply, for one of those impudent fingers had stroked its way, through the crisp hair, down to the seam of my sex lips and now pressed lightly against my bud. I felt the skin of my clitoral hood slide over the little nub, as Anne's knowing finger rubbed its way between the moistening lips of my sex. Slow, delicious tingles spiralled lazily up my spine, like bubbles fizzing along the stem of a straw, and my hips rocked unconsciously with the flares of pleasure produced by Anne's manipulations. My cheeks brushed against the silky fronts of Anne's hips, and the realisation of her total nakedness poked through the fabric of pleasure that her finger was weaving in my mind. She was wearing no knickers, and the fleeting contact of her pubic hair against the crease of my bottom confirmed this. I pushed my bottom back more firmly, to feel her nakedness better, and the front of her melded into the back of me like we were made of plastic. Her breasts bulged against my shoulder blades. Her stomach sucked against the sweaty hollow of my back. Her thighs flexed in hot, muscular contact against the straining backs of mine.

I felt cool air slip in between us as she moved her left hand away, out from the restriction of my panties, and into the warm space where my buttocks pressed against her taut inner hip. Her fingers curled around the full flesh of my bottom, where it tensed beneath my cotton pants. She gathered up the material and, in one smooth movement, pulled it up into the tight cleft between my cheeks. It felt oddly, uncomfortably sexy, to have my bottom divided in such a way. The pressure on my clit increased as Anne's hand was pulled tightly against my cunt by the drawing up of my knickers at the front, by the tugging at my behind. I tilted my upper torso away from Anne, to ease the pressure between my cheeks, and the heavy globules of my swollen-tipped breasts hung like ripe fruit. I moved my right arm over Anne's, so that she could twist around my hip, and burrow even deeper between my thighs. I felt a finger slip wetly into me, between my puffy lips, and wriggle like a little snake along the crease.

The edge of Anne's hand kept the pressure on my clitoris, as her fingers squirmed up into my pulsing slit. I bent forward, rudely opening my legs to strengthen the stance, and braced my upper body by clutching the corded muscle above my knees with both hands. The hand at my rear was adjusted, and I felt the slim fingers joining in the seeking of their fellows at my front. A sudden stretching sensation in my sex heralded their entry, and I groaned in utter abandon as Anne smoothly pushed a couple of fingers in. She leaned away from me a little, and her right hand ceased to play around the entrance of my cunt, and concentrated on the pearly nub

19

that was the centre of my pleasure. Her other hand had found a rhythm that was clearly pleasing to us both and, with each inward movement, I felt the entrance of my vagina yield a little more.

'God, you're so fucking tight!' Anne murmured, even as I felt her attempt to add another finger.

'No, too much,' I protested, as the finger joined the others within me. She slowed her pace, and shortened the movement of her hand, and I trembled on the edge of acceptance. She kept me there, on that delicious precipice, by the perfection of her knowledge. She knew, by the shudders of my hips and the shivering in my legs, that I was close to coming.

Moving swiftly, she withdrew her hands and rolled my cotton pants down, over the swell of my hips, until they were stretched taut across my widespread thighs. She rubbed her whole forearm down my perineum and over the swollen lips of my cunt, then back up, to fiercely enter me again with three bunched fingers. My brazenness increased with my excitement, and I tilted my hips up to her, so that she could push her hand more rudely into my stretched and slippery pussy. I groaned, and squeezed the walls of my vagina against the insistent press of her slim fingers. She slapped me, once, twice across my broad cheeks, and I came against the thrusting, beak-like intrusion of her hand. My head snapped up, and I howled with ecstasy.

'That's it! Come,' she cried, and slapped me once again in delirious arousal. I felt her hand slip out of me, as I fell to my knees, with my pants tangled around my lower thighs. I turned my head groggily, and her figure swayed above me as my eyes struggled to focus. I watched as she sat down before me and lay on her back. Her brown thighs lolled wide, and the slit below the thin stripe of her pubic hair gaped pinkly out at me. I saw her hands float down, dreamlike, to flirt with the glistening opening, and watched, fascinated, as the pale ovals of her fingernails disappeared into the puffy crack. She had no ring on her fingers, and her right hand slipped up, unhindered, until only the last knuckles could be seen. Her other hand had slipped beneath her, and she raised her hips up so that she could delve between her plump cheeks. I clearly saw her pink and hairless anus accept the probing of the middle finger of that hand.

I rolled over on my naked hip to her, so that I could lie on my side and watch her masturbate. My eyes had adjusted to the dimness, and every detail of what she was doing was plain to me. I was especially fascinated by what she was doing to her arse, and my gaze was concentrated there. I lay as if in a dream and devoured the sight of her anus sucking at that slim finger. It bulged a little outwards as the slim stem withdrew, shining from the juices that were dribbling from the workings of her other hand.

The noises of Anne's panting mingled with the wet sounds of her masturbation, until it was difficult for my ear to separate the two. I saw her arsehole tighten, and her cheeks bunch ever tighter against the hand between them. It looked like some kind of sandy-coloured spider crouched in the seam of her bottom, probing with one jointed leg into the crinkled hole that they framed. Her huffing and puffing changed to low animal groans, and the firm muscles of her inner thigh strained so that the tendons were thrown into sharp relief. Her upraised stomach rippled with contractions as she jerked her hand inside herself. My own stomach tensed as her crisis approached, until there was a knot of tension under my heart. All at once she collapsed, letting her bottom thump down on to the spider. Its legs fluttered weakly under the bulge of her cheeks, while her other hand slipped out to dangle against her inner thigh. I hauled myself over to her on shaking limbs, until I was crouched on all fours above her. I gently let my upper body down to rest on hers, and felt the answering clasp of her damp thighs around my waist. My knickers were in a tangle round my ankles, so I kicked them off, and drew my knees up under me again, so that my bottom swayed loosely to the cool air that drifted in the open window. I lay like that, with my head on her sweat-beaded chest, and listened to the heavy thumping of her heart. My head rose and fell gently, with her breathing, and her hand eventually walked up the wet coils of my hair to rest on the crown of my head. Her heartbeat was slow and steady before she next spoke, and I smiled into the golden skin of her chest.

'You are going to have to return to that house, Jessica,' she said, 'but don't worry. I shall be going with you.'

I murmured some sort of thanks against the firm mound of one breast, but I was lost in the feeling of the coolness in my cleft and the loose, lazy sensation in my bottom.

'I have a plan,' she continued, 'and I think you're going to like it.'

I listened to her outline of what we would do. Her voice rumbled pleasantly up from her chest, and I felt the first warm stirrings of hope light a stray ember in my stomach. The slide into depravity began there, and I would love every minute of it.

THE BOND

Lindsay Gordon

Forum said of *The Bond*, Lindsay Gordon's third novel for Nexus, that it 'rescues the vampire novel from the lush clutches of Anne Rice and gives it a modern, adrenalin-fuelled spin.' We'd say it was one of the most original, challenging and stimulating erotic novels we've published in a long time.

The first two are *Rites of Obedience* and *The Submission Gallery*, and Lindsay followed *The Bond* with *Angel*, *See-Through* and *Domination Dolls*.

In the following extract from *The Bond*, Missy gets hungry . . .

There was a lot of talent in the bar where I met Charlie, but I know he was the right choice. I needed some vigorous loving after the long journey to La Posada.

'May I sit down?' were his first words.

Narrowing my eyes and blowing a plume of smoke across the table, I wore my best look of disinterest. Dressed in a black suit and silk shirt with no tie, he stood before my table, smiling. His self-assurance made me suspect a cocky side if he became too comfortable in my company. I liked his smile, though, and I dug the retro style to his clothes; it reminded me of happier times. I did suspect Charlie of being vain, but knew I could work that to my advantage – vain men make me aggressive and I was in the mood for something hard.

'Sure,' I said, curious about him. If he was a fool I could easily get rid of him.

He pulled up alongside me in my booth, but didn't get too close.

'What's your name?' he asked.

'Bonny,' I answered, still looking straight ahead, already having decided that I'd like to be Bonny for the night. My real name is Missy, but Bonny suited the place I was drinking in. It had a swing band, red leather bar, dim lights and layers of smoke drifting above people's heads.

'Can I get you another drink?'

'Thanks. Bourbon, straight.'

He signalled for the waiter and introduced himself as Charlie. While he messed around opening a packet of smokes and cracking small talk, I stretched my mind to take a closer look at him. Late twenties, I guessed, gym freak, was probably self-employed, and had no worries about being single because he needed plenty of time to stand before a full-length mirror admiring his body, and although girls came easy few were that patient. Although he enjoyed a good run with the ladies in his small and knowable town, he loved to see a new face in one of his haunts. Especially mine, with a beauty spot and cherry-red lips, like a vision sent from the past.

Across the lounge, Hank sat in shadow, watching us from his booth. Through the dark I could see the end of his cigarette and could feel his eyes on my bare shoulders and cleavage, framed by the black dress I had on. He'd been to this bar before and had brought me down here after we ate steak in a diner. Once I'd finished my second dessert of ice cream and lemon pie, I told him I was hungry and he said he knew a place.

Light from the lamp on my table, shielded behind green glass, allowed my date to check me out; the way guys do when they think they're being discreet. But for a guy who was so self-assured, his speech broke up when he took a good look down my dress and at my shiny thighs crossed beneath the table. Saying little, I nodded at his comments and occasionally answered a question. Around the room I saw another four guys who had waited too long to come over and ask if I wanted company. On each of their faces something had dropped; the hope had disappeared from their eyes and been replaced by longing. Still, I was happy with this Charlie character and my appetite increased every time I got a whiff of his scent under all that aftershave. Wondering if Charlie's muscle cut was deep and tanned, I gave him a little more attention. As I turned my eyes upon him, he stared at me like he would do anything not to blow it with me.

'Bet you're all of eighteen,' he said.

'Close,' I replied, smiling at last.

'You studying up at the college?'

'No, I never took that route. Fell in love instead.'

'I know that story,' he said, nodding. 'Did he turn into a louse?'

'No, he turned into my husband.'

'You're married?'

'Afraid so.'

'Sorry. I didn't see anyone with you.'

'No harm done,' I said, enjoying the smell of his anxiety.

Confused, he gave me more space in the booth. 'Want me to beat it?'

'You'd know by now if I did.'

'What you doing out, then?'

'Playing a game.'

'Don't see any cards,' he said, and then laughed nervously.

'There are other ways to gamble.'

'Like?'

'Maybe I'll show you.'

He looked uneasy.

'See all those people out there?' I said.

He nodded.

'One of them is my husband.'

Charlie started to look around.

'Don't look. That's one of the rules. Look at me instead. Why change the habit of your entire evening?'

Picking up his drink, he knocked it straight back and looked like he was ready to split. Only he couldn't; despite the alarms screaming inside his head he was unable to leave my side.

'Thought you were the type who liked a game,' I said.

'You might be the prettiest thing I've seen outside of a magazine, miss, but losing teeth is another matter.'

'He'll thank you for it.'

Charlie exhaled. 'You're shitting me.'

I shook my head and giggled. 'My husband's older than me. A lot older, and he likes his young wife to be happy.' With that I gave him a wink and he relaxed a little. 'Interested?' I added, and uncrossed my legs. He said nothing, but began to rub his mouth. In his lap, I could see the rise I had made out of this lounge Romeo.

'Want to dance with me?' I invited, when the band began a good slow Red Simpson tune.

He swallowed and I watched his Adam's apple move up and down his clean-shaven throat. 'More than anything,' he whispered.

For some reason that story gets most guys horny. I use it often when I hunt younger guys because it keeps Hank sharp too, on account of him liking the sweet pain of my betrayal. You see, later on, after my thirst is slaked, I'll tease Hank with the story and if I'm lucky his love will leave bruises. Hank seemed distracted for a few days and I lacked the energy to try levering details from him. In hindsight, I guess he'd been dreaming about the Preacher and that is never a good sign. As we drove in the late afternoon, when the sun turned red, Hank's hand was near my puss as he steered the car with the other, and my need to play began to boil beneath my skin. Uncomfortable, I became sassy and snapped at him in the car. Being preoccupied with his dreams about the Preacher, it was probable he deliberately whisked me into feeling restless, not only because he liked to watch me hunt, but because he wanted to be punished in this passive way for being unable to shake that bastard from out of our lives for good. Tonight, he wanted to twist and burn over me while I took another man. And after he'd taken my bottom without permission that morning, Hank deserved to ache for me. If I was lucky, maybe he'd weep over my digression too; reassurance a girl can never get enough of.

As we danced, Charlie held me close and let me sample an impression of his thick pipe, hard as wood, and waiting for me down there. Pressing through my thin dress, I could even feel the shape of the big head. Raising myself on to my toes, it rested against my puss and I decided I loved the feel of it. Wondering about his fit inside me, I imagined it passing through the slit in my sheer panties. I let him hold me closer.

'Do you have a place?' he asked, and a shudder passed through him.

'Mmm,' I moaned, close to his smooth cheek. 'A motel room. My husband rents it for me, just out of town, so our neighbours never get wise.'

Charlie pressed his pipe against my belly, made firm by a white corselette. 'Girl, you're too much.'

'Want to see my fuck pad?' I asked.

Charlie couldn't speak but his hands clenched on my buttocks.

'But let me be honest, I want to fuck, nothing else,' I said.

His breathing became hoarse, but there were no words, and his exhalations began to hang like low clouds over my bare neck. Feeling his energy build up was exciting. In anticipation of having him splashed all over and up inside me, I decided to make things worse for him and better for me. 'I'm real tight, though, so don't rip anything.'

With a dry hand, he pulled my face before his lips and I could see the devil in his eyes. 'Now,' he whispered.

I kissed him long and deep, giving him tongue and leaving smears of red across his mouth. 'My husband is watching, so kiss me good.'

Charlie raped my mouth right there on the dance floor. Among all those dancing couples and under the hot lights, I explored his body through his thin shirt. When my claws found his back he broke from the kiss to gasp. Lining his skin, I let him know our love would be hard. 'Maybe I can't wait,' he said.

'Then maybe you should take me outside.'

Whisked from the dance floor, Charlie pulled me through the tables and out into the parking lot. As we left I looked over my shoulder at Hank, who was slouching against a pillar by the dance floor. Through the murk of smoke and the lightning of strobe, I caught sight of simmering eyes in a drawn face. I smiled and blew a kiss. Charlie held my hand and led me from the bar.

Behind the kitchens, in long shadows, I enjoyed Charlie's fury. Panting his desperation all over my upturned

29

face and white shoulders, his hands became busy below. He slapped his belt from the buckle and flopped his stiff meat into the night. When my cool fingers entwined around his length to massage the veins and ridges of his girth, Charlie raised my dress up to my navel. Cold air washed across my thighs, taut with suspenders, and lapped around my waist, braceleted by a corselette. Squinting through the dark, and trying not to whoop with joy, he surveyed the treasures he never expected to glimpse when preparing himself earlier in the evening.

As I squeezed his fat pipe and pushed my hand, vigorously, up and down his length, Charlie's breathing found a rhythm. 'I'm damp,' I said. 'And my panties are slit under the corset, so get this inside me, quick.' Gripping the rear of my thighs and spreading his feet, he measured my weight and then lifted. His biceps swelled and his face trembled. Passing my hands over my shoulders, I grasped a window sill. My heels left the tarmac as Charlie raised me to the right height. 'Fuck me,' I whispered to his wild eyes.

Inside my head, waves slammed and broke apart on a cliff face. Thick as a python, Charlie's fat cock stretched me so wide I thought I heard something tear. Resting my head against the rough bricks of the wall, and stiffening my shoulders to form a solid base into which he could smash, I readied myself. When he came through me I squealed like a feeding piglet. Long strokes to the very back of me made me feel as light as a feather. At the pit of my womb, where all the velvet waited to slurp his milk, the head of his cock felt like an apple. Hard and round, it slipped down to pack my box, then withdrew to the squeeze of my lips, before rifling back through me to push the air from my body. Grinding himself in hard, the flat muscles on his pelvis squashed my clit-pip and I started to croak.

Across the lot, two girls climbed from a Pontiac Firebird and stopped dead in their tracks. Over Charlie's shoulder I could read the shock and delight on their pretty faces. Staring at our bouncing silhouettes, they giggled silly, excited things to each other. Deep down, I knew both of them envied the strange girl the local tough thrust up and down the wall.

Spiking the back of his thighs with my heels, that glinted like shiv blades in a street fight, I spat right into Charlie's face. My spit dripped from the black arch of his brows and in his eyes I could see a murderer's glee. 'Want to play hard?' he said in a hissy, pissy voice and his mouth went all fierce; not ugly, but savage and snarly. When I'm fucking I like to see that, and it makes me push my luck to find a man's limit. Afterwards, they always weep like babies and hold me like they're sorry, but I only smile and enjoy the bruises they leave, as if the black marks are kisses left by a movie star's lips.

'Go on,' I said to him, and widened my hips a fraction to take the blasting from his groin. Dipping his head, he groped a mouthful of brassière and the soft flesh it suspended and almost bit my breast off. After half a dozen thrusts that made me see stars, he paused and groaned. I felt two strong pulses in my womb. Pushing his floppy body away, I dropped to a crouch before him. While I made ready to collect, a thick rope of cream landed on my cheek and it felt hot. The next three ejaculations I managed to pull into my mouth and they hit my tonsils before slithering into my tummy. I suckled hard, until his brown cock waned against the inside of my clinging cheeks, and Charlie had to clutch his chest with one hand and support his weight by pressing the other into the wall.

After my own dizziness passed, I fingered the stickiness from my cheek and rubbed it over my teeth in preparation for drinking something more salty. As I pulled my stockings back up to the lips of my puss and straightened my dress, I watched the two girls from the Pontiac walk past with their noses pointed at the moon. I felt their sudden disapproval and hoped they would stay quiet.

The taller blonde girl whispered 'slut' to her busty friend. Whether she intended me to hear or not, she had no idea that I could hear her thoughts if I chose. When I'm aroused I can catch a quick heartbeat in my ears from the other side of a room; I can smell a fresh slice on a finger in broken glass three blocks away; and I want to tear skin apart like pastry to lick out the filling beneath. Never fuck with me when I'm roused.

'Fuck you,' I said, real loud, and patted my hair flat where it stuck out at the back.

Busty gasped at my language but the tall bitch with the mouth said, 'Against a wall, not likely.'

They only enjoyed a few seconds of laughter before I was beside them. While Busty cried, I took Lanky back to her car, slapping her tight arse all the way to humiliate her into being my bitch. Stunned by the strength in my hands, and unsteady on her pencil-thin heels, she was manoeuvred against the rear door of the car so I could shove her over. When her long legs were stuck in the air and her head slid about on the leatherette of the back seat, I took a peek at her puss.

'Leave her alone!' her busty friend shrieked from behind. 'I'll call the cops.'

Lanky looked frightened and her fight was gone. I smiled down at the peroxide-softened beauty before me and I stroked her lean, tanned legs. Terrified, she clamped both of her hands, palm down, across her pussy; somehow understanding that was where the truth lived. Fixing her frightened doe eyes with my own, I said, 'From now on, bitch, you'll roll with every slut in boots who rides through your town.'

'Sorry,' she said, trying not to cry. 'I didn't mean it.'

'That's right, you didn't. You only said it to cool your own heat. It turned you on to see me against that wall and it disgusted you too. But we both know what you'll be dreaming about tonight between your safe, crisp sheets. Don't we?'

I didn't expect her to answer, but she moved her hands away from the silk and moisture between those gazelle legs.

'Stop it! What are you doing to my friend? Harriet, please get up. Don't let her hurt you,' Busty whined from behind me. But Busty's cries petered out to whispers and then nothingness, when her lanky friend, Harriet, clasped the back of my head with her athlete's thighs and began to moan. From behind, I guess the fat-chested friend could see my slim body, elegantly dressed, dipping its perfect blonde head between the rangy legs of her best friend. Enough to cut anyone's tongue out, I guess.

Charlie watched the whole thing from the shadows. Freaked out by the girl that had lured him from the dance, he seemed to be entertaining second thoughts about going home with me. But as I teetered towards him across the lot on my slingbacks, all sweet as apple pie and Marilyn wiggly, he fished a set of car keys out of a pocket and nodded in the direction of his car.

As we drove to my motel, I caught him peeking at me. Not at my legs or chest like before, but at me – the idea of me. After discharging himself so furiously, I guessed he now had the clarity of mind to think things over, and what I had done to the lanky girl worried him. Once or twice he was about to say something but stopped himself.

'Charlie,' I said, and when he looked me in the eye, I dabbed some of him from the side of my mouth. He swallowed and nearly ran a red light. 'When I'm excited,' I said, 'I sometimes go too far.'

Charlie nodded.

Crossing my legs at the thigh removed his last misgiving.

Back in the motel, I poured Red Label Scotch into the tooth glasses I found in the bathroom, while Charlie sat on the bed and eyed Hank's things that were folded on a chair.

'Relax,' I said, and stretched myself out on the bed behind his back. The clattering sound of my high heels when they hit the floor encouraged him to lie alongside me, propped up on one elbow.

'You live near here?' he asked.

Sipping my Scotch, I ignored him.

'Sure I would have seen you before.'

'Not scared are you, Chuck?' I said, and he looked away, feeling silly. 'I'm seventeen, the door is locked and no one is going to disturb us until I'm finished. No one.'

Taking quick gulps from his drink, Charlie watched the door for a while and I surveyed my prize. Fat cock and a hard body; I had chosen well. Moving closer to him, I placed a finger beneath his chin and made him look at me. Slowly, I untucked his shirt. When my red fingernails brushed against his skin, he closed his eyes. Deftly, I popped each button from its hole on his shirt and he accommodated my hands when I shed it from his body. Along each side of his spine, beneath his shoulder blades, there were welts that looked tender, like the pink gills of a fish.

Seizing me by the elbows, he held me away from his body and I could see the muscles trembling around his mouth. Lowering my eyes, I spied his cock poling his trousers out like a tent. I made a little humming sound that vibrated off the bones of my face and I smiled at him. 'You want that?' he said, and I could see the brown skin on his shoulders goosing. Stretching out my tongue, I wet my lips and made a noise like a small animal. Charlie yanked me forward and on to his chest.

Our kisses were clumsy at first because we were trying to eat too much of each other, but I withdrew a fraction and he followed my lead until we settled into an easy embrace of the lips that seemed to employ my whole body. As he sucked my tongue in and out of his mouth and I enjoyed the scratch of his stubble on my face, I slipped a hand down to his cock. With only the tips of my nails making contact, I ran my hand up and down his length and felt his thighs and buttocks tense.

Our kissing became heated again and I wished Hank had been watching; it's really hard on him when I kiss another man's mouth. Perhaps it's more intimate than penetration: This time, we could sustain the kiss without clicking our teeth together or pinching each other's lip skin. We vanished into the kiss; became absorbed from ourselves into the union of mouth. As he pressed my face down, like he wanted to swallow my head, I felt my dress start to move up my body. His hands became impatient when the hem caught under my buttocks, and he hoisted me off the bed to yank the garment up to my armpits.

'Steady,' I warned, suddenly concerned for the thousand-dollar dress, but Charlie was lost in me. He unclipped my brassière and plucked the gauzy cups from off my chest. As his mouth encircled one of my breasts and the palm of his hand rubbed the other, so my nip would tickle his skin, I peeled my dress over my head and let it fall to the rug beside the bed. His mouth and hands swapped from one breast to the other while I watched, enjoying the sight of a stranger busy with my chest. I'm lucky to have a good hard bosom – not unwieldy, but prominent naked or clothed, with sensitive nips.

Sliding my legs around the bed and raking my nails through his hair, I encouraged his feeding, and when he tried to remove his mouth from my wet skin to take a breath, I commanded 'No' and squashed his face back into my softness. Pleasure began to blind me; I closed my eyes and stared into the dark red things that swirled inside my head. Empowered by my arousal, I felt as if I could raise Charlie above my head or trample him beneath my angry feet.

When he stuck a hand under my corselette, I wondered whether my glowing puss burned his fingers. 'You're so wet,' he murmured, with a mouth full of nip and puppy-fat tit. 'Can I take a sip? Just a taste, little lady?'

Arching my back off the bed, I spread my thighs and rolled my eyes back, knowing he would pay for his goading. The bed shook as he hurried around me and the mattress dipped under my bottom as he arranged my legs over his shoulders. 'I'm going to suck you through these slut panties,' he told me, and then I felt his breath on my inner thighs, followed by his whiskers in the place where my puss meets my buttocks. Twisting my wrists so my hands would lock at a right angle to my forearms, I pressed my palms against the wall, between the brass rungs of the headboard.

Charlie licked the dew from my panties and then he whipped my lips and trimmed floss with his tongue. Soon I lost patience with his teasing and jammed my groin against his face. There was a moment of resistance from Charlie, but I strangled his neck with my slippery legs and seized the cold metal of the headboard – two-fisted – to pump his face. Fastening his jaws over my hole, he made long, measured laps at my lips with his broad tongue, slipping through my furrows, passing across my opening and meandering back to my pip.

Trying to move my bottom so I would only receive his tongue on my special spot, Charlie seized my garter straps and held me still by those harnesses so he could continue collecting my moisture with his tongue. I had to respect him for making me wait for a while, but I guessed he wouldn't be able to restrain himself for long. He would want to hear my music; my bird sounds and my baby-crying noises when my pip is under the lash of a tongue.

Holding his head fast by using my thighs like a vice, he licked me to my second peak of the evening. Only when my legs seemed to fall away from the rest of me did I allow Charlie to disentangle himself.

'That was good. So good, you bastard,' I said, between breaths. Charlie had risen to his knees, and from his nose to the cleft in his chin I could see how my honey had made his skin shiny. Raising my head off the pillow, I peeked between his legs and liked what had risen to gut me. Shuffling my bottom up and down the bed, and sliding my feet up his chest, I let him know I was ready.

'Pretty girl,' he whispered, 'you're gonna suck me first.'

Giggling, I opened my mouth and rubbed the tip of my tongue over my front teeth. Charlie clasped my ankles and then rubbed his hands, fiercely, up and down the outside of my legs, creasing my nylons. He even dipped his cock towards my puss as if he couldn't wait to skewer me. 'Thought you wanted to fuck my mouth,' I said, lost to my new lover, and my love of this game.

Throwing my legs to one side, Charlie loomed over my body. With an excited sigh, I pushed myself down the bed until his cock and balls and their meaty odour hung about my face. Gripping himself at the base of his thick stem, he jammed himself at my mouth and missed. Pinching his purple berry of a phallus between finger and thumb, I planted him in my warmth. Greeting his organ with my curling tongue, I stretched my jaw and let him pass to the back of my throat. Angling my head back and fighting the involuntary urge to gag, I took three-quarters of him inside my skull and gripped his hard buttocks to hold him there. Before allowing him to withdraw, I was content to consume him and measure his length and weight with the bones and flesh of my head. When he finally slipped back, I hugged the bumps of his meat with my lips until the salty tip was cradled between my pursed lips.

'That's the greatest,' he said, real quiet.

I flashed my eyes at him – eyes still heavy with dark paint and luxurious with false lashes. He slipped back inside. Overjoyed with my catch who played along with everything, I moulded the shape of his manhood with my fingers, squeezed its putty with my hand and sucked its briny beads into my stomach.

'I'm going to come,' Charlie said.

'No,' I commanded, holding him away from my mouth. Even though he tried to push his cock back into my mouth, I held him firm. Desperate to splash wave after wave of relief down my throat, he then tried to beat himself in and out of my fingers, but I gripped him, refusing him the friction he required. When the safety catch was back on and the moment of danger had passed, I used my tongue to cleanse him of dew. 'I don't want you shooting off and then passing out. I have a need tonight.'

'You want to be fucked good,' he said, torturing himself with the pain of anticipation.

'Mmm,' I encouraged. 'Like a pretty slut wife who picks men up in bars.'

He tried to press his cock back into my mouth again but I would not relent. 'Let me come in your mouth, Bonny,' he pleaded, and said it so sweetly I nearly gave in. I laughed at him instead, slipped through his legs, and sat up behind him. Charlie looked angry when he turned to face me; desperation clouded his reason. I'd made him mindless – the way I needed him for what I had planned.

'You want to fuck me, tough guy, then you better do it good. Understand that. You don't want me going back to town tonight, do you?'

'How did a kid like you get such a smart mouth?' he said.

I smiled.

'Had much practice?' he said, angry and jealous, but delighted too.

My smile stiffened and, behind my back, I unthreaded the thick leather belt from his trousers. Welling up inside me came the strongest urge to both love and destroy.

'Where you going?' he asked, when I moved off the bed. Before the wide mirror on the dresser, I stood looking at myself, entwining Charlie's belt around my hands.

'Turn the main light off,' I said.

He sat in silence.

'Go on.' The certainty in my voice made him obey. Inhaling the dark like the aroma of good food, I said, 'Now switch the bedside lamps on.'

With heavy shades angled downward, the lamps covered the bed with a reddish glow. In the mirror, I watched Charlie move behind me. Understanding, he gently bent me over so my hands rested, palm down, on the top of the dresser. From my left hand he removed the strap of leather trailing from my fingers. His breathing sounded louder.

In the mirror, his reflection was obscured with shadow but the cut of his physique was more defined. From his hands there was a sudden snapping sound and I realised he had flexed the leather. 'Wait,' I said, and unclipped all four garter clasps from my stocking tops. Nylon, coloured like Sahara dunes, slithered down my legs until only my feet were covered. After stepping from my corselette, I peeled both stockings off the pinky soles of my feet.

'Now,' I said.

Before the echo of the word died in my head, it was drowned out by the scream of pain in my body. When the leather roped around my buttocks it made a wet sound. *Plat!* I shuddered and held the air in my lungs.

Plat!

Moaning, I cantered from one foot to the other.

Plat!

Fisting my hands on the dresser, I lowered my head between my shoulders.

Plat!

My knees began to give way and through my tears I saw Charlie hesitate and then suspend his next stroke.

'Do it!' I cried out.

He delivered, lashing me against the dresser, and shouted, 'Why?'

'Fuck you,' I said.

Again and again, he whipped me and the blows spanked the hard walls with echoes that hurt my ears inside.

'I want you,' Charlie said. 'You're going to be mine.'

Sniffing, I smiled, glad it was dark because my reflection would have revealed what I can be. Sometimes I don't like to see my own face.

Charlie's breath laboured. 'Does your old man whip you, girl?'

'Everybody does.'

The next blow was harder than the others and I sucked my hair into my mouth and bit down on it, before laughing through gritted teeth.

'Slut,' he swore and came up behind me. I turned around and slapped my hands against his chest, making him flinch and blink. He grabbed my shoulders but I bit his wrist. When he recoiled I fell to my knees and swallowed him. With rough, kneading fingers he scruffed my hair into fuzz and strands that stuck out at all angles.

Losing his balance from the force of my suckling, he staggered away from me to keep his feet. I followed on foot, my thin body flashing white in the gloom. Charlie cupped my tender cheeks with his hands. I slipped my arms around his neck and crossed my legs around his waist, locking my ankles in the small of his back. Like Hank, he had the strength to cradle the blonde demon bound to his body. Taken to the bed, I was thrown upon

39

the mattress and then covered by his body, raw and slicked with sweat.

He made me claw his face like that. What else could I do with him shunting me across the bed, slapping his body against mine, and crying out for salvation in this dark place I had made for us?

Like a thirsty dog, he licked my face from chin to forehead. No one had ever done that before and I knew my memory of Charlie had formed; whenever a tongue touched my skin, I would think of this boy who tried to dissolve my beauty with his broad tongue.

Squeezing my breasts until the breath had gone from me, he fucked me into the bed. A hard sound, like I was clearing my throat, came out of my mouth when he touched the back of my womb. Harder and harder he fucked, until I had moved to the other half of the bed and gone over the side, where my weight was supported by my shoulders and the back of my tousled head. With a fleshy thump, our still-grinding bodies joined our snatching mouths on the floor, where the violence of his thrusts were like flashes of murder in the dark.

'Fuck–' he slammed into me and then withdrew '– me.' My voice warbled and he threw himself back into me. 'Yes, yes, yes,' I cried with every quick pump from his hips until I came and became wordless. Pushed across the floor, the carpet burned us, but we didn't care. When my softness was jammed against the skirting board, he thumped clots of warmth against the sides of my womb and whispered, 'Love you.'

Stroking his head against my breasts, where the slowing tempo of my heart lulled him to sleep, my eyes flashed open so wide I could see a spider emptying a fly on the ceiling.

'Could you love me?' he asked.

'For ever,' I said.

'Can we be together?'

'For ever,' I replied, and he hugged me close, making me feel insignificant with his hard arms.

'Do you want me in every dream?' I asked.

'Yes,' he said, and nuzzled his head between my breasts.

A warm current of goodness pumped through my pet. He brimmed with wealth: iron-stock, rust-pepper, broth-spice. 'This won't hurt,' I whispered, lowering my gleaming smile to a part of him that was as soft as a shorn lamb.

THERAPY

Maria del Rey

Maria del Rey is one of Nexus's most established authors, described variously as 'the queen of SM' (*Caress*) and 'mistress of the stylish SM scenario' (*Forum Erotic Stories*), and she remains one of the most imaginative and explicit.

Maria's novels and short story collections for Nexus are as follows:

The Institute
Paradise Bay
Obsession
Heart of Desire
Sisterhood of the Institute
Underworld
Eden Unveiled
Dark Desires
Dark Delights
The Pleasure Principle

Therapy, meanwhile, is a stand-alone story you won't find anywhere else.

I felt nervous as I lay back against the leather couch. The muted hum of the traffic filtered through the slatted blinds which sliced the sunlight into long, thin bands of yellow. The room was cool and comfortable but I was still tense.

'Just try and relax.'

The calm authority of Dr Evans's voice felt reassuring, doing something to dispel my nerves. I shifted slightly, trying to make myself more comfortable.

'Just close your eyes and try to relax,' Dr Evans suggested.

With my eyes closed I could block out the distractions, focusing instead on the rhythm of my breathing, on the flow of air through my nostrils and the steady beat of my heart.

Dr Evans judged the moment perfectly. 'Where are you?'

I hesitated for a moment, trying to picture the time and the place, to re-create the moment just as I remembered it. 'I'm standing in front of a door . . . I'm waiting.'

'Why are you there?'

I hesitated once before answering. 'Because I've been delivered . . . No . . . Because I have to be there . . .'

'Why?'

The question seemed to float up from my consciousness, as though the question came from me and not Dr Evans. 'Because I need to be there . . . I have to prove . . .' I let the sentence drift into silence. The images were so strong now. I was there, not in a consulting room in a private clinic, but *there*.

'How are you dressed?'

My question or the doctor's? I couldn't tell any more. 'I'm wearing a short pleated skirt, black or dark blue, well above the knee . . . A tight white top under a denim jacket . . . Sports shoes, no socks . . . The white top contrasts so well with the dark skirt and my long black hair . . . I feel nervous.'

'Why?'

'Because I don't know what to expect on the other side of the door . . . I'm trembling slightly . . . I'm scared but excited too . . . I want to check myself in the mirror but there isn't enough time . . . My lips are glossed up and I've only just applied liner to my eyes . . . I want to look good.'

I stop, as though I am there again and I have to catch my breath.

'Go on now,' Dr Evans whispers, 'tell me what happens, let the story unfold and don't stop until it is over.'

I knock on the door and step back a little. The laughter and the music that were seeping through the door suddenly quieten down. I swallow hard just as the door opens. For the life of me I don't know what to say or what to do as the man at the door looks me up and down. He's aged around thirty, tall, muscular, with dark brown eyes and a cruel, sneering look on his face.

'Well, looky here, boys,' he calls back into the house, 'looks like this little lady's lost.'

He laughs and I hear it echoed back by the other men inside. He must be Jim, I realise belatedly. I had imagined someone more refined, someone less aggressively masculine.

'What do you want here, girl?' he demands loudly, silencing the laughter from the rest of the room. The door is still only half-open, he is blocking my view, I can barely see inside.

'Jasmine sent me,' I report softly. I know that I can turn away. I can stop things going any further by simply walking away from the situation. But I can't.

'Jasmine sent you, huh?' Jim repeats loudly. 'And d'you know what Jasmine's sent you for?'

His question is loud and lewd and delivered with a leer. I nod, nervously.

'Well, baby,' he says, 'better get in out the cold.'

There is silence as I step into the room. The light is low but I feel like I'm walking into a spotlight, all eyes are on me. I try to take in the picture without having to meet any of the eyes that are fixed on me. The room looks like it is full of men, but part of me says that there can't be more than seven or eight of them sprawled around the room. The air is thick with the smell of cigarettes, beer and sweat. I can almost smell the testosterone in the air.

The door closes and I know that I am alone, that there is no way out and that I have to go through with it.

'Well, baby, what do you say?' Jim asks, breaking the tense silence.

What can I say? This is what I have to do, this is what Jasmine wants. The men in front of me range in age from late teens to late thirties or early forties. Most of them are white, but there are a couple of black guys there too, both of them staring at me. They all seem to be nursing cans of beer or cigarettes; they're all psyched up, I can feel the vibes from right across the room.

'Come on, man,' one of them says, 'show us what we've paid for.'

His comment draws yells of approval from the others. I am stunned. Paid for? Is this why Jasmine wanted me here? Is this really what it's about: money? I feel a little sick but I don't have time to react.

Jim comes up behind me and places his arms around my waist. I can smell the beer on his breath and the sharp, acrid smell of his sweat. 'Just relax, baby,' he says quietly, his voice so soft suddenly that I understand that the others can't hear him. His arms are muscular, I can feel the flex of his biceps as he pulls me close, enveloping me in his arms.

I breathe in sharply as he slips my denim jacket off my shoulders. I look up into his eyes, seeking comfort and

47

safety and for a moment I feel that he is there to look after me. My jacket is dropped unceremoniously on the floor, cast away with a flourish that draws raucous yells of approval. Jim's fingers slip under my top, I can feel the rough grain of his skin against the smooth white flesh of my stomach. My face brushes his and the stubble is hard and spiky against my soft, white skin.

My top is lifted up slowly, exposing me inch by inch. The men around the room are chanting, hollering, filling the room with a noise that seems to vibrate through into my skull. Jim pulls my top over my shoulders, over my head and then throws it across the room. Instinctively I reach to cover myself, to shield my breasts from those leering, prying eyes. Jim takes my wrists and pulls my arms down to my sides. I look up for a moment, knowing that every single man is eyeing my breasts, encased in a lacy white bra.

'Nice, yeah?' Jim remarks. 'You guys like?'

Whatever else Jim says is drowned out by the chorus of beery approval.

'Nice packaging, let's see the contents,' is the only clear comment that I can make out.

Jim releases my wrists and I try to cover myself up again.

'Be a good girl now,' Jim cautions loudly. 'Be a bad girl and I'll have to put you over my knee, understand?'

His comment is greeted with laughter. My face colours red as I imagine myself being publicly punished. There is something cold in Jim's voice and I know that he hasn't just made an empty threat. He pulls my arms down again and then he simply unclips my bra and whisks it away. My face is burning with shame as I stand there and let myself be ogled by so many men. I am trembling and I can feel tears welling up in my eyes, but at the same time I don't want to give them the pleasure of seeing me cry. I close my eyes and wait for the sound to die down.

Jim reaches around and cups my breasts from behind. His rough hands squeeze and he flicks his thumbs back and forth over my nipples, making them stand out. I feel overwhelmed by his presence, by the heat from his body, the smell of beer and sweat, the feel of his fingers exciting my nipples. Despite myself I lean back against him, unable to resist the unexpected tremor of pleasure that passes through me.

'More! More! More!'

I open my eyes and see myself: half-naked, on display, the only female in a room full of men straining at the leash. I have never felt so vulnerable in my life. This is how Jasmine wants me to prove myself. This is how she wants me to prove how much I love her.

My skirt falls to my ankles and the room is silenced again. I am wearing nothing but a pair of skimpy white briefs, a thin film of lace that is pressed between my pussy lips. They can see that I am bare, that my pussy has been shaved clean in readiness. The thin covering of lace seems to accentuate the swell of my pussy lips. I have never felt so exposed before, never.

'Jasmine do this to you?' Jim demands, lewdly rubbing his fingers back and forth over the lacy briefs.

'Yes . . .' I whisper as he presses my panties between my lips, his fingers working back and forth, pushing gently into me. I am wet.

Jim nods appreciatively. He slips his fingers under my panties and into my sex, finding the wetness that betrays my excitement. He strokes me for a moment, working his fingers back and forth so that they brush my clit as he seeks the moisture that leaks from inside me.

'This girl's wet,' he announces loudly, taking his fingers from my sex to his mouth. 'Tastes good too,' he adds, laughing coarsely.

My panties are yanked down and then left to fall to the floor, a tiny bundle of white around my ankles. I am naked, exposed, on view to the voracious men around me.

'It's party time!' Jim announces. He steps away from me and starts to unbuckle his jeans. His eyes are fixed on me, and as I gaze at him I feel a tremor of fear and excitement. My nipples are hard, standing proud of my firm breasts and aching with arousal. My long legs are still trapped at the ankles by my skirt and panties. My bare sex is exposed and now every man in the room knows that I am wet with excitement. They know that I am wet, but do they understand that my excitement is tempered with fear? Do they care that I feel shame as much as anything else?

In moments Jim is naked in front of me, his hard cock jutting out obscenely. His body is muscular, his flesh clothed with fine dark hair, a tattoo etched across his chest and more on his arms. I can't take my eyes from him, yet I know that around me other men are also undressing.

'On your knees,' Jim snaps.

I obey instantly, dropping down on to my knees. I lay my skirt on the floor and crawl on to it, seeking safety and comfort with my own clothes. Jim steps forward, his hand ringed tight around the base of his hard cock. He reaches down and takes me under the chin, urging me closer.

'Come on, baby, this is why you're here,' he hisses.

I can smell the sweat from his cock and his balls, it overwhelms me, making me dizzy as I respond to it. I press my lips to his hard flesh, my tongue darting from my mouth to taste him for the first time. He is urging me on, mouthing obscenities as I start to lick him. There is a hushed silence from the rest of the room, but I have no time for them.

'Open your mouth!'

I open my mouth and he pushes his cock between my lips. His hard flesh powers into my mouth and I struggle to breathe, struggle to cope. He holds me in place as he starts to pump into my mouth, thrusting hard between my lips. I lap at his hardness, wetting my lips so that he can slide in and out. I almost slip at one point and instinctively I reach for him for support.

I hold on to him and start to bob my head up and down with his thrusts. His hard flesh fills my mouth repeatedly, thrusting into me, penetrating with a tense rhythm that I struggle to match. Each time he fucks my mouth my face is pushed into the wiry hair of his abdomen, filling my nostrils with the musky aroma of his sex.

'That's it . . . That's it . . .' he grunts repeatedly. Somehow his cock has swelled even more and his thrusts

50

are sharper, jabbing into my mouth again and again. He grips my hair in his hand and forces my face down as his cock explodes into the back of my throat. I gag as waves of come spurt into my mouth. I choke and try to get away but he holds me in place, forcing me to swallow his seed.

At last he releases me and I fall back. His cock is still semi-erect and coated with spit and spunk. He is smiling, looking pleased with himself. I feel dazed more than anything else. My mouth is suffused with his taste and my lips and face are splashed with sticky come.

'My turn now,' a voice snaps.

I look round to see that one of the other men is beside me. His thick cock is hard and leaking a jewel of fluid from the slit.

'She's not finished yet,' Jim objects. He motions for me to get down on hands and knees again. 'Look,' he says, squeezing a thick droplet of whitish fluid from his cock, still almost hard.

'Greedy bastard,' the second man objects. 'This is for all of us,' he complains.

Jim laughs. 'She's not finished with me, yet. But look, she's got plenty of other holes to be filled.'

The other man turns to his friends. 'I get her pussy first,' he announces.

As Jim grabs me and pushes his cock back into my mouth, the other man takes his place behind me. His fingers go straight for my sex, pushing in roughly between my bare pussy lips. I am already wet, but the roughness of his approach seems to amplify my desire, making me wetter and more aroused. The pleasure pulses through me, a jolt of sensation that makes me moan softly as I suck the last drops of semen from Jim's cock.

The man behind slicks his fingers through my sex and then grips me tightly by the waist. Jim pulls away, sated at last, and his place is taken by one of the younger men. I glance up at him and he smiles and licks his lips. My eyes sweep the room and I realise that most of the other men there are watching intently. A couple of them are already half-undressed, the others fully clothed, but from their rapt expressions I know that they are no less turned on than the others.

I manage to look back just as the man behind me presses his cock against the lips of my pussy. He looks at me and grins. 'You're nice and wet for me,' he says, 'just the way I like it.'

I sigh with pleasure as he slides his hardness into the wet heat of my pussy. He has been rough with his fingers but he is surprisingly gentle as he pushes his cock into me. He pulls me back as he presses forward, filling my sex with his until my backside is pressed down on his abdomen.

'Nice and tight,' he calls to the rest of the room.

The man in front of me touches my face and I turn back to him. His erection is inches from my face, nestling in a bed of wiry, black hair. My mouth still tastes of Jim's come, but as I start to suck on the younger man's cock the taste merges with his. I half-close my eyes and let the pleasure pass through me. Two cocks. I have never done anything like it before, not even in fantasy. I picture myself on hands and knees, being fucked roughly in the mouth and in the pussy, and I feel a wave of pleasure surge through me. The man behind me is fucking me harder, pulling way out and then slamming all the way in again, penetrating to the hilt and making me quiver ecstatically.

I suck greedily on the cock in my mouth, swirling my tongue around it, closing my lips tight, taking the hardness deep into my mouth. The younger man's motion grows more urgent, thrusting faster and faster. I cup his balls in my hand, holding him for a moment before he lunges forward one last time. I take his length as his body tenses hard and then he climaxes. I let his come pool in my mouth, trying to hold it, afraid that I'll choke again. He holds my face down, pushing his cock deeper into my mouth until I can hardly breathe. I start to swallow his spunk but when he withdraws his cock my lips open and I feel it dribbling down my face.

The man behind me thrusts into me one last time and then he too climaxes. I can feel his cock throbbing and twitching as he pumps his seed deep into my pussy. He pulls away and yanks me round. 'Suck this,' he orders. I turn and as I do so I am aware that his semen is dripping from my pussy and down my thigh. He still holds his cock in his hand, coated with his juices and my secretions. I lean forward and start to gingerly dab at his flaccid cock with my tongue, tasting myself on his flesh.

'Look at this, guys,' the younger man says. He reaches down and shifts my backside round so that the rest of them can see. He opens my pussy with his fingers, letting the warm spunk spill from within. I can do nothing to stop him displaying me so shamelessly as I am still sucking the other man's cock clean.

'My turn now,' announces the next man. He is tall, with dark blue eyes and blond hair cut short. He positions himself behind me and presses his erect prick against my pussy. He enters me quickly, sliding in and making me sigh with pleasure. His fingers seek my clit and I also shiver to climax as he strokes me there. I have finished sucking the man who has fucked me and as I look round I see that two of the other men are arguing over who is going to take me next.

'Don't look at them,' warns the man who has started fucking me. I must have hesitated because the sudden hard slap takes me by surprise. I yelp and turn to see that his palm print is imprinted on my backside, the pattern of his fingers a vivid red against the pale white skin.

'That's it,' Jim urges him from across the room, 'if she's bad then you put her in her place.'

I turn to Jim and pay for it with another hard smack. The intense pain seems to connect with my excitement, however. The sharp pain merges with the current of pleasure in my sex. The man who is fucking me pulls away suddenly; I feel the break in his rhythm and a twinge of disappointment. He has been fucking me so well.

'This way,' he orders.

He wants my mouth. I crawl around to him, eager to please him, aware that both my buttocks are still smarting red where he has spanked me. He is on his knees and pulls me forward so that my backside is high in the air. I look up into his eyes and see a cruel glint of pleasure that makes me feel nervous once more.

'Suck,' he snaps.

I begin to gently nibble the purple glans of his cock, lapping up my pussy taste, wanting to appease him more than anything else. There is movement behind me but I daren't turn round or falter. Somebody touches my pussy and I feel a thrill of desire once more. I need to be fucked. I need it more than anything. Fingers stroke across my pussy lips and down my thigh, tracking the dribbles of semen that have poured from me. And then the wetness is applied to my tight rear-hole. I try to shy away from the unexpected intrusion but am rewarded with a flurry of hard slaps across the backside.

'Keep still, honey, or you'll get a whole lot more,' a gruff voice warns me.

My bottom is smarting but the pain only seems to inflame my desire. Again my anus is stroked and touched, lubricated with the spunk from my pussy. I can do nothing but concentrate on the cock in my mouth, taking it as deeply as I can. My stomach is a knot of fear and excitement. Suddenly my hair is yanked hard and I am pulled away from the beautiful hard cock I have been sucking.

'Turn around.'

I turn to look at the man who has been lubricating my anus. He grins as he presses his fingers to my lips. I look at him and realise what he wants. 'Do it,' he orders. I take his fingers in my mouth and suck away the semen that coats them, trying not to think about where he has been pressing those fingers.

I have been lubricated for a reason, however. The man behind me stands over me and aims his hard cock between my bottom cheeks. I know that I have to relax, that it would be the only way to take pleasure from the pain of being sodomised. He presses down on me and I feel his penis pushing against the tight ring of my behind. I gasp as he starts to penetrate.

'This your first cock up the ass?' the man in front asks.

I close my eyes and nod as the man behind me pushes into me.

'This'll take your mind off it,' the man in front says, laughing, pushing his stiff erection towards my mouth.

I start to suck on his cock as the man behind me pushes deeper still. The man behind me is taking it nice and slow, inching his hardness into my rectum. When he stops I know that he is all the way in; the thought of it is supremely exciting. Soon he starts to fuck me, slowly at first but then speeding up as I relax into it. I have expected nothing but pain but that is not what I feel. I suck greedily on the cock in my mouth, sucking in my cheeks so that my mouth is nice and slippery.

The man behind me pushes his fingers against my clit as he fucks me harder. I shudder and climax suddenly, the thrill of orgasm transmitted back to him so that he gasps and climaxes too. As he rolls away the cock in my mouth erupts and I try to swallow more mouthfuls of come, but I am not allowed to. He pulls his cock from my lips and starts to pump it savagely with his hand, spurting thick arcs of sperm across my face and into my hair.

'Suck me now,' the man behind me commands.

I turn to him, unable to believe what I have just heard. Vaguely I am aware that my anus is glistening and still leaking his come, and that being on all fours means that it is distended and visible to everybody in the room. My face is dripping with streams of warm white come, thick droplets of it caught in my hair and the taste of it filling my mouth.

'Go on, bitch,' he whispers, 'do it.'

Bitch. That is what I have become. That is what Jasmine has wanted for me. I look back across the room: they are all watching intently, waiting to see just how far I'll go. I cannot resist.

There has been no lessening in the strength of his desire. His cock is still hard, coated with the slimy come that he has spurted deep into my rectum. My heart is pounding as I move slowly into place, lips half open, face down low, backside high in the air and fully exposed to an audience of strangers.

I open my mouth and take his hardness, smoothing my lips down along the glistening length of his flesh. I swallow my taste, the taste of my backside and the taste of his semen that has penetrated it. There is silence as I clean him up, lapping and licking up every trace of his juices. When I look up I see the looks of excitement on the faces of the other men. I am the bitch they have always dreamed of, the woman who will do anything, the slut who debases herself in the service of men. That is how much I love Jasmine, that is what I have to prove to her.

A moment later one of the black men is in place. His thick erection is soon in my mouth, lovingly licked and sucked, pleasured without complaint. I work my mouth and lips back and forth, greedy for the explosion of come that nestles deep in his balls. He withdraws, turns me over and begins to fuck me, pushing me flat on the floor and taking me roughly from behind.

While he fucks me another two guys are in place, pushing their cocks into my face. I suck first one and then the other, driven mad with desire as I service three men at once. I climax again, shuddering and crying out as the black man fills my pussy with his hardness. One of the men comes in my mouth and I suck greedily while the other masturbates himself over my breasts.

When the black man has climaxed in my pussy I am rolled on to my back and another takes his place. As I am being fucked on my back somebody else kneels beside me, turns my face towards him and takes my mouth. One of them massages my breasts, kneading the flesh and then pinching the nipples until I cry out in pain.

For a while there is nothing but a blur of bodies and pleasure. Somebody else fucks me anally, working his cock in and out until he climaxes. When he has finished he uses his fingers to feed me his come from my anus. Still another makes me kneel so that he can wank his cock between my breasts until he sprays me with thick waves of come that dribble down my chest and dangle like jewels from my nipples.

I do not know how many men use me. I do not care. This is what Jasmine wanted. This is what I have become for her.

Finally, I am faced with the second black man. He has been watching and brooding all night. Where some of the others have used me more than once he has held back. Now he stands above me, a tall, imposing figure, ebony-skinned and with a large erect cock that juts threateningly from between his thighs.

'Look at you, slut,' he murmurs menacingly.

He has been drinking and there is an angry contempt to his voice. Suddenly I remember myself. I have been so lost in the pleasure that I have forgotten myself. All of my inhibitions, all of my fears, come flooding back. I shrink back on myself, covering myself up with an arm across the chest and another between the thighs. My body is wet and sticky. Spunk pours from my pussy and leaks from my anus. It is smeared across my breasts and down my thighs. My lips are wet with it and my hair is matted together in places. I am worse than a whore. He is right. I am a slut.

'Come on, Clyde,' one of the other men says, but his heart isn't in it.

Perhaps Clyde has brought them all to their senses too. I feel the anger radiating from him.

'Look at you,' he repeats. 'Covered head to foot in spunk. You're a slut, aren't you? The worst kind of slut there is.'

'Please . . .'

'Open your mouth,' he demands.

I hesitate and then do as I am told. I have been spanked more than a few times and I do not relish the prospect of being punished by him.

'You've still got a face full of spunk.'

'Clyde . . .' Jim says.

'Look at her,' Clyde repeats. 'You expect me to put my cock inside her?'

'Please, let me go now,' I whisper.

Clyde shakes his head. 'I need to fuck you,' he tells me. 'But you're too dirty. You need cleaning up, woman.'

He stands in front of me, legs parted, looking down on my cowering figure. As I gaze upwards he takes his semi-erect cock in his hands and holds it towards me. I cry out in shock as the water bursts forth, a thick, warm stream of it aimed directly for my face. He pisses on me. Over my face, across my chest, in my hair. He bathes me in the warmth of his spray, covering me so that my skin glistens as it sweeps away the dried semen that has been caked on me.

'Open your mouth,' he orders.

I gaze up at him and he pisses over my face again, across my lips, my cheek, my forehead and into my hair. Slowly, hesitantly, I begin to open my mouth. The first droplets of his fluid pour between my lips and into my mouth. I swallow a mouthful and feel a frisson of arousal ignite deep inside me.

Jim steps forward a moment later. I get up on hands and knees, pushing my backside up, offering myself to him. I half-turn as he too lets loose, drenching my backside with his golden spray. I feel it running down my back, over my buttocks, dribbling sensuously over my anus, splashing against the bare lips of my sex. I touch myself and cry out with the most intense orgasm of the night.

I know that I will be fucked again. I have been pissed on to cleanse me so that I can be used once more. My anus, my pussy, my breasts, my mouth. Every part of me is theirs. This is what Jasmine has wanted for me. I seek oblivion in pleasure, and as I lie there, shivering with pleasure, glistening with moisture, I know that I will never be the same again.

My heart was still pounding as I opened my eyes. The visions were so strong, I could see myself so clearly: naked body glistening, bathed in pleasure and ready to be used again and again.

Dr Evans was behind me. For a moment there was silence and then I heard a movement. A hand reached across to touch me on the shoulder.

'Don't say anything,' Dr Evans whispered.

A hand reached down to touch me. Fingers skilfully worked their way down to unzip my trousers. I gasped softly.

'Just relax,' Dr Evans said softly.

My hard cock flexed powerfully as her fingers slipped under my shorts.

'That's a very powerful fantasy,' she whispered. 'I know that you need this.'

I closed my eyes and tried to picture myself as a woman once more as Dr Evans began to massage my aching hardness.

NAOMI'S SECOND TALE – HENS

Lucy Golden

Thanks to her short story collections, *Displays of Innocents* and *Displays of Experience*, Lucy Golden rapidly acquired a reputation for deliciously perverse – and often wet – tales of submission, domination and humiliation.

The following story is taken from *Displays of Experience* . . .

W endy shuffled uneasily, rattling the ice cubes in her glass and avoiding my eye until she could finally come out with it. 'Is this true what I've heard about Paul's last Friday?'

'I don't know. What have you heard?'

Her eyes opened wide. 'You want me to go into details?'

'No.'

'Well then? Is it true?'

'Probably.' I knew I was sounding childishly sulky and Wendy's silence was eloquent criticism. 'Yes.'

'For heaven's sake, Naomi! Why?'

'They made me!'

'Oh, come on! You're an adult. You could have refused.'

'They made me.' Repetition of the pathetic excuse only confirmed its inadequacy, but I carried on talking to hide the weakness. 'How did you find out?'

'Chris told me,' Wendy said. After a short pause, she continued. 'It's not the end, you know. Carrie's going to invite you to her hen-night.'

I frowned. 'She already has.'

'Yes, but now you're going to be the entertainment.'

Alec drove me there, to the wine bar where they had all gathered. We could hear voices and laughter from far down the street and found the door propped open with a chair to let in some cool air and the crowd of them clustered round a table at the far end. Alec pushed me inside, said he would collect me from Carrie's flat later, and then walked out. I turned back, utterly alone, towards the table of eager, grinning faces.

I only knew three of them: Wendy, Carrie of course and Natalie, her flat-mate. That was it; the rest I had never met before. It was only just seven o'clock, but the party had obviously been going for some time and they had effectively taken over the whole bar.

Carrie was full of herself, but she could afford to be: she would soon be off out of it all. She jumped up when she saw me and called me over. 'Right now, this is Naomi, who you all know about, and for tonight, she's all ours!'

Then she went round the table, introducing everyone I didn't know and ending with the one sitting in the corner, a pretty girl who was by far the youngest of the group and looked barely old enough to be there at all.

'This is Anna. She's Natalie's baby sister and only turned eighteen last week. She's down staying with us for the weekend and we've got to look after her, because she's very innocent.'

The little face wrinkled briefly before turning back to inspect me again. She had looked intrigued at Carrie's comments about me and in spite of the frequent giggles, there was an unsettling hardness about the girl. 'So what do we get to do with her?'

'Anything!' Carrie answered. 'Anything we like! From what I have heard about what happened at Paul's last week, she is game for anything.'

'What shall we do first?' one of them asked.

Almost immediately Anna piped up, 'Let's make her take her clothes off!'

'Anna! We can't do that here!'

'In the ladies' we could!' The girl's enthusiasm was childish, but there was no doubting her determination. Clearly she was not the least intimidated by being the baby of the group and a good eight years younger than me and it was her simplicity, her directness that really worried me. Whereas with most people lack of experience means they do not know how to start, with her it meant she did not know when to stop. I turned to Carrie.

'Look, I don't know what you have in mind or what Paul may have said, but I am certainly not doing anything like that.'

Anna carried on as if I hadn't spoken a word. 'I did it once to a girl at school; I took her clothes away and she had to stay there for hours!'

'Carrie!' I protested again. 'I mean it!' but it was as if I wasn't there. Anna's cheery excitement was frighteningly infectious, and when nobody else objected, I looked round the circle of faces and realised no one would. To suggest anything less would now just seem cowardly.

Anna turned to her sister. 'Nat, have you got those handcuffs?'

'They're in Wendy's car.'

'There you are, then!' Anna was far too pleased with herself. 'We can put her in them! Come on!' She leaped up, caught hold of my arm and started dragging me towards the back of the wine bar. Her sister, Natalie, and Carrie both followed, and also another girl, whom I didn't know.

Anna didn't let go until we were all crammed into the tiny toilets. Then she turned to me. 'Right then. Take your clothes off.'

I again looked to Carrie for help. She and I were roughly the same age, easily the oldest ones there, and I felt that made, or at least ought to have made, a bond between us. She seemed to feel nothing, indeed while Anna bubbled in eager excitement, treating the whole affair as little more than an entertaining schoolgirl prank, Carrie stayed menacingly silent. Anna was playing a game; she intended to win, but it was a game none the less. Carrie was in earnest; her eyes brooded with rigid expectation, displaying an explicit understanding of the situation and of the erotic implications which their plans held for me.

In contrast to both of them the third girl leaned calmly against the door as if bored; so far she had said nothing but when our eyes met she spoke. 'You might as well do it, you know, because if you don't, we'll only tear them off you anyway. Besides, my husband was at Paul's last weekend, so I know you're an exhibitionist little tart: you needn't come over all coy and innocent.' The calm frankness of her tone made the words all the more menacing.

When I still didn't move, Anna grew impatient. 'Right, you two hold her and I'll do it.'

'No!' I said quickly. 'It's all right. I'll do it.' I reached up to the buttons of my shirt and froze. I suppose I could have refused, I could have resisted and struggled but what would that have achieved? There were plenty more of them outside and if they needed more people to hold me, they would get them. Besides, if they already knew what I had permitted last weekend, on what basis could I pretend outrage now?

I trembled, looked round the waiting faces and was lost. When both Alec and Paul had beaten me last Friday, it had been glorious. I had felt so totally alive, so fulfilled, but it had been the presence of the other people that made it so. If no one had been there, had seen me being humiliated, and seen how aroused it made me, and how much that increased my humiliation in a magnificent accelerating spiral, the pleasure would not have been comparable. But they had all been men, and now my captors were all women. The evil of so perverted a persecution raised me higher than ever; I was even less a friend, even more a victim, surrounded here by my own sex than I had ever been before. It was that discordant stretching which held me in its grip. Shame and degradation, even the anticipation of appalling pain, pulled me back. Exhilaration, desire and pride pushed me forward.

So I unbuttoned the shirt, feeling their eyes scrutinising me as my skin and the neat white bra were revealed. The instant I took the shirt off, Natalie grabbed it out of my hand. My bra came next, though I held the cups over my breasts a moment allowing the briefest, lightest caress across my nipples before she snatched that away too, tearing the thin straps over my skin.

I unzipped the skirt next, slid it down my legs, stepped out of it and handed this to Natalie as well. This left only my knickers, modest enough at the front, but cut high and very revealing across my bottom. Knowing what they would see when I took that last item off, I stepped back until I met the unforgiving cold rim of the basin. Every day I had been checking in the mirror and I knew full well that the evidence of last Friday's caning was still clearly visible in thick red lines across both cheeks of my bottom. They were a less brilliant scarlet than they had been at first, but they were still undeniably there, clear irrefutable proof of what had been done to me. It could only make me the object of yet further derision.

Anna was impatient. 'Come on, take your knickers off. I want to look at you entirely naked.'

I pushed my knickers down and off, then just stood there clutching them. I didn't want Natalie to add this final trophy to her bundle, because there was no mistaking their condition. They felt sticky to my touch, and I would not have been surprised if she opened them out to inspect them thoroughly. Nor could I step forward, because although it was bad enough having them all standing in front of me, all unashamedly staring at my breasts and my pubis, it would be worse once they saw my bottom.

Anna, inevitably, insisted on more. 'Turn round. Let's see what the lads did to your bum.'

I turned slowly and it was Carrie, standing by my side, who immediately gasped.

'God, look at this! Look at the state of her! Here, turn right round and show them.'

Anna was equally enthusiastic. 'Wow! That's brilliant!'

I don't know how long they would have spent admiring the fading stripes if Wendy had not come in with the handcuffs. Natalie pulled the knickers out of my hands, but when she remarked how disgusting they were, Anna immediately wanted to see. She carefully peeled them open to peer in at the incriminating gusset and was enraptured and intrigued at the wet stain now revealed.

Meanwhile, Carrie and Wendy pulled my hands round behind my back before clicking the handcuffs tightly round my wrists. They closed with a firm solid click; obviously real ones, not some flimsy plastic toy.

Then Natalie went to the door, taking my clothes with her, and called out to the rest of the girls who all trooped in, laughing and jeering to see me standing there. I was made to turn round so that they could all inspect the marks across my bottom and several reached out to feel them, running their fingers along the raised lines that still crossed both cheeks. Some of them circled right round me, prodding and tickling and several pinched me: my thighs, my bottom and even my breasts, but they all kept coming back to the cane marks on my bottom.

Eventually Carrie led them back to the bar to eat, leaving me standing alone in the small tiled room, listening to the high voices and low music from the other room. Over the next half hour several came back and they all taunted me. Once another girl, not one of our party, came in. She stopped in shocked surprise to see me standing there, handcuffed and naked, and even asked if I was all right. A few seconds later she returned and held the door open while a man put his head round, grinning at the sight I presented.

Eventually, inevitably, when the door opened, it was Anna who sidled in. She didn't go into either of the cubicles, but stood at the basin studiously washing her hands and watching me continuously in the mirror.

Finally she turned round and tossed away the paper towel. 'Sit down on the floor.'

'Why?'

'Just do it.'

She tried to sound strong and decisive and if the nervous tremble in her voice betrayed her, it didn't defeat her. Her evident determination to overcome her own nervousness gave her an authority that I could not oppose. Unable to use my hands to support myself, I knelt down with difficulty then dropped on to my bottom on the cold tiles and sat with my knees together in front of me.

She squatted down in front of me. 'Open your legs. I want to see your fanny.' For all her nervousness, it was still just a game to her, and perhaps that was what gave her the assurance and confidence to press on. I slid my legs open as she stared down at everything now revealed between my thighs.

'More!'

I pushed my legs further apart still and she settled down right between my feet, leaning forward to peer at me closely. 'Have you peed yourself?'

'No!'

'You're very wet, you know.'

I said nothing.

'Is it true that you're an exhibitionist?'

'No.' Yet we both knew I was lying.

'Then why do you get so wet when you are naked in front of everyone?'

'I just do. I can't help it.'

'I think you're an exhibitionist.' She was considering, like a curious, precocious child as she stretched out the tips of her fingers to push my outer lips further to one side. 'Your fanny's ever so big. Has it always been like that?'

'I don't know. I suppose so.'

She now carefully eased the inner lips open. 'And all ragged,' she mused. 'How many men have you slept with?'

'I don't know.'

'Well, guess.' Her head tipped to one side as she continued her examination.

'I suppose about ten.'

'That's not very many for someone as old as you. How many times altogether have you shagged someone?'

'I don't know. I mean I've been married for nearly five years, so quite a few.'

'I've never done it at all; I'm a virgin. Maybe that's why your fanny looks so battered and used compared to mine.' She was still casually opening and closing my lips with the very tips of her fingers as she contemplated my answers.

'Five years? That's about, what? Two thousand nights? I suppose in all that time you must have done it, well, at least a thousand times. That's a lot. A thousand times. A man's cock going in there.' And as she spoke she slowly pushed her finger inside me, right up until her hand was squashed against me and she could push no further. Then she slowly pulled it back out, gazed at its new sheen and even raised it to her nose and sniffed.

She stood up and stared down at me. 'I'm glad I came tonight. You can get up now if you like.' The door banged as she left me.

It was about twenty minutes later that Wendy and Carrie returned carrying a long khaki mac and announced that I was being taken down to a pub. They didn't unfasten my handcuffs, simply draped the mac round my shoulders and buttoned it down the front.

The pub was already crowded, but we found a semi-enclosed corner where we settled round a table. I was pushed right inside with Carrie on one side and Wendy on the other. A huge mirror emblazoned with an advertisement for some whisky or other hung directly opposite me so that every time I looked up, I caught the reflection of our little group. Eight girls were dressed up for an evening out; one sat nervously in the middle, the empty sleeves of an incongruous and rather grubby mac waving about her like flags. I looked ridiculous, wearing a huge mac on such a hot summer evening, but at least I was covered.

Two men up on stools at the bar kept glancing over at us and as soon as Natalie went up to get our drinks, they tried to pick her up. They were quite scruffy, as if they had just stepped off a building site, and looked entirely out of place in what was mainly a young persons' pub. Their matching thinning hair, huge beer guts, and sagging jeans were so similar they might easily have been brothers: Tweedle-dum and Tweedle-dee.

I was given a pint of lager, but as I couldn't pick it up, one of the others periodically held the glass to my lips. Then Anna reached across from the far side of the table and tipped it so far that much of it spilt round my mouth and ran on to the mac. They found this very funny, and would deliberately tip it further and further. Wendy then held up the glass with one hand, pulled out the collar of the mac with the other, and tipped up all the rest so that it ran, ice cold, down my face, my chin, my neck and chest and trickled all the way down my stomach to form a pool on the bench between my thighs.

As one of the men returned from the toilets, he paused by our table; he knew something was going on, but couldn't tell what it was. 'Your friend must be bloody hot in that mac!'

All the eyes turned on me as Natalie answered. 'Well, yes, but that's all she's wearing. I've got all her other clothes in here.' She held up a carrier bag. 'See?' And she took them all out, dropping them on the table one by one. 'Skirt. Blouse. Bra. And here are her knickers. Would you like to keep them? They're pretty well creamed.' They dangled from her fingertips for a second before being snatched away and engulfed in his huge fist.

I could hardly hold my head up, could feel my face blazing red as he stared down at me, mesmerised, licking his great red lips. 'She's a cracker, she is!'

He returned to his friend at the bar, and I saw them pawing over my knickers, but still continually looking over in our direction. Once, when Carrie knew they were watching, she turned and unbuttoned my mac, all the way. She didn't pull it open, but lay it loose across me, threatening at any moment to fall away. The mirror opposite now showed a thin strip of white skin down the middle of my body, which widened fractionally with every movement. With my hands still held behind me, my movements were restricted, but when I lifted my shoulders, the mac slipped more until the gap between my breasts was almost a hand's width across. Beneath the table, I swung my knees apart briefly and, above the table, the whiteness was visible down to my waist. When I looked down, my pubis was exposed.

The other man climbed down off his stool, and strolled down towards the toilets. As he approached us, Wendy started to replace the mac properly over me, but just as he passed, Carrie, on my other side, turned to help, and made sure that in doing so she had to pull it right open briefly so that for a few seconds one of my breasts was fully on display. All the girls burst out laughing and everyone else in the pub turned round to glare at us, and stare suspiciously at me.

When the pub closed, we set off to walk back to the flat that Carrie and Natalie rented. The night was warm and fine, and as we crossed the open car park behind the new shopping centre, we found a figure hovering furtively in the corner of the stairwell. It was one of the men from the pub who had obviously stopped to relieve himself.

Carrie called to him. 'Hey, mister! Do you want a blow-job?' All the others immediately screamed with laughter, while the man tried to squeeze even further into the darkness. Carrie grabbed hold of my arm, dragging me across to where he was now hurriedly refastening his trousers.

'Here! You've been eyeing her up all night. Have a proper look!' and she lifted the mac right off my shoulders and away, leaving me entirely exposed in the middle of the open square, unable even to use my hands to cover myself. The man finished fiddling with his trousers and turned suspiciously. Slowly he crossed the short space towards us, his eyes never leaving me, and stopped, a little unsteadily, a couple of feet away. A broad grin developed, spreading stupidly from ear to ear.

'Very nice! Very nice indeed. Nice big round titties. I like that.'

Carrie turned and looked appraisingly at me, then reached up and pinched my nipple. 'Yes, they are rather nice. Would you like her to suck you off? She will if you want.' Her smirk betrayed that the deliberate crudeness wasn't for his benefit, but just to cheapen me.

His grin widened even further, and then suddenly switched off. ''Ere, you 'aving me on? You the law, or something?'

'No! Not at all. It's a genuine offer. We're just playing a game and my friend Naomi would like to suck your cock. If you don't believe me, you feel her. I bet you'll find she's sopping wet. You feel her cunt.'

The man's piggy eyes narrowed and he took a step forward as his huge grimy hand landed on my stomach and crawled down. He dug his way between my thighs, roughly pushing his fingers along my tender lips before one thick stubby finger was suddenly thrust right up inside me. He laughed stale smoke and beer fumes into my face.

'Well, you're right about that, darlin'. She's fuckin' drippin', she is!' He continued rummaging his fingers through my pussy as I tried to pull away. 'Well, I gotta admit it's been quite a while since I've had anythin' but my own fist round my cock, so if she wants to give me a little suck, I ain't gonna stop 'er.'

Without removing his right hand from between my legs, he started to fumble at his zip with the other. The girls circled eagerly round us and young Anna pushed in so close she could have reached out and touched me. The man finished undoing his filthy trousers and finally pulled his hand away from my sex and held it out.

'Bloody hell! Soppin' wet, she is!'

'Where? Let me see!' Anna grabbed his wrist and inspected the evidence shining across the man's filthy fingers. 'God, so she is! Look! Gross!'

When she let go, the man laid his hand on top of my head as if blessing me. 'Down yer go, then, darlin'. Down yer go!'

I allowed myself to be pushed down until I was squatting in front of him, glad to be away from his groping hands, glad to be able to open my inflamed pussy to some cooler air, but sickened at the sight and smell of what was dangling there waiting for me. Like the man himself, his penis was short, stubby and pasty, and he held it in one hand, waving it at me as I tried to bring myself to put the revolting object in my mouth. Anna was leaning down, watching intently, fascinated revulsion on her childish face. She glanced eagerly from me to the man's cock and then back to me again.

'Come on, Naomi. I want to see you actually do it.'
When I didn't move immediately, she put her hand on the

back of my head and pushed me forward until the man's cock was brushing against my cheeks and lips.

I opened my mouth and let the foul thing plop in.

'God, she's doing it! She's actually doing it!' Anna was ecstatic, beaming round at the others, but suddenly she stood up and addressed the man. 'You mustn't, you know, actually come right in her mouth. I want to be able to see all your stuff coming out.'

The man smiled and chucked her under the chin. 'If that's what you wanna see, little girl, then you shall.'

She squatted down again beside me to be on a level to see better exactly what I was doing, utterly enthralled and utterly repulsed.

At first I couldn't move. I could feel his cock, only half warm as if it were only half alive, lying like a slug across my tongue. His sour smell filled my nostrils and a rancid unwashed taste filled my mouth. But although I hadn't moved, it was stiffening of its own accord and lengthening steadily in my mouth. I ran my tongue once round the thing and it twitched and swelled. His foul wiry pubic hair was no longer tickling my lips and nose, because I could no longer get the whole of his cock in my mouth. It was fatter now, too, and as I finally made myself work my tongue round beneath the slimy ridge it inflated rapidly. The head was so large that it was difficult to breathe and finally I released him and pulled away. Anna looked aghast as the thing waved glistening wetly in the twilight.

'God! It's huge!' The comment was mostly to herself, but she reached out to grab hold of it in her little fist, her fingers barely reaching round it, and pushed it back into my mouth. From the corner of my eye, I saw her hands disappear under her skirt.

The man reached down himself and gripped his cock round the base as I worked my lips over the head. He was starting to grunt now and his free hand gripped my hair, pulling and twisting painfully.

'That's the way, darlin'. Fuckin' magic.'

The ring of girls sniggered and pressed closer.

His breathing was becoming noticeably laboured and his grunting and encouragement more continuous. Suddenly he grunted even louder, a single strangled 'yes!' and pulled away. I quickly shut my eyes and my mouth as the fountain of cold slimy semen splashed down all over my face.

Anna was absolutely fascinated. 'Ugh! Gross! Look at her. It's all over her face! God! Let's find someone else and make her do it again!'

The mac was draped round me again and we moved off, the others laughing and singing as they danced their way through the empty shuttered streets while I stumbled after them with the man's sperm drying on my face and the sour taste of him still in my mouth. At a Chinese takeaway, Anna found two more men and got her wish.

We waited in the garish lights, peering in at the two customers inside, while Natalie went in to speak to them. We couldn't hear the words, but the meaning was all too sickeningly clear so that when they all turned towards us at one point, Anna knew immediately what was required and calmly pulled my mac wide open. I watched the expressions flow over their faces as I was displayed again, and as I saw the desire in their eyes, I felt the need reciprocated through my own body; utter uncontrollable lust that shook me and a feverish longing to be displayed completely and not just displayed but abused.

It was obvious that they took little persuading as they followed Natalie out and I was directed down an alley at the side of the building where we stopped beneath a security light. The girls gathered round again as one man unzipped his trousers and reached in to pull out his cock, already semi-erect, and wave it right in front of my face. He quickly fed the tip between my lips and was soon fully erect and grunting as he clutched my head and forced himself deeper and deeper into my mouth. When he shoved his hand down inside my mac to maul at my breasts, Anna, who had again pushed up close beside me, immediately pulled the mac away entirely so that everyone could watch his huge hands clutching at my breasts and squeezing my nipples as he pulled and clawed at me.

75

Anna again asked him to pull out before he climaxed so that she could watch, and he pulled back almost immediately as thick jets of semen erupted right in front of me and spattered over my eyes, down my cheeks and even in my hair.

Anna was jubilant. 'Ugh! It's just so gross! Look at all that stuff!' She was brazenly clutching at her own sex with both hands and almost jumping up and down with excitement. 'Now the other man! Now the other man!'

He slowly, nervously, unfastened his jeans and pulled out his cock. It was quite long but entirely soft, and although I licked him, sucked him and tried everything I could, his cock just didn't erect. Soon it was clear to everyone, including him, that he had had too much to drink to be able to get an erection. Carrie started to scoff, but Anna pushed her way to the front again.

'I know! Slap her with it! Slap her across the face!'

The man seemed a little bemused at first, but he stepped back and swung his long penis from side to side, slapping me across my mouth and cheeks, still wet with his friend's ejaculation. Five or six times he spattered against me before the first man called out from the mouth of the alley and this one rezipped his trousers and hurried away.

They wouldn't give me back the mac as we continued on our way. The other girls ran on ahead, laughing and singing, waving the mac in the air as if determined to wake people up and encourage them to peer timidly from behind their lace curtains at the spectacle I presented as I hobbled after them, handcuffed, naked and defenceless through the empty street. My face was covered with the drying sperm of two strangers; my legs were smeared with dirt and mud. But, as we came in sight of the flats where Carrie lived, my pussy was running with the juice of utter, unbelievable, arousal.

Her flat was on the second floor, and I could see everyone hanging over the balcony watching for me. They cheered raucously as I appeared at the front entrance and began to climb warily up the open concrete stairway through the centre of the block to where they waited for me at the top, crowded on to the little balcony.

'Look at her! She's filthy! Look at her face!'

I was led through the little hallway and straight into the living room where they finally took off the handcuffs and let me rub the angry red weals round my wrists. Music was already blaring out, several wine bottles had been opened, and glasses were scattered around. Carrie came right up close to me, slopping wine from her glass with every step, and reached up to pinch my nipple, pinch it hard.

'You're disgusting, Naomi. Look at you! You'd better have a shower, while we prepare for your party.'

I was grateful for the chance of a shower, but the implication of her other comment was less reassuring, and I walked through to the bathroom trying to work out what she could mean. I had assumed that I would be allowed to shower alone, but Natalie, Anna and one of the others decided they wanted to come with me.

They didn't even let me draw the shower curtain across, insisting that they wanted to keep an eye on me all the time, so I stepped into the bath, took down the shower head and turned the water on. The cascade running down my skin was wonderful. At last I could wash off the ejaculation of the two men and all the dirt that I had collected during the evening and I played the jet all over me, rinsing my hair as well as my body and getting rid of the sticky beer that had been poured all over my breasts. But standing under the running water made me discover that I desperately needed to pee, and although I put it off for as long as possible, the drinks that had been forced on me during the night were becoming too much. I finally admitted my need to the three girls.

'Well, go on then,' said Natalie, taking the shower head out of my hand. 'You might as well do it there. Sit on the end so we can see.'

'No!' I protested. 'Come on, Natalie, please at least let me use the toilet.'

'No,' Anna interrupted. 'You can do it in the bath; I always do.' Her directness, her total lack of shame still took me aback but, with no choice, I sat down as I was told, but even this was not enough.

'Hold your fanny open. I want to see the piss coming out.'

How could anyone be so callous? How could a girl so young and, by her own admission, so inexperienced, be so completely shameless and depraved? I couldn't act like that now and at her age had been painfully shy and thoroughly naïve. Yet it was her look of innocence that enhanced the humiliation of debasing myself at her command. I pulled my lips open while she leaned over to watch intently as I urinated down into the bath.

After I was done, Natalie kept hold of the shower head and as I continued sitting there with my legs wide apart and my lips held open, she played the spray of water over my sex and down as far as my bottom. The intense silence as they watched was broken by Anna. 'Nat? Stick it up her bum.'

'Don't be daft! It wouldn't fit!'

'Take the handle off. It unscrews.'

I am sure the others were wondering, as I was, how this young girl knew so much, but she was right. When Natalie had got the handle off and the weak spray had been reduced to a pathetic dribble, I was made to kneel down on all fours on the bottom of the bath.

I felt Natalie's thin fingers and sharp nails pulling and tugging at me as she pressed the metal ring against my anus. I had never in my life had anything pushed into me there and the muscles naturally closed to prevent any entry. It was Anna, again Anna, who had the solution.

'Squirt some shampoo in first. That should lubricate it.'

The small sharp round nozzle of the bottle was pressed against me and then a sudden squirt of it shot inside. The shampoo bottle was removed and this time when the shower hose pressed, it slipped through the ring of muscle and suddenly the hard alien shape was crawling up inside me, a cruel invasive presence that lacked any sympathy with my own warm and yielding body. The flood of water emphasised the foreignness and maliciousness of this encroachment, and I shuddered, pushing her hand away as I felt myself being bloated and filled.

Once she withdrew the tube, the need to expel the water was paramount. I needed to get up, somehow to stagger over to the toilet and relieve the unbearable pressure, but I couldn't do it. I couldn't risk stepping out of the bath and had only got up into a squatting position when the need became too strong and, despite the gloating audience, despite the shame, despite the ridicule of the baying girls watching me, I let myself go where I was.

Their howls of laughter brought all the others running in from the living room to see what they were missing. They arrived just as Natalie was rinsing round the bath.

'You should have called us!'

'Yes, do it again!'

So a second time I was made to kneel down in the bath and they all watched avidly while a little shampoo was squirted into my bottom and then the long hard end of the shower tube slithered deep inside and a second slow jet of warm water filled my guts.

The bathroom was too small to fit everybody so this time they insisted that I go out on to the balcony. I stumbled out, doubled over but so desperate to release the churning contents that when Carrie set down a small plastic bucket in the middle of the balcony, I no longer had the stamina to protest. They all stood round in gales of laughter as I was led up and allowed to squat over it and could finally release all the water from inside me. So public a display of so intimate a process was alone almost enough to flood me to orgasm.

When I was led back into the lounge, dry again, the chairs had all been pushed out to the edges of the room, making space in the centre where a large towel was spread out.

Carrie giggled when she saw my reaction. 'Don't be shy, Naomi. Come and lie down here, on your back, right in the middle where we can all see you.'

The girls all filled their glasses, perched on chairs or took up positions on the floor, and settled back to watch although, after I was arranged to Carrie's satisfaction, I noticed that several changed their positions, shuffling down to somewhere they would get a better view between my legs. Even little Anna, who had been given pride of place in the centre, edged up closer.

Carrie returned to her seat and called to one of the others to begin. She came out, knelt down beside me and made me part my legs and raise my knees so that I was completely revealed to everyone, as if I were at a doctor's surgery. She remarked at how wet I was, and then the others laughed because I was blushing, but every sneer, every humiliation heaped on me only made it worse. My clitoris was swollen; my lips were swollen and now I was lying spread-legged in front of all these people, most of them strangers, while they probed and toyed with me as they wanted.

The girl started applying some sort of roll-on gel all over my pubis, but when I asked what she was doing, she wouldn't tell me precisely. 'Just making you pretty.'

She smeared it all over my triangle of pubic hair at the front, and even between my legs, right on to the lips themselves. For this she had to pull them open, and the continual pressing, pulling and squeezing inevitably made them swell and moisten even further than they already were. Even this, an entirely automatic reaction, led them to mock and jeer, so she continued for some while, deliberately prodding and teasing just to disgrace me.

Next the girl had a cloth and a bowl of water and she started to wash me. It was the cheers that met this which caused me to look down again, trying to find out exactly what was being done to me. It was then that I discovered that what she had been putting on was a depilatory cream and as she wiped away the cream, all my pubic hair was coming away with it. I was being left as bare as a newborn child.

When she was done, all the others crowded round to see, to touch, to feel the smooth delicate skin. Even Wendy came over and peered down at me, before reaching out to run gentle fingers across the smooth hairless surface of my swollen sensitive lips.

Carrie was delighted. 'That's much better. Now we can see what you've got and now it's play time. In a minute I want to watch you frig yourself, but first, we're going to blindfold you so you won't know who's doing what and spank you. Four from each of us, I think. Turn over on your hands and knees.'

I pleaded with them then to let me go. I really begged and pleaded, literally on my knees, to be excused that. Last week I had received twenty-four strokes with a cane and the pain had been unbearable. Yet I would have preferred to receive that again, even double that, to the utter humiliation of being their toy, to be spanked like a naughty child, to suffer every indignity they could dream up and finally to have to masturbate in front of all of them, in front of friends, work colleagues, strangers and even little Anna. In truth, I knew even before I started that they would not listen to me. And maybe I was not convincing enough, because even as I knelt there, I could feel the growing arousal that belied my tears and that was welling up deep in my pussy. I knew that when they spanked me I would scream and sob and make an exhibition of myself just as I had done the week before, and I began to suspect that they wanted to show that they could better the men in what they put me through.

I was made to kneel on the floor while they all gathered in a semicircle behind me but as the blindfold was placed over my eyes, I was lost. I could feel my sex, newly exposed and vulnerable, throbbing in anticipation of the pain to come and the blindfold was soaking wet with my tears even before I was kneeling in position, my forehead resting on the floor, my bottom straight up in the air.

The first four slaps landed in quick succession straight across my cheeks. They were not nearly as hard as the cane and as I waited for the second four, I began to think that I might survive this. Then the second girl started, much harder and her blows were more accurately placed together in one spot on one cheek of my bottom. I heard my own crying as I waited for the shuffling that told me the next girl was ready. I leaped up the instant the first

81

landed, for she had deliberately aimed much lower, right across the tops of my thighs. The rest of hers were the same, a band just below my bottom that stung worse than anything that Alec or Paul had ever done.

I thought at first this was probably Anna; such a cruel variation seemed characteristic of her, but I was wrong because Anna was next. I heard her innocent voice (she didn't care if I knew which one she was) telling me to kneel up straight and I knew she had something evil in mind. Even so, when her first vicious slap landed not on my bottom but across the side of my left breast, I screamed and my hands flew up to protect myself at the same time as I tore off the blindfold. She just told me that if I didn't take my hands down, she would put the handcuffs back on me. I hesitated before dragging my hands away, and then knelt there, my hands at my sides as I waited to receive the remainder of the child's cruelty. My degradation now seemed complete, and I bore the remainder of her slaps, a second on my left breast then two across my right, with few tears. Someone I didn't know followed Anna and she hit me on the front of my thighs. After that came Wendy, my friend, but she avoided my eyes as she smacked me at least as hard as any of the others, aiming one stroke at each cheek of my bottom and one to each breast. The last girls followed Wendy's pattern as well and as the final stinging slap burned across my nipple, I collapsed on the floor in tears, my thighs twisting and quivering with a longing I was given no opportunity to satisfy.

They did not replace the blindfold after that but made me kneel back on all fours again as they all crowded round me. Immediately their hands were swarming all over me; nipping and squeezing, nails scraping across the tenderest areas, scratching at the hand prints, pinching at the bruises. My swollen and tender breasts hung beneath me, aching for some tenderness and Anna again focused on my breasts. I remember wondering whether it was jealousy because of the minuscule swellings beneath her own sweat shirt, for she was blatantly bra-less and if it hadn't been for her tiny nipples poking out, she could have passed for a boy. She was carefully examining my face as her fingers pulled and tugged at my breasts, dragging out my nipples as far as she could stretch them, and always watching avidly to gauge my reaction. Suddenly one of my nipples was clamped viciously tight and I looked down to find she had attached a wooden clothes peg to the delicate nipple. The instant shock as the peg closed completely winded me, so that I couldn't cry, couldn't speak, couldn't breathe. She smiled when she saw my agony and calmly took a second peg, stretched out my other nipple and then for a few racking minutes held the jaws open around the nipple and then smiled even wider as she slowly let the spring close on to me.

Within seconds, my nipples had gone so numb that the pain was surprisingly bearable, but it returned the instant she took the pegs off again and Carrie told me that they now wanted to watch me masturbate.

I tried refusing and I tried pleading again, but they ignored all my pleas and settled down to watch again, a comfortable and respectable audience waiting to be amused by the naked entertainer who was spread out before them. Yet I was wet, visibly and undeniably wet and lying on the floor as I was with all of them gathered round me, they could all see the evidence. It was so shameful and the worst part was that I knew what effect their presence would have. I was already aroused from everything that had already been done to me and, as my fingers slid down between my lips, to have them there witnessing my own self-abasement was the final glorious straw that destroyed all my self-respect.

Still, they all watched me closely, and each time I was nearly there, when I was tantalisingly close to coming, they made me stop and only allowed me to play with my nipples until some of the urgency had died down. Then I was permitted to touch my clitoris again, until I was once more nearly ready to come.

Ultimately it was Carrie who fetched a carrot from their kitchen and ordered me to use that to bring myself off, but they all giggled at the obvious ease with which the thing slid inside me and the way it immediately triggered my complete loss of self-control as I climaxed so loudly.

And it was Natalie who then fetched a plate of butter and a second carrot and insisted that I push this one into my bottom. The utter humiliation of being made to masturbate seemed insignificant compared with what they now demanded. The thing looked huge, although in truth it was not much thicker than a man's cock, but I pushed it deep into the yellow butter, and it looked even more disgusting and threatening once it was shining ready for its sickening purpose. Yet it was also more alluring, and the prospect of being publicly stretched in so intimate a place by so huge and obscene a phallus made me tremble. I did finally succeed as they all sat watching in rapt attention.

And it was finally Anna who demanded that I pull it back out again and put it in my mouth and lick it clean.

And at the end, they carefully replaced the blindfold and settled me down on my back again. And as I lay there, still naked, each of them came in turn and squatted over my face while I licked them. I could see nothing, just felt each of them come to take up her position; the feet either side of my head and then the person squatting and a vulva was lowered down and pushed on to me. I had never in my life kissed a girl like this, and had never considered how different they might be. Some had masses of thick hair; some had none, although whether these were completely shaved or just underneath, I don't know. Some had huge lips, thick fleshy curtains that filled my mouth; some lips were so small I could hardly find anything there at all. Some held themselves above my mouth; others pressed down and rubbed themselves against me. Some were wet and flowing the instant my tongue reached up to them; others were relatively dry. Some climaxed almost at once; some were slow and demanding but they all stayed until they were satisfied. Some were sweet and fragrant; some were bitter and sweaty and I am certain that one of

84

them had only just been to the toilet and hadn't wiped herself at all, not in either place.

And every one of them came to me, all eight presenting themselves in a steady succession. Each aroma that filled my nostrils was subtly different but all unmistakably feminine and all pungently aroused. I had no idea which was which, and I was sorry for that. I would like to know which was Anna: one of them had seemed not only small and closed, but also clean and sweet, and I could imagine that as being Anna, barely eighteen and, as she had confessed, a virgin. But had she meant just with men or was I the first person of either sex who had tasted her vulva and brought her to orgasm? Equally, Anna could as easily have been the one who came to me straight from the toilet, dirty and sour. In many ways that seemed more likely.

And I would like to know which was Wendy. We had been friends for many years and she had taken my side several times earlier in the evening. Yet when the opportunity had arisen, when I was lying there on the floor, naked and helpless, when she had the chance, she too followed the lead of all the others, coming to squat over my face, compelling me to lick her sex, to push my tongue into her vagina, to nibble at her clitoris and accept her juice smeared across my mouth, added to the juices of the others. Whichever position she had taken in the queue, even if, out of some last vestige of loyalty or sympathy, she had hesitated as long as she could, she had ultimately taken her place above me and forced me to lick her to orgasm. Someone, and maybe this was Wendy, had also presented the tight bitter ring of her anus and required me to lick her there as well. Just because we were friends, it hadn't stopped her adding to my humiliation, but I would have liked to know how far she had gone. I needed to know how to react the next time we met as friends; whether I should say nothing about it, whether I could ask for an apology, or whether she would order me to take my clothes off again, lie down on the floor and lick between her legs until she climaxed.

And which of them was last in the line? Who had lowered herself over me when she was already so wet that I almost drowned in the river of her arousal? Who was it who then leaned down and pulled my legs so wide apart and slapped me? Who had known that after the first vicious stinging blow across that most tender part of my body that I would lift up my hips in a wordless appeal for another? And a third and then a fourth landed straight across my open sex, until I again made so shameful a spectacle of myself by losing control as I was convulsed in another racking screaming climax.

THE DISCIPLINE OF
NURSE RIDING

Yolanda Celbridge

Yolanda Celbridge is our most prolific author, and her books have so far fallen into several distinct groups, all devoted to the joys of corporal punishment. The Maldona series is an extraordinary chronicle of erotic fantasies revolving around the complicated Rulebook and the physical upbraiding of miscreants according to its strictures.

Meanwhile, novels such as *Memoirs of a Cornish Governess* are an 'erotic Baedeker of the UK', to use her own phrase. Along with its sequels, such as *The Governess at St Agatha's* and *Miss Rattan's Lesson*, it is set in a pre-war world of corsets and chastisements, in which the essence of ladylike deportment can only be instilled through the unsparing use of disciplinary implements.

The Discipline of Nurse Riding and *Police Ladies* are further examples of Yolanda's growing feel for uniform fetishism – incorporating more than a few bizarre treatments and unusual punishments, of course.

A list of Yolanda's Nexus novels also includes:

C loughton Wyke Health Hydro was approached by a winding road up to the clifftop, from where the dusk lights of Cloughton sparkled seductively in the distance. Beyond that were miles of reeds and waving sand-dunes, and the grey twilit ocean. The property was surrounded by a tall hedge, backed by rows of poplars, and there was a small gatehouse at which the taxi halted, to announce their business. The attendant – a lady dressed in a black fur coat against the evening chill, and with legs in black dress nylons – picked up a telephone and spoke briefly. Wearing black shiny boots, she emerged from her cubicle with a bucket and spray-gun, and sprayed the wheels of the taxi before raising the heavy barrier pole and allowing them to proceed. As they approached the great white crenellations of the mansion, through wide lawns, gardens and orchards, Prue looked back and saw that behind the poplars was a wire fence about twelve feet high, ringing the whole property. Even in the darkness, everything looked immaculate, and the wire fence gleamed. As she stood by the front door in the comforting nest of her cases full of clothing, Prue watched the taxi chug into the night, and nervously rang the doorbell.

'You are late, miss!' were the first words Prue heard at her new home. 'The Mistress of Hygiene takes a dim view of unpunctuality.'

She looked up and saw a young woman of about her own age holding a clipboard and dressed in a cross between a maid's and nurse's uniform. She said the 'new nursemaid' should follow her. She introduced herself as Nurse Heckmondthwaite and, without offering to help Prudence with her cases, she about-turned, flicked her pretty rump and strode briskly off on clacking high heels. Her uniform was white: a very short skirt and a tight blouse, under which her torso seemed unfettered by underthings. At her waist was coiled a curious tube of black rubber, with a knobbly bulb at the end.

Her blouse and skirt were made of thin, shiny rubber, although her stockings were cream-coloured, of finely meshed nylon, with a chocolate-brown back seam. Prue could see bare white thigh above her plain stocking-tops and suspenders, but could not see if she was wearing rubber knickers too, or any at all. The nurse had slim and finely muscled legs beneath her shiny cream stockings. They walked along a polished tile corridor, in pastel pink, and smelling medicinal, with vases of pretty flowers livening the pink walls, on which mural paintings depicted naked, or nearly naked females at various hygienic exercises. Prue asked the nursemaid if only females were treated here.

'Why, no, maid!' exclaimed her companion tartly. 'You'll see plenty of males – and not just pictures.'

Prudence was shown into a long corridor, this one painted white, like a real hospital. All along it were doors with little windows, like cells, and into one of these she was shown. It was a pleasant, if spartan room, with a bed, washbasin, table and an easy chair. The floor was dark-green linoleum with a little fluffy pink rug, and there was a steel-frame hospital bed, with crisp fresh linen and dark-grey blankets. There was a little vase of peonies on the table, which Prue thought nice, and the curtains were a cheap but bright flowery cotton; the window looked out over the grounds, and in the distance the night sea glinted.

'You can unpack later,' said Nurse Heckmondthwaite. 'I expect you'll want to get straight to bed, as reveille is at six in the morning. First, I'll take you to Matron's office, and have you enrolled.'

They proceeded down the corridor, at whose end the nurse pointed out the 'privy'; Prue glanced in, and saw a row of open shower stalls, equally open Turkish squatter commodes, a plunge pool, and cabinets which the nurse said were steam and sauna baths, and were in service twenty-four hours a day. A hot, acrid smell emanated from the privy, and Prue asked what a sauna was. The nurse explained that, like a steam bath, it was a hot cabinet, to cleanse the skin and revitalise the inner organs, only it had dry instead of steam heat. During a bath, the skin was stimulated by beating with birch twigs, beneficial to the circulation and 'moral wellbeing'.

'The sauna and steam bath are an essential part of hygienic therapy,' she said, 'alternated, of course, with an ice plunge. And the birch treatment is most important, for male and female subjects alike. It is Finnish: Finland is not very far away.'

Prue shivered, and said she believed the birch was a very painful punishment, and that there was a certain baleful magic about the word *birch*, and she had read of schoolboys being birched naked as punishment. She blushed when she said it. Nurse Heckmondthwaite smiled with thin lips, and replied that the birch in bathing was therapy, not punishment, but that therapy and punishment were truly the same thing.

'There *is* a magic to the kiss of the birch, above all other instruments of healing,' she said, 'and it is wonderful, not baleful magic. The cane kisses with one tongue, the birch with many.'

She recommended Prue take a short sauna before bed, as it would relax her after her journey.

They entered Matron's office, where Nurse Heckmondthwaite curtsied; Prue did likewise, and was introduced to Miss Bream. The Matron was a woman of about thirty, with a crisp white uniform of starched cotton, a pink pinafore over it, and, like the nurse, a very short skirt which rode up above embroidered cream stockings which appeared silk. Unlike the nurse, Miss Bream did wear a very obvious corselage under her blouse, for her bosom

91

struck Prue as quite . . . inordinate. The woman's breasts were massive, and cunningly supported and thrust outwards by what must have been a very stout corset, which also pinned her waist to pencil thinness. Even under blouse and pinny, her nipples stuck out so huge and pointed that they seemed to wear a separate little corset of their own. Her hair was cut severely short at the back and sides, a lick of hair curled back from the forehead, in a boyish style. She too wore alarmingly high shoes with pointed toes and heels. Miss Bream looked over her pince-nez spectacles and nodded at her, then looked at the paper Nurse Heckmondthwaite handed her, and frowned.

'Late, eh, Nurse Riding?' she said, in the blunt accent of the north. 'Can't have that. Unhygienic behaviour has to be nipped in the bud, my girl. Tenner fine, I'm afraid.'

Prue looked puzzled.

'Nurse Riding . . . that's you, girl.'

'O . . .' Prue beamed, then frowned and said in embarrassment she was not sure she could afford so much.

'Out of your wages, then,' said Matron, 'only it's four pounds extra for the paperwork. Of course you may take a treatment instead – four strokes of the cane. I dare say you'd prefer that.'

Prudence gasped, but neither the nurse nor Matron seemed to think this anything extraordinary.

'A . . . a caning?' she exclaimed. 'On my first day?'

'Certainly. But four is hardly a caning. Don't tell me you are unaware of our hygienic rules, and don't tell me you've never been caned before. This isn't the namby-pamby Home Counties.'

'Of course I have, Matron,' Prue exclaimed proudly.

'Well, then. Four is only a tickle. Think it over; if you opt for treatment, you can take them in the morning after breakfast.'

'I . . . I think I will take the treatment, Matron,' said Prue, her heart beating. 'Since I am a nurse, now.'

'Very well. Four, then. On the bare, of course.'

'O! Of *course*, Matron,' murmured Prudence.

The rest of her interview did not take long; she signed some papers, was given a rulebook to study, and her basic uniform, a pile of clothing which smelled lovely and crisp and fresh. Matron said her training would take a week, but that she would be learning 'on the job'. Prue blurted that she was so looking forward to being a kind nurse, and wearing her lovely crisp uniform, and healing patients . . .

'Nurse Riding,' Matron said crisply, 'we do not have "patients" at Cloughton Wyke, we have subjects. And our subjects need no kindness from their nurses: they need, and get, hard and proper discipline.'

At her room, Nurse Heckmondthwaite bade Prue goodnight, and said that after breakfast, she would be shaved and given her deep cleansing, before being sent straight to her apprenticeship. In the morning, she had only to follow the other nursemaids to the breakfast hall.

'Shaved?' said Prue.

'Your whole body,' said the nurse, 'lady's place and all. Unless you are already shaved down there. Nursemaids may keep their fluffy heads, the Mistress thinks girlish vanity is not unhealthy, within limits. Goodnight, nursemaid.'

Prudence stripped, looked at herself in the mirror before wrapping herself in her towel. She ran her fingers through her curly mink, and looked at the fleshy pink lips peeping coyly beneath. What a pity it had to be shaved! And yet . . . there had been something curiously exciting about Miss Macardle's bare mons. To be bare seemed suddenly desirable, with the lips of her gash no longer coy . . .

The privy seemed deserted at this midnight hour, but when she opened the door of the sauna to a blistering wave of hot air, she saw another body in it, lying face up and naked on the upper bench. Prue grinned and felt a bit silly – she had her towel, but, of course, one bathed naked, didn't one? Gingerly, she unfolded her towel and sat on it, on the lower bench by the other girl's toes. At once, the heat caressed her like a glove. The other girl sat up.

"Lo, nursemaid,' she said. 'Be a duck and fling some water on the stove, will you?'

There was a bucket and ladle, beside a selection of sponges and birch flails, which Prue thought looked more like branches than mere twigs. She obeyed, was rewarded with a ferocious hiss and gasped as a wave of hot humid air seemed to flatten her. The other girl laughed.

'First time?' she said gaily. 'New, eh? I'm Jess. My real name's Jezebel Rise, but everyone calls me Jess.'

Prue introduced herself. Jess was a brunette, her hair neatly pinned back in a bun, and her body glistening with droplets of sweat. Her breasts shone like dew, and they were deliciously formed, thrusting out full, and hanging quite proudly to her ribcage, as though stretched and inflated. Prue was reminded of Miss Bream, and wondered if some mysterious hygienic process was at work. Between Jess's legs, the fount gleamed like a polished vase, smooth as her whole bare body. Her shoulders and buttocks were impressively broad, as her waist was narrow. Pinned in her pierced nipples were two large silver rings.

'Still got your rug, eh?' said Jess boldly. 'Well, you'll feel better once it's off. Any hair under the pits?'

'Just a little,' said Prue nervously. 'I shaved the other day, and waxed my legs too, but —'

'I shave every day,' said Jess, 'usually in the sauna, 'cos you don't need lather. Doesn't take long once you get used to it. Surprising how hairy a girl really is, when you look into all the nooks and crannies. The Mistress Hygienic says we may be descended from apes, but shouldn't look like them. My bumhole gets so hairy! It's so much nicer now – smooth and slippery and more efficient if you see what I mean. I'll razor you here, if you like, once the sweat softens you up. Save the trouble tomorrow morning, dry shaved in full view of the nurses. Usually they do it after your bumsquirt, or "colonic irrigation", in hygienic parlance, which we all must have.'

Prue sighed with the pleasure of the heat seeping into her, and began to rub her hands over her sweating body.

She felt quite wet very suddenly, and Jess said it was the steam: one did not want the heat to be too, too dry. Eager to make conversation, Prue said ruefully that it was her first night, and already she had incurred punishment, and was to get four strokes of the cane, on her bare.

'Four,' said Jess. 'Why, that's not punishment, it's a tickle. Surely you've been caned before?'

'O, dozens of times,' lied Prue.

'Well then! Bum up and bear it! I had two sets of eighteen, in rapid fire, a couple of days ago, with only five minutes' pause between sets. My, it smarted! And still does! Here, look.'

She twisted round and showed Prue her buttocks, which were mottled deep crimson.

'How awful!' said Prue, forgetting her thrashing of the male, which did not seem awful. 'Is it always on bare?'

'Always. What other caning is there?'

'Nurse's discipline does seem strict. What had you done?'

'Had to bathe a lady subject, and I didn't have the water cold enough. One set for that, and then to excuse myself I explained there weren't enough ice cubes in the fridge, and that got me an extra set, for whingeing. Can't say I didn't deserve it. Actually, I got my own back 'cos, on our next session, I gave her forty with the tawse, as part of her hygiene – *and* made her wear a discipline after – that's a hair shirt. Here, do you like my nipple rings? I got them last week, when I passed my test for second level. If I make third level, I'll be able to have my quim pierced too, and have a ring there, and maybe even a *guiche*, you know, a nice little ring between your gash and your furrow. The more tin, the more respect! And a tattoo . . . mmm!'

Prue said she felt quite faint, and Jess said it was time to take a plunge. She took Prue's hand and led her from the cabin to the pool, where she pulled her into the icy water. Prue shrieked at the shock, then broke out in giggles and sighs as she realised how lovely the cold was. They splashed in the water and she felt her nipples go all

hard and tingly; Jess's nipples were hard too, and big, like
little brown teacakes. Suddenly she touched Prue's fount.

'You don't mind if I have a feel?' she said. 'Just to see
how thick you are, for your shaving. My, you do have a
big mink! When you're bare, you know it will always grow
again, and even thicker – should you want to look like an
ape.'

Prue said she did not want to look like an ape; it seemed
taken for granted that the vivacious brunette was indeed
going to shave her now, and Prue felt attracted towards
the young nursemaid, and was in no mood to resist. They
returned to the cabin, and Jess invited her to join her on
the top bench, where it was hottest. Before she sat, she
picked up sponges and birch rods, and said that it was
good fun to 'loofah' each other, then tickle with the
'twiggies'. Prue felt the sponge scrub her belly and breasts,
then her back, then thighs and when Jess came to her
quim, she scrubbed quite tenderly and for quite a long
time, until Prue felt all tingly down there.

'That is nice,' she said dreamily, and began to do the
same to Jess, finding that her sponge lingered most on the
stiff nipples and fleshy quim-lips, which hung quite wide
and showed the neat glistening pink within, in pleasant
harmony to the pink of their lathered bodies. Jess quite
brazenly put her fingers to her gash and opened the lips
further, inviting Prue to 'scrub deep'. Prue did so, and felt
the hard little button of Jess's damsel tremble as her
strokes brushed her. Jess breathed deeply.

'I think we are ready for twiggies,' she murmured. 'I'll
show you how it's done.'

Prue turned round, and felt the birch rods sweep lightly
across her back, making her shiver with a stimulus that
was halfway between pain and tickling. Then she turned
to her front, and received the same treatment on her
shoulders and belly, and then full on her breasts – to her
surprise, she liked that best, and felt her nipples harden
even in the wilting heat. Seeing her arousal, Jess began to
beat her harder, and Prue did not object, not even when
Jess parted her thighs and began to flagellate the soft inner

skin, and allow the birch tips to brush the lips of her quim, which were now noticeably swollen and standing free from their tousle of mink-hair. Jess whispered that the cane was a sweet kiss, but the birch the embrace of love itself. Then she said it was time for her shaving, and Prue waited, sorry that her 'birching' was over, while Jess fetched her razor.

She made Prue lie down on her back and spread her thighs wide. Prue shut her eyes and drifted into blissful dreams as she felt the cool swish of the razor against the tender skin of her lady's place, and then she opened her eyes and saw Jess intent on her task, feeling the nipple rings stroke gently over her belly as the razor purred at her fount, and thought only of Jess. She reached down and began to stroke Jess's hair, and then was ordered to lift her thighs right up to her breasts.

Now Jess applied the razor to her furrow, and her bumhole itself, and Prue gasped as the razor tingled right on the tender skin of her arse-bud. She did not object, nor flinch, but felt her juices begin to trickle on her thighs and mingle with her copious sweat. Jess signified her work was over by planting a single kiss, with closed lips, right on Prue's gash, and, in passing, her chin brushed Prue's tingling damsel, making her cry 'oo!' and sigh. When it was her turn to birch her new friend, her hand trembled.

Jess opened her thighs, and held up her breasts, inviting Prue to 'tan teats' first of all. Prue did so, gingerly at first, but then harder and harder at Jess's insistence, until the breasts were deep pink and the nipple rings jangled loudly at each birch-stroke. Jess asked if Prue liked her teats, and were they big enough from the vacuum treatment, and soon she would be able to 'wear the lyre' like Miss Bream. She said Prue had lovely firm teats, and treatment would make them a dream. Prue concealed her puzzlement.

'O! O!!' Jess moaned. 'It's so nice. Who needs men, when we girlies can have such lovely fun together? Jerks, the lot of them, only fit for having their bums whipped and squirming with the spuling tube in their holes. How I love the wet slap of a cane on a male's bare croup! Don't you love to spank boys, Prue? You must have done, a bit. And that is why we are all here, really, isn't it? Because we love nurse's discipline, the harder the better.'

Prue lied cautiously that she had never spanked a boy before, but said that the idea did excite her. She asked what a spuling tube was, and learned that it was the same as an irrigation – the Mistress loved German hygiene, with all these fearfully scientific names, and *Spültherapie* was one of her favourites.

'You will make a very thoughtful nurse, Prue sweet,' Jess purred. 'The teats are so sensitive, in every way. To kisses and strokes ... and when it's done right, a teat-whipping under the lyre is pure beauty. How I long to feel it myself! Now let's have a taste on my thighs and my gash, and don't forget my bum. You know, when you pass the test for level three, you are permitted to take vinegar baths, like the subjects. Balsamic vinegar is wonderful for cleansing and toughening the skin. I've had one – sneaked in after Mrs Shapiro had hers, and had a whole half-hour before I was caught. Got thirty with the cane for that! – balsamic vinegar is costly, and supposed to be reused for the next subject, you see. But it was worth it, my bum hardly felt a thing. And I had my revenge, the next time *la* Shapiro got a vinegar bath, I had a really big pee in it first! O, yes, *that*'s good –' as Prue swished Jess's thighs and swelling quim-lips.

'Now for the juiciest bit,' said Jess, her eyes heavy with pleasure. 'My bum, please, and make her smart well.'

She turned round and spread her buttocks wide so that her clean-shaven furrow and anus bud were fully exposed.

'All over,' she whispered, 'and hard, nursemaid.'

Prue had lost all pretence at 'hygienic' treatment, and began to flog Jess's naked fesses with all her might. The birch rods, soaked in their sweat, were quite heavy, and dealt a resounding wet slap at each impact on Jess's trembling bare, which began to crimson very rapidly, the new caress overlaying her older colouring. At each stroke, Jess shivered and gasped, 'Yes ... yes ... harder,' until Prue's sweat was as much from her flogging exertion as from the sauna. She was scarely surprised to see Jess's fingers flick down between her open thighs and across her quim, where she quite blatantly began to caress her hard little damsel.

'You don't mind me diddling,' she panted, 'it's just that you whip so beautifully, Nurse. We're not supposed to – hygiene isn't supposed to be pleasure – but everybody does. It is all hypocrisy ... O yes, up there, catch my bumhole, *how* it stings! Who is to prove we take pleasure? O, lord yes, that's good, I'm going to spasm ... O yes, yes, beat me, Nurse, beat my bum, sweet Prue!'

Prue continued her flogging which was now more than dutiful, as she felt her own quim and belly fluttering in the excitement of the other's pleasure, and her own fingers found her clit as she watched Jess tremble in her spasm. Panting, Jess sat up and turned to place another kiss on Prue's gash, this time open-mouthed and with her tongue flicking on Prue's distended nubbin.

'Such a big clitty,' she exclaimed. 'Do let's diddle.'

She began to lick Prue's damsel with rapid and expert flickers of her tongue, sending shudders of pleasure up Prue's spine. Prue's fingers now began to rub and tweak her own tingling stiff nipples, and she felt herself close to orgasm. She heard Jess pause to whisper:

'Northumberland, such a strange place, with all the legends of the sea. Sometimes, at night, you can hear the foghorns calling to ancient drowned ships, like *this* – it's called a mermaid's kiss ...'

To Prue's surprise and pleasure, she began to moan, or chant, softly at first then louder and louder, her open mouth fully cupping the lips of Prue's quim as the tongue continued its devilish flickering on her stiff clit. The vibrations seemed to shake every atom of Prue's body, as Jess bellowed with a mournful yet voluptuous sound that was just like a sonorous foghorn! Prue shivered in approaching ecstasy, and as Jess moaned her hymn of worship, she spilt over into a gasping luscious frenzy of orgasm.

No words were necessary; the two women paused to kiss full on the mouth, their wet tongues embracing, and then Jess pushed Prue's head between her own parted thighs. Prue did not resist, but fastened her mouth on Jess's quim-lips and with her tongue found the stiff damsel. Flicking against it, and causing Jess to shake with her pleasure, Prue began to moan softly against the swollen quim-lips, filling her lungs and roaring as she felt Jess flutter and moan in her new climax. Prue's fingers were busy on her own clit, still throbbing and stiff, and as her moans grew to a bellow, and Jess clutched Prue's hair and pressed her head to her quaking belly, both women climaxed a sweet second time.

Suddenly the door clattered open, and the two shocked tribadists saw, wreathed in steam, the glowering figure of Nurse Heckmondthwaite.

'This noise!' she cried. 'Enough to waken the drowned. Caught in flagrante, you wicked maids! You, Riding – I knew you were a bold one, arriving late. Well, it seems you have more to look forward to in the morning than a mere scratching of four. Four dozen will be more like it.'

'It was my fault!' cried Jess. 'I'll take the flogging.'

'Shut up, Nurse Jezebel,' snapped Nurse Heckmondthwaite. 'You shall take *a* flogging, but Miss Riding here shall take *the* flogging, along with her nursemaid's irrigation.'

She uncoiled her rubber tube and stroked the bulb insolently under Prue's trembling chin.

'And if I'm nice to Matron, I think she will permit me to administer both at the same time.'

'Redheads!' whispered Jess. 'They are all the same. Vitriol is so unhygienic!'

'I didn't know Miss Heckmondthwaite was a redhead,' said Prue. 'Her hair is brown, like yours.'

'Didn't you see the roots?' sneered Jess. 'She's embarrassed – why, I don't know, she is just as much of a goop whatever colour her hair is.'

The two nursemaids squatted beside each other in the privy, amidst the bustle of early morning ablutions. The women all wore their nakedness easily, and few bothered even to wear bathrobes for the short walk from bedroom to privy. Some who carried themselves proudly were adorned like Jess: with body piercings, metal armbands on waist, arm, thigh or ankle, variously gorgeous earrings or necklaces, or tattoos on their buttocks, bellies and even breasts.

There was a momentary hush as a new nursemaid entered the privy, and all eyes turned to her. She was nude like the others, but her nudity was so adorned that her body seemed almost clothed. She sauntered amongst her comrades as though inspecting them, and flicking a wet towel playfully at an occasional rump or bosom, which was greeted either by a pleased simper or a sullen scowl. She was dramatically tall, a good six feet in her heels, and her upswept hair was jet black. She was very slim, and her body rippled with lithe muscle, except for her fesses and teats, which actually jutted from her body in a way that looked like a surreal artwork, had it not been for the sensuous quivering of their firm, distended flesh. Alone amongst the nursemaids, she was not barefoot, but wore black shoes with sharp heels and toes, which seemed to be waterproof, of rubber Prue thought.

On her forearms and upper thighs she wore golden bands like an apothecary's snake, and the same on her left ankle, extending up her calf like a boot. Her extruded belly-button was pierced, and wore a black jewelled brooch, with a little gold tongue and eyes, and this was the head of a tattooed snake which grew across her fount and belly from her wide, thick quim-lips. In the centre of her swelling buttocks, she wore an array of sparkling studs, each one seeming separately pierced, and around them a tattoo which was whorls of stars and moons, growing from the cleft of her furrow and embracing her fesses like a swirl of gold dust. She wore a ring through her quim-lips but, as well as that, they were held apart by two clamps attached to tiny gold chains which fastened to the bands on her upper thigh.

Her open quim showed bright glistening pink within, and the effect was not so much shocking as proudly intimidating, as though daring a challenge of some sort.

Jess whispered that being 'tent-pegged' was a rare privilege: by baring her quim so boldly, she was proclaiming her sovereignty. Chains criss-crossed her belly, leading from her quim ring to her nipples, which seemed very wide, like young apples, and were encased in black metal covers like pointed thimbles. Two further chains looped round her neck from her nipples and supported her conic breasts, although their quivering firmness suggested no need of support. They were duly pert, but at the same time so ripe and heavy that they should hang: but they did not. The waist above a flat belly was a pencil, and her naked flesh showed deep indentations, as though she slept in a corset. Her skin was pearl white, and glowed with fragile translucence that belied the taut frame beneath, and the cruelty of her wide, disdainful lips.

'That's Henrietta Farle,' murmured Jess, 'she's third level. She could easily make fourth, and be a Sister Surveillant like Heckmondthwaite, but she prefers to stay here in barracks, as we call it. I think she just likes to lord it over the rest of us scrubbers. She's so proud of her body, the hag! All the treatment she's had . . . she can take the lyre, with those teats.'

Prue asked if all the adornments meant something specific, and was told no, nurses like Henrietta simply enjoyed certain tolerances. As for the lyre – well, Prudence would soon know: it was the most hygienic of treatments, being at once stern discipline and subtle beautification.

'Watch out for Henrietta, she's easy with her affections when you least expect, then tight when you want her to be easy. Power like hers is not just rank, it is aura.'

Prue whispered mischievously that she supposed Henrietta had a tent-peg for her bumhole too; then asked Jess if she had ever been in Henrietta's power. Surprisingly, Jess blushed and looked down.

'Sometimes . . . it is hard to resist naked power,' she whispered, then shivered and shifted on her commode.

As if summoned, Henrietta Farle stalked towards the two squatting nursemaids and glared haughtily down at them through the steam.

'Well, Jezebel,' she said, flicking her towel right against Jess's quim, 'I hear you have been up to tricks – corrupting a new nurse, and letting her bum smart for your naughtiness. Scarcely ladylike, my dear.'

She peered at Prudence, and then more specifically at her bare breasts, holding her gaze quite impudently on her nipples; Prue suddenly blushed.

'You're lucky, nursemaid, that it's only Heckmond-thwaite who's going to beat you. If it were me . . . why, you'd be making commode standing up! And you couldn't bear the touch of your tunic against those teats for quite a while . . .'

Suddenly she flicked her towel against Prue's nipples, very sharply. Both nursemaids watched the curl of Henrietta's ripe bare buttocks as she swaggered away.

'The vicious bitch!' Jess swore quietly. 'I'd like to tan her bum – and that Heckmondthwaite. Each wants Miss Bream and hates the other . . . intrigues are like that here, Prue. But I promise you'll always have *my* affection.'

Solemnly, as though to demonstrate her sincerity, Jess made a great fuss of wiping Prue's bottom for her, which made them both giggle. Then they showered hot, plunged into the icy pool, and scampered glistening and naked to their rooms to dress. Jess cheered her by saying she would be issued with further clothes in due course, once settled in – 'they may not pay much, but the kit is quite decent.'

Prue unfolded her new uniform, crisp and clean and starched. She had a white skirt, very short, like Nurse Heckmondthwaite's, and a pair of dark blue nylons, with matching rubber-soled 'sensible' shoes – evidently, the wearing of high heels was for the senior nurses only.

But she was pleased at the frilly blue bra, suspender belt and lacy nylon panties which were flimsy and almost see-through. Her blouse was white nylon, and her blue bra was quite daring and visible through it, as it pressed quite tightly against her breasts. Over that she had a thin blue cardigan which she allowed to hang open. Her ensemble was completed by a pretty blue starched bonnet. Jess said she looked tight, meaning it as a compliment, and said they really were good about kit: if a nurse did well, she could get oodles of nice things, silks and cottons and leather, and even latex, like Heckmondthwaite. Prue laughed, and said she already had such things, quite daring ones too, in her cases, and hoped she would get the chance to wear them. Meanwhile, she said she felt lovely in her tight things, the casing of her uniform like a shell, protecting her and at every move reminding her of her body.

They proceeded to breakfast in the refectory, a large hall with tables seating a dozen nurses at each, and with the meal served from trolleys by 'skivvies' as Jess called them: nurses who were purging some imperfection or other with this minor penance. There were perhaps fifty nurses; a dozen of them sat adorned in their fineries at high table above them. Jess said that the High Mistress of Hygiene rarely dined in hall, and in fact rarely appeared at all.

'What if no one has committed any imperfections?' asked Prue innocently. 'Who serves the food then?'

Jess's only reaction was to laugh and shake her head. They tucked into their breakfast of thin toast and margarine, plentiful tea, salami, and hard-boiled eggs, with pots of acrid rhubarb jam. Prue was assured this was very hygienic. Jess said the piquant salami was reindeer meat, 'from over there', gesturing across the North Sea.

'Much more humane than eating battery-farmed stuff,' she said between mouthfuls. 'The reindeer gets a jolly good life and plenty of reindeer snogging, before he pops his clogs. Not like our poor pigs and chickens, cooped up and tormented their whole miserable lives, as if they were human beings!'

After the meal, the nurses scurried off to their duties. Prue reported to Miss Bream, for her novices' examination, along with five other maids for their weekly irrigation.

The Matron was brisk and her smiles were brief as she ordered the nursemaids to strip and fold their uniforms neatly. Miss Bream paid especial attention to the neat removal of the girls' panties and bras, telling them not to tear them off hurriedly, but to slip them over thigh and breast with ladylike calm and precision. She first complimented Prue on how smart she looked in her new kit, and then Miss Bream unhooked her bra for her, and put her finger into the elastic of her panties, at the cleft of her bottom, to help her draw them down. Miss Bream said that the others should take their irrigations first, under the surveillance of her assistant, Miss Gageby, while she gave Prue her medical. Prue was asked to lie down on a sort of operating table, while in the bathroom she heard whooshes, gurgles and squeals of the girls at lavage. Matron prodded and poked her, inserted her rubber-gloved fingers into every orifice, pressing quite long and hard in her holes to establish that she was 'vaginally experienced'.

'But your bum is nice and tight, Prue,' she said, 'so I guess you are an anal virgin.'

Before Prue could react, she added that nurses were grown-up maids, and were free to organise their own affairs, as long as they observed hygienic principles. She felt Prue's breasts, squeezing her nipples quite thoroughly, as though she were a mere subject of scrutiny, to be handled like an animal, or naked slave girl. Miss Bream said that she had lovely firm teats and, with training, she might be privileged to take the lyre. Prue asked what that was, and Matron said it was a device for the enhancement of the breast, which caused considerable discomfort.

'The principles of the Hydro,' she said, 'say that the controlled pain of discipline is the cleanest beauty.'

Then it was time for Prue's irrigation. She was strapped to a small table which spread her arms and legs wide, with her furrow and buttocks stretched wide on a raised platform. The other nurses, their irrigations complete, were allowed to stand and observe. Matron inserted two rubber tubes into both her holes, and turned on a jet of hot water whose pressure at the root of her anus made her buck fiercely. This was sucked out, then a new jet entered her hole, now of freezing cold water. As the irrigation went on, she no longer tensed her sphincter muscle in resistance, but relaxed to welcome the spurts which filled her to brimming.

The fillings grew longer and longer, and each time Prue was ordered to hold the liquid inside her before evacuating. She said she felt about to burst, but Matron said that after a while she would get used to it, and even enjoy it, and that she should enjoy, too, the privilege of being bound for treatment. On her nakedness were fastened the eyes of the sullenly beautiful Miss Gageby, who kept brushing an errant lock of hair from her brow as she manipulated the taps. The door opened and Nurse Heckmondthwaite entered, bearing a long knobbly cane with a splayed tip. Miss Bream sighed, and said that they came to the matter of Prudence's chastisement.

'It was Nurse Heckmondthwaite who reported your imperfection,' said Miss Bream, 'so it shall be she who administers correction. I have determined the sentence, of course, after consultation with the Mistress of Hygiene, who graciously conferred with me on this matter. She thinks it healthy, Prudence, that you should so soon experience public correction of your own person, as a first lesson in the harmony of hygiene and stern discipline, which we ourselves must welcome even as we administer it to our subjects. The sentence, Prudence Riding, is twenty-one strokes of the cane, on bare. Normally, for such an offence, you would be stripped and bridled, and led through Hydro to refectory to bend over the high table. However, as you are a novice, you shall be chastised before these nurses only. Instead of public bridling, I am going to apply an irrigation of chilled oil, and you will please hold it in for the duration of your chastisement.'

There was a ripple of laughter from the nurses as Prue squirmed on the rush of freezing liquid which spurted forcefully into both her holes. Trembling, she tightened her sphincter, so as not to let the slightest dribble escape her anus and slit. She heard Nurse Heckmondthwaite lift the cane and swish it twice through the air, and then suddenly the implement caught her squarely across her naked buttocks. She jumped, and her sphincter tightened involuntarily with the searing lash of pain on her bare flesh. Tears leaped to her eyes but she did not cry out.

She looked round helplessly as her head jerked in her pain; she saw the nurses smiling, or else pressing fingers to mouths agape; Miss Bream had one hand inside her Matron's tunic, as though scratching her breast-flesh, but her fingers seemed to linger on her noticeably swollen nipple; Nurse Heckmondthwaite's face was flushed, her eyes heavy and her lips twisted in a rictus of ardent pleasure. The caning was slow, clever agony, like a white-hot sword crushed into her naked flesh. The strokes took her expertly, at every part of her croup and tender furrow, the cane's tips stroking with cruel precision a hair's breadth from her quim-lips. But she did not protest, not even when the terrible twenty-first stroke caught her cruelly on her anus bud.

'Good,' said Miss Bream.

Prue sighed in relief that her punishment was over, until Nurse Heckmondthwaite respectfully reminded Misses Bream and Gageby, unctuously careful to address them properly as 'Miss', in deference to their rank: the nurse-maid Riding was previously sentenced to take four.

'Deliver four,' said Miss Bream. 'Tight ones . . .'

Four more strokes! The cruellest of her beating cracked on Prue's bare buttocks. Her insides full to bursting, she squealed through clenched teeth at each cut, while the other nurses giggled, and Heckmondthwaite grunted in cruel satisfaction, at the frantic wriggling of her buttocks and swollen belly. At last, she heard Matron's instruction to evacuate, and now she sighed long in relief as she let the freezing oil spurt from her holes. She was unbound, and stood trembling before her tormentor, her eyes misted with tears. She thanked Nurse Heckmondthwaite and Miss Bream for their thoughtful punishment, and de-clared herself truly cleansed. Nurse Heckmondthwaite seemed a little disappointed, but Miss Bream smiled, and told her in a brisk voice to shower and dress, as her tasks awaited.

'You have to assist in the treatment of two subjects today,' she said, 'one female and one male. As you already seem sympathetic to the matter of correction, Prudence, you might be permitted to do a little more than assist.'

ROUGH SHOOT

Arabella Knight

Arabella Knight is one of our most popular authors, specialising in delightful tales of dominance and discipline. The judicious use of the cane and tawse abounds in her special correctional academies, as wayward young women are taught how to behave and soon develop something of an appetite for the pleasures of punishment. Her settings and themes have included an all-female community on a remote Hebridean island (*Candy in Captivity*); a specialist fashion house with a unique way of training students to be *corsetières* (*Sisters in Servitude*); a wartime team of young Wrens using novel means to interrogate their quivering subjects (*Conduct Unbecoming*); a spoilt girl being sent by her despairing guardian to an education establishment with a difference to learn the penalties for disobedience (*The Academy*); and the heiress to a large mansion disguising herself as a maid to discern its true value, and discovering that beyond the oppressively strict regime lies a world of delicious torment (*The Mistress of Sternwood Grange*).

The following story is taken from Arabella's second collection of Nexus short stories, *Brought to Heel*. The first collection is *Taking Pains to Please*. Arabella has also written a number of Nexus novels:

The Academy
Conduct Unbecoming
Candy in Captivity
Susie in Servitude
The Mistress of Sternwood Grange
Intimate Instruction

Lady Alice strode purposefully down the draughty corridor along the east wing of Strachayle Castle. Approaching a large, mullioned window, she stopped abruptly, turning to instruct her maid scurrying in her wake.

'As for the Godolphin girls, Miss Edwina will have this bedroom and I shall place Miss Charlotte in there. During their visit, as their personal maid, you shall occupy the box room at the end of the landing, girl.'

'Yes, ma'am.' The maid nodded obediently.

'Strictly speaking,' Lady Alice continued as she fingered the window sill for traces of dust, 'the rough shoot is a gentlemen's sporting weekend but I am obliged to Lady Godolphin and so have agreed to receive her daughters. It will complete their coming-out season.'

Heather, the maid, relieved to see that her mistress had failed to discover any dust, merely nodded. Lady Alice would have dispensed brisk discipline if her finger had detected any evidence of a lazy maid. But the moment of danger, and the threat of a sore bottom for Heather, had passed. She sighed.

'London debs frequently prove to be as spirited as they are inexperienced,' Lady Alice pronounced as she inspected the curtains closely. 'See to it that there are absolutely no nocturnal adventures. Understand me, girl? No midnight excursions.'

'Yes, ma'am.'

Lady Alice drew her lorgnette swiftly up to her piercing eyes. The lenses flashed as the mistress inspected her maid. 'Girl,' she barked, 'did not the housekeeper issue you with a clean, starched apron this morning?'

Heather blushed. Squirming under the glinting lorgnette, she nervously palmed the crisp apron at the curve of her thighs.

'You have managed, I see, to soil it already. I shall see to it that tuppence is deducted from your wage this sabbath to defray the extra laundering costs. I will not abide slovenliness in my maids. Go straight down to the housekeeper's office and ask her for a clean apron, girl.'

'Yes, ma'am.'

'And for two strokes of her tawse.'

Heather bowed her head, meekly accepting the prescribed punishment. Behind her back, her hands fluttered before instinctively cupping and shielding her buttocks.

'And, girl –'

'Yes, ma'am?'

'Come back upstairs to me directly you have been punished. I wish to see your stripes. I want you properly punished and so I will examine your bottom for my own satisfaction.'

'Yes, ma'am.'

Three hours out of London and four hours from Inverness, the powerful train thundered northwards, its thick ribbon of smoke curling away over the flat Fenlands.

Watching the gold and brown patchwork of autumnal fields flash by from the luxury of their first-class carriage, the Godolphin sisters lapsed into companionable silence. Since leaving London, their excited chatter had been of the Season so far. Dances, suppers and more formal dinner balls. Their presentation at Court – before a diminutive, plump little Queen dressed in funereal black. Goodwood. The opera. Encounters with virile men ruined by the oppressive vigilance of chaperones. Equally thrilling for the debutantes was their introduction to bustiers and corsetry that squeezed and to the cool kiss of silks and satins upon their trembling young flesh.

Now they were heading for Scotland and the weekend rough shoot. To Strachayle Castle, which would be bristling with desirable males. Their hearts hammered behind their heavy, swollen breasts. To be alone amongst men at last. Alone, unaccompanied and unchaperoned.

Edwina closed her eyes and recounted the intimate highlights of her coming-out season so far. She shivered as she remembered the fierce mouth, and the warm, probing tongue, of a Hussar. He had twirled her away from the dancefloor during a waltz, kissed her savagely out on the balcony and then spun her back into the respectability of the ballroom that night in Cadogan Square. She had, later that night in bed, played with her pussy properly for the very first time, the memory of his hard lips and punishing tongue soaking her frantic fingertips.

Edwina flushed at the memory, then shivered with pleasure at the thought of other waltzes, other gallant officers. Dominant men who had gripped her fiercely, held her closely, their proudly erect manhoods urgent against her moistening maidenhead. And that evening in the opera. Yes. She shuddered and moaned at the delicious remembrance. A decorated Major in the Blues, his leathery face masterfully stern, bending down in the darkness to retrieve her gloves. She had held her breath and squirmed as his hands had caressed her upper thighs. She blushed and grew pleasantly hot at the thought of his sure and certain touch, at the bold impudence of his hand sliding beneath her buttocks to squeeze and fondle them throughout the entire second act of *Turandot*.

Edwina, a brown-eyed, softly lisping brunette, delighted in the easy arrogance and supreme confidence of older men. Experienced, mature men. Melting in their presence, she often felt the soak of her excitement at her silk cami-knickers. She yearned to know their power more intimately. But during the Season, the rules of engagement between the sexes were strict and the codes of propriety severe.

As the train thundered onwards, she lapsed into a waking dream. Behind coyly closed eyes whose lashes frequently flickered with excitement, she conjured up deliciously naughty dreams and desires for the weekend of rough shooting. But Edwina scorned the dubious pleasures of roaring guns, barking dogs and chill mists on freezing grouse moors. For her, the game to be bagged was men. Preferably older men. Worldly men of experience. A Tory grandee, perhaps. Stern and accustomed to command. He would curtly insist upon a midnight assignation, instructing Edwina to attend him in his chamber. Risking the shame of scandal if discovered, she would rush on tiptoe to him. Behind his locked door, he would remain attired in his black velvet smoking jacket, sipping brandy as she shrugged her white lawn chemise off and stood in its puddle at her feet, naked and gleaming before him. He would approach, judging her as he would a horse or dog. Inspecting her intimately, he would run his firm finger from her chin down her throat to her bare bosoms. The fingertip would close into a cruel pincer with his thumbtip at her nipple. Gazing dominantly into her wide eyes, he would tease and tame the painfully peaked flesh-bud then bring his cruel lips down upon it to suck, then bite.

Moaning slightly, Edwina tossed and turned in her sumptuously upholstered leather seat. At the join of her thighs, a warm ooze signalled her delicious distress. Despite her tight clothing, the corset and crinolines, she managed to spread her buttocks wide, almost crying out softly as a dull ache burned deep in her cleft. Lulled by the rhythms of the wheels and seduced by her waiting fantasy, she drifted back into her dark reverie: her wicked desire for naked submission and meek surrender to the sharp appetite of a mature, dominant male.

Behind closed eyes, she imagined him once more, still attired in his velvet jacket, in stark contrast to her soft nakedness. The contrast rendered him more powerful, more masterful. Naked, she would be his plaything for an idle hour. She would uncover her body for his perusal and pleasure. Yes. But, withdrawing his brutal hand from her punished breast, he would ignore her and return to sip his brandy. In her daydream, Edwina whimpered her soft sigh of pleasure. To be naked and ashamed before this man, this silver-haired statesman who forsook her breast to bring his lips to his brandy. She thrilled to the imagined humiliation – and her pussy wept with joy.

'Put your hands up behind your head, my girl,' he would instruct her.

Burning with both pleasure and shame, Edwina saw herself obeying with reluctant eagerness. Her breasts would swell and burgeon as her arms rose up, elbows angled, in obedience to his command. At her coiled, dressed hair, her fingers would undo her careful locks, spilling them down in a wanton tumble. Utterly naked now, and lewdly exposed, she would inch her thighs apart. Like a harlot. A shameful harlot one furtively read about in the Bible or the lurid Sunday papers taken by the servants below stairs. Dizzy with the thrill of her sinful lust, and shyly eager to be deservedly punished for that sinful lust, she would name for him – touching them, as she did so – her maidenly parts.

'And what does my little whore call these?' he would demand, tapping her nipples with the tip of his crop.

Cupping her breasts and offering them to him submissively, she would whisper her shameful response.

The crop would rake down across her belly and drag intimately through the dark nest of her curled body hair below.

'And what name has my little wanton tart for this?' he would growl, probing the sticky fleshfolds of her private place.

Rising up on her tiny white toes, she would confess the name.

'Not fanny?' he would counter sharply. 'Or cunny?'

Then, at last, the hoped-for – dreaded – command. 'Kneel.'

Bowing her head down so that her lips kissed the carpet at his feet, she would crouch, quivering, awaiting his pleasure and her pain. Treading her down with his foot upon the nape of her neck, he would guide the tip of the crop down along her spine to the soft warmth between her raised buttocks. Soon, he would ply the crop less tenderly, more violently. With a vicious affection, to slice-swipe her naked cheeks and kiss them with crimson that would burn to a deeper red. But before the sweet strokes across her helpless buttocks, she would have to endure the bitter-bliss of abject humiliation as she knelt, naked, in his thrall.

The mournful screech of the train's whistle opened her large brown eyes instantly. Blinking away her fantasy, Edwina gazed out through the carriage window. In the far distance, just visible against the purple smudge of the horizon, she saw that a hunt was up and in full cry. Red-jacketed riders on tiny horses were following a speckled pack of miniature hounds. The master of the hunt saluted the train, acknowledging its whistled greeting with two muted notes on his horn. Thundering on, the train gave a farewell blast. The hunt vanished from sight. Edwina closed her eyes, her mind dwelling on a set of sepia prints she had glimpsed when staying with a great-aunt who rode with the Quorn. Sepia prints of huntsmen erect in the saddle, their crops alert and aquiver. Conscious of the wet seethe between her thighs, a moist warmth that rendered her fluffy little pubic fringe soaking, she seized upon the conjured image of her nocturnal visit to the lair of the silver-haired politician, her Tory squire, in Strachayle Castle. She wanted him still fully dressed, to sharpen her sense of his mastery over her trembling nakedness. A nakedness he would straddle as he flexed his cruel crop. Soon, the pleasurable pain would commence.

Down on the carpet beneath him, she would clench her small fists and willingly inch her bare bottom up. *Crack*. The first swipe of leathered cane across her waiting cheeks. Taloning the carpet, she would jerk in anguish at the bite across her rounded buttocks. Then, almost immediately, another short thrumming hiss as the crop lashed down. *Crack*. Another searing swipe – one of many, many more to blaze down and bite-slice her flesh. She would grunt her response into the carpet, the shrill yelp softened by a sweeter note of dark joy. Between the strokes, she would squeeze her cheeks together as if to extinguish the tiny tongue of fire licking the length of her cleft. But nothing, she feared, would damp down the blaze deep in her tiny anal whorl.

Sitting opposite her sleeping sister, Charlotte Godolphin remained wide awake. Her summer months had been long and lonely ones and her Season had not been a success. With short, bobbed blonde hair the shade of pale champagne and glittering green eyes, Charlotte was almost exactly the opposite of her younger sister in every respect. Where Edwina was shy and timid, Charlotte was bold and strong-willed. Where Edwina sought maturity to take her firmly in hand, Charlotte desired to dominate youth.

Early nursery experiences with a tough nanny had allowed Charlotte frequent glimpses of naked male buttocks being firmly chastised. With two brothers and Thomas, a cousin, in the nursery and later at their small desks in the school room, Charlotte enjoyed the spectacle of nanny being fierce with the unruly boys. She had frequent cause to relish the ritual of their bottoms being bared to receive the flurry of stinging spanks.

The intervening years had afforded few crumbs of comfort to feed her growing appetite for the punishment and strict discipline of males. Three summers ago, she had contrived to get her cousin Thomas whipped when he was down for Michaelmas from Eton. She had lied, telling her mother that it had been Thomas who had introduced the grass snake to cook's bed. Lady Godolphin had plied the dog whip across the howling boy's bare bottom behind closed doors – but Charlotte had listened at the door, her pulses racing and her breasts feeling inordinately heavy in their sweet ache.

There were rumours, of course. Whispered asides between visiting dowagers. Whispered accounts of the caning of pantrymen suspected of stealing claret – and kisses from squealing maids. Charlotte had also overheard mention of a salon in Ebury Street where young bucks were tied up and flogged with bundles of birch twigs. Charlotte would bring these scraps and morsels to bed with her at night to feed her hot imaginings as her fingers flayed her pussy.

Charlotte was sure that there existed a private world within London society, a secret world where young men sought pleasure in being punished by ladies who found pleasure in dispensing discipline. But the doors to that world remained closed. Not so the doors to the library. She had passed many instructive hours among forbidden books, poring over Sadean texts and alighting, by chance, upon the poet Swinburne. She became acquainted with his professed penchant for pain, for strict punishment. In his confessions, the florid rhymster freely owned his need for cruel stripes to inspire sweet strokes from his pen.

Now, at last, she was heading for Strachayle Castle and the possibility of adventure. Such weekend gatherings always included poets and painters. Yes. There would be several young men, foppish in their long hair and peacock attire. Pale young men who would be eager for her strict attentions. She pictured herself in a drawing room, alone, perusing a small book of French verse. She would be smoking a small, slender cheroot and sipping a pink gin. One such young man, timorous, with delicate hands and shyly averted eyes, would enter. Avoiding her gaze, he would approach the pianoforte, seat himself before it and commence playing. It would be Mozart. She would join him, allowing the ash from her cheroot to spill down upon the white keys. Her presence would make him increasingly nervous. His fingering would become less sure. At his third blunder at the keys, she would sharply rap her folded fan down across his knuckles. With a soft moan of delight, he would bury his fist between his thighs. The bond would be forged between them. Later, in the moonlight of her bedroom, he would be naked and kneeling – hers entirely to do with as she pleased.

Charlotte concentrated hard, just as she did when reading German novels. Concentrated hard, anxious not to miss the slightest nuance. She imagined her bedroom after midnight. They would both be naked, young debutante and kneeling youth. He would be begging to kiss her

118

breasts, belly and below. She, like La Belle Dame Sans Merci in the book in her father's library, would only deign to allow him to lick and lap at her feet. Whimpering softly, he would obey, his hot, wet tongue busy at her toes. After a strict spell of this delicious homage, she would turn languidly and offer her bare buttocks to his eager, upturned face. Further homage would then be paid, his flushed face buried between her soft, rippling cheeks.

Her sovereignty established, they would enter into the night of discipline and domination. She would select a silken stocking to bind her kneeling slave, bind his ankles together into burning helplessness. Another silken stocking would visit his wrists and render them useless and immobile above his naked buttocks. Whimpering with fearful anticipation, he would writhe. Stern and silent, she would motion to him to be still, and out of pity allow him to peep as she donned a crisp white basque. His eyes would widen in wonder as she drew the laces tightly, squeezing her breasts until they bulged. Smoothing her belly and thighs, she would gaze down, smiling contemptuously at his thickening manhood raised in a smart salute. Capturing it between her knees, she would squeeze it as tightly as the satin at her bosom squeezed her ripe flesh. She would feel the warmth throbbing between her controlling flesh.

The train clattered over a set of points, jolting Charlotte out of her vivid reverie. Opposite her, her gloved right hand scrabbling fitfully at the silk dress stretched across her lap, Edwina dozed. Charlotte watched the gloved fingers suddenly splay out like a starfish as Edwina, in her turbulent dreams, palmed her inner thighs.

Charlotte studied her younger sister's face. The mouth was slightly open, the lips moist, the pink tongue-tip protruding as it would to lick at the ripeness of an oozing plum. Edwina was clearly enjoying a very wicked dream. Charlotte closed her glittering green eyes and returned to hers.

She revisited her boudoir in Strachayle Castle, where her naked slave-lover would beg for his pain. As he became both loud and impatient, she would have to kneel down before him and silence his pleading whine. Charlotte clenched her small paw-fists twice and purred as she anticipated finger-forcing her slightly soiled cami-knickers into his mouth. Further dark joy would flow from the binding of his imploring eyes with calico. Silenced, and denied sight, he would be all hers – the green-eyed cat had captured her quivering little mouse. Let the tantalising teasing and exquisite torments commence.

With a gloved hand, of black velvet and stretching tightly up to her elbow, she would finger her captive intimately: rubbing, stroking and then probing as she explored all the secrets of the naked male so far denied to a well-bred debutante. Fear and excitement would bead the temples of her willing victim. The only sounds audible would be her panting breath and the soft creaking of her crisp basque. Utter wickedness. She would then experience the forbidden delight of his hot erection nestling against the soft curves of her bosoms and then, guided by her gloved fist, his twitching length between her satin buttocks. Would she dare to press the glistening tip of his captive shaft into that hot little hole buried deep between her cheeks? Squirming in her carriage seat as the train sped on, Charlotte grunted thickly. In her imagination, her night of perverse pleasures in Strachayle Castle was yet young.

Pain. That was what she desired to delight in – punishment and pain. The punishment and pain of a submissive male. She anticipated every single moment of her impending dominance. After undoing his blindfold to gaze down into his fear-clouded eyes, she would show him the instrument of chastisement. With neither crop nor cane to hand, it would have to be her silver-backed hairbrush, stiffly bristled and glinting with the promise of pain. Then she would slowly bind a pink ribbon around the knout of his erection to stem and stay his spurt of vital juices elicited by the severe strokes of brush on bottom.

Forcing his head down into a cushion, and pinning him firmly as his gagged mouth mutely kissed the velvet, she would palm his upturned buttocks with her gloved hand. The sweep of the controlling hand would grow firmer. She would pause, briefly, to finger-stroke his cleft. As his sac swung gently between his splayed thighs, the time would come for the gloved fingers to close around the handle of the silver-backed hairbrush, grip it tightly and raise it aloft. The chastisement would commence: again, and again, the polished surface would crack down mercilessly across his punished buttocks. Her bound slave would writhe before buckling under the savage onslaught but, helpless in her thrall, he would not be able to escape her vicious tenderness.

After nine strokes, she would quickly invert the bristled face of the brush to tap the ribboned knout of his pulsing cock. The dancing pink ribbon would signal his desperate need for release but, cruel mistress that she was, Charlotte would deny him his desire and revisit his suffering cheeks to blister them harshly with the spanking brush. As his bottom reddened to an almost unbearable shade of pain, she would thrill to the knowledge that her own cami-knickers were silencing his howls of anguish.

And when the prinked fingers of her velvet-gloved hand released the ribbon? What then? Charlotte had as yet no direct knowledge of the erect male organ exploding and ejaculating. Forbidden texts in her father's library had prepared her but she enjoyed only a vague notion of how her punished slave would respond. The pink ribbon, dancing excitedly at the end of the twitching erection. With her dominant gaze quelling his submissive eyes, she would talon his hair and force him to worship her as her gloved hand slowly teased the ribbon loose.

Candle wax. Hot, sticky and quicksilverish. That was what it would be like. A squirt-splash of his seed up on to the swell of her bosom. Perhaps a pitter-pat upon her face. Would she dare to tongue-tip catch a pearl of his liquid devotion? It would be warm and creamy and waxy to the touch. The forbidden books had prepared Charlotte for the wet excitement of a whipped man. But no book yet printed, she acknowledged, could ever prepare her for the muffled scream of agony torn from her punished worshipper's gagged lips.

With a long, unbroken screech of its whistle, the shuddering train plunged into a long, dark tunnel. Charlotte gasped and sat bolt upright, blinked then twisted her face towards the black carriage window. Her green eyes glimpsed their own cruel reflection in the darkened glass. The eyes of a cat, hungry for her mouse.

The pony-cart trundled up along the mud track slowly. Shivering in the back, exposed to the chill mist, the Godolphin girls suffered the delights of a rough shoot. Heavy tartan rugs around their knees failed to keep them warm. Soon the moorland rose up too steeply for the labouring pony. Dismounting – cursing softly as they slipped and shivered – the sisters trudged the final mile to where the guns had assembled. Higher up, where the mist was thicker and more penetrating, the men stood in a ragged line, muffled in tweeds and frequently sipping from hip flasks.

On the crest of the rolling moor, beaters appeared, advancing slowly down towards the guns. They were shouting and waving sacking and thrashing the heather with long sticks. Rabbits bolted down into the bark and blaze of the guns. The beaters advanced, fanning out to cover the hillside. Small, fat grouse whirred up from the wet cover. Another salvo reverberated across the moor, bringing the dead birds down into the heather.

It was a dreary, dull sport for the girls. They shrank back from the noise of the guns and the reek of acrid cordite. They soon grew numb from both the boredom and the cold. They recoiled delicately from the sight of blood-spattered grouse being bundled and trussed as the game was bagged – and shuddered as rabbits were held aloft to have their necks stretched and their full bladders squeezed dry. The interminable Saturday shoot had not been a sparkling success. The Godolphin sisters bumped back in the cart to Strachayle Castle in the chill of an autumn dusk.

★ ★ ★

'Shall I run a bath, ma'am?' Heather enquired, helping Edwina out of her mud-spattered attire. 'Or would you prefer to wash and dress your hair before dinner?'

'I think I had better bathe, please.'

Please. Heather's eyes widened a fraction at the word. It told her that the young lady she was briskly disrobing was not the customary assured daughter of the aristocracy. Haughty young debs never used 'please' or 'thank you' to their maid. This girl, Heather mused, unlacing the strings of the corset and allowing the trapped breasts within its strict confines their freedom, was a shy little thing. The maid smiled as she stripped her mistress bare. Her shy, somewhat submissive mistress.

Edwina, her soft buttocks joggling as she trod the carpet, murmured a shy question to the maid.

'Oh, no, ma'am,' Heather replied emphatically. 'You'll not be seeing any of the gentlemen this weekend. Most strict about that, Lady Alice is, ma'am. Gentlemen dine separately, then retire to their port and cigars. It's billiards for them, ma'am. The ladies read religious texts or sew their pretty samplers.'

'Oh.' Edwina's sigh could not conceal the deep note of disappointment.

'Any particular gentleman, was there, ma'am?' Heather prompted.

Edwina replied guardedly that she had hoped for some instruction from Sir Julian Fox, one of the weekend guests.

'Instruction, ma'am?' Heather echoed, retreating to the bathroom. She shivered as she remembered the old roué's consummate skill with the cane during a brief visit earlier in the year.

'Yes,' Edwina replied, hurriedly explaining, 'I need to be schooled. I remain such a novice and he is surely a man of rich experience.'

'Bath's ready, ma'am. Look sharp. Mustn't be late to table.'

The maid assisted her mistress into the bath tub and, unrequested but not refused, used the soap flannel

123

vigorously. Edwina surrendered to the deft, capable hands of the busy maid, submitting her soft, pink nakedness to the soaped yellow sponge. Heather exchanged the sponge for a loofah. Edwina gasped aloud as it raked her shoulders and spine. Heather grew bolder with the loofah, using it at first in the cleavage between the wet, shining breasts and then angling it down to nuzzle the dark patch of pubic hair beneath the curdling soap suds. Edwina, grinding her buttocks into the dimpled rubber bath mat, shyly opened her thighs to receive the rasping length.

The snout of the loofah teased her labial fleshfolds as the eyes of the naked mistress met those of her attendant maid. Heather saw in Edwina the disappointment and the yearning. Reaching down, she caressed the bather's naked thigh as she insinuated her hand to wrench up the plug.

'Up,' she ordered, her tone crisply polite.

Edwina rose up as instructed, the creamy suds anointing her breasts and belly.

'I'll rinse you then dry you.'

The 'ma'am' had been dropped. The maid was now in control of her mistress.

'Turn around.' The curt command brought a slight flush to Edwina's cheeks. Her shining buttocks wobbled as she obeyed.

'Close your eyes.' Heather mounted a small foot stool and emptied the ewer of ice-cold water in a sluicing cascade over the nude.

Edwina gasped and squealed, hugging and squeezing her breasts protectively. The cold water raised her thick nipples up instantly.

'Stop that silly noise.' *Spank*. Heather slapped the wet bottom sharply. 'Hurry up and get out.'

Edwina half turned towards the maid, her lips parted in wonder. Her left hand was at her spanked buttock, soothing the reddening cheek.

'Leave that alone or there'll be another,' Heather snapped.

Edwina dropped her hands, exposing her bare bottom to the whim of the maid's spanking hand – the maid who

124

was now utterly in command of her mistress shivering before her.

Roughly towelled dry, during which operation her breasts suffered cruelly, Edwina trembled eagerly as she waited for the fine sprinkle of dusting powder to be applied. Heather guided the nude girl to the bed in the adjoining chamber and arranged her captive face-down upon the bedspread. Cupping her right hand, she sprinkled the rose-scented powder until her palm was pale. Applying the dusting powder gently at first, Heather's touch became increasingly dominant as it swept down the dimpled spine and firmly caressed the proffered buttocks. Moaning into the pillow, Edwina inched her hips and thighs up so that her bare bottom could enjoy the delicious sensation of the sleek palm at her swollen curves. *Spank*. The sudden blow caused her heavy cheeks to wobble. Edwina hissed her pleasure – the necessary signal for the punishment to begin in earnest.

Heather mounted the bed, dimpling the bedspread as she knelt, using her left hand to pin her naked mistress down by the nape of the neck while her right hand cupped and squeezed the buttocks beneath its controlling touch. Edwina wriggled and squirmed in a token show of resistance, rubbing her nipples and pussy-lips into the rasp of the bedspread. Four harsh spanks rang out, the small, firm hand cracking down across the helpless cheeks. Edwina writhed in delicious pain, her sinuous jerking and sensuous wriggling immediately inflaming the hand into a furious, blistering staccato. The quickened hand caused the pink cheeks to redden as the crimson flush of pain spread across their delicious curves. Tiny red blotches betrayed the harsh imprint of the spanking hand's fingertips along the outer buttock's swell.

Squealing loudly, Edwina tried in vain to twist out of the maid's pinioning grip.

'Be still,' Heather commanded. 'I know when.'

Slumping down in submission, the mistress moaned as the maid ravished the bare buttocks with her spanking hand. Curving her hot palm, Heather shuffled her knees a fraction and stretched across to reach the outer cheek.

Edwina writhed as the unblemished flesh burned pink then as uniformly crimson as its already punished twin. Satisfied, the maid addressed the soft sweep of the lower buttocks at the point where they melted into the swell of the upper thighs. Her angled hand swept up into the helpless flesh, causing her victim to scream.

'Silence.'

Obediently, Edwina bit the pillow to muffle her moans. In a swift test of her sovereignty, Heather relaxed her grip, releasing the spanked nude from her thrall. Edwina remained prone and still, squeezing her reddened cheeks spasmodically. Whimpering softly, she gestured for the return of her punisher's controlling hands. Smiling, the maid cupped and sharply squeezed both of the crimson buttocks then, lowering her face down into their inviting swell, licked and softly bit the chastised bottom.

Edwina's fists pummelled the bedspread. She jerked her nakedness against its rough weave, rasping her pussy so that the juicy outer lips splayed wide and her tingling inner fleshfolds raked the fabric deliciously.

'No. Stop that,' Heather warned, tapping the naked bottom with an admonishing forefinger. 'Not now. You must not be late for dinner. Tonight,' she murmured, fingering Edwina's sticky cleft lightly before scratching at the hot sphincter within, 'I will come to you. And I will bring something special. Something special for your naughty, bare bottom.'

Dinner was dispiriting. Lady Alice's fare was in itself quite acceptable – oyster soup, turbot, a baron of beef, a baked, spiced ham, Orkney cheese and fruits from the hothouse – but the company was dull and the conversation duller. The men dined separately. From time to time, gusts of coarse laughter bellowed from their secluded lair. Later, they would withdraw for cigars, brandy and ribaldry behind firmly closed doors. Lady Alice conducted her table with crisp propriety. Tomorrow, she informed her female guests, there would be a bracing walk to the kirk with religious texts and samplers to sew after lunch.

Edwina, her bottom still stinging after the severe spanking, squirmed and squashed her hot cheeks into the hard seat of her wooden chair. To her delight and shame, her belly tightened and her juices flowed freely as the baked, spiced ham was brought to the table. Its pinkness was just like that of a freshly chastised bottom; as the succulent meat surrendered to the carving knife, she felt her inner muscles spasm and implode.

Between the removal of the Orkney cheese and the arrival of the fruit, Lady Alice saw fit to complete her young guests' social education, launching into an interminable disquisition on the etiquette of rough shooting. Edwina fiddled with her ivory-handled fruit fork. Would midnight never come?

'It's a tawse. For your backside. Like I promised.'

Edwina shrank a little from the brutal length of leather. Her sudden movement caused the candle flame to flicker.

'Touch it,' Heather urged, offering the supple tawse to the young lady in the bed.

Edwina stretched out a curious finger and traced it along the shining hide. Emboldened, she accepted it across the palm of her upturned hand. Feeling its weight, she shivered.

'Smell it.' The maid's tone was curt. Only her eyes betrayed her fierce excitement.

Edwina obediently sniffed.

'Taste.'

Her flickering tongue-tip darted forth, retreating instantly from the haunting tang.

'Face down. I'll take the pillows,' Heather grunted softly as she gathered them up, 'and put them here.'

Edwina, turning over in the bed, felt the pillows between her naked hips and the cool linen sheet beneath. She nestled her pussy into their softness.

'Makes your bum nice and big and round,' the maid remarked, dragging the top sheet and blanket down to the end of the narrow bed. 'Hands up to the bedstead.'

Edwina's fingers blindly sought and found the brasswork at once. She gripped the dull metal tightly.

Crack. The broad belt whistled down, searing the proffered cheeks viciously. The punished nude squealed and clenched her whipped cheeks in a reflex of sudden agony. A second, then a third sharp crack followed, the swift strokes lashing down harshly across the naked bottom. At the brasswork, the gripping fingers splayed in an ecstasy of anguish. The punisher's grunts of exertion were drowned by the punished nude's choking sobs of joy.

'Silence,' Heather warned, raising the tawse once more above the quivering buttocks. 'Especially when you reach your satisfaction.'

Whimpering softly, Edwina tightened her grip on the brass bedstead and buried her face in the mattress.

The maid teased the hot buttocks of her mistress with the tip of the dangling tawse. Edwina jerked her whipped cheeks up and tried to capture it in her cleft. Heather grinned, snapped the leather aloft then swiftly cracked it down. The broad belt lashed the buttock's rounded swell, briefly flattening the double crimson domes. Edwina shuddered in response.

She'll be loud, this one, when she boils over. She's simmering nicely now, Heather thought as she fingered the tawse. Simmering nicely. Another three'll bring her to the seethe.

Crack. The leather barked. The nude jerked and squealed, her reddening cheeks wobbling deliciously.

Two more, Heather mused, and this little rabbit will be done to a turn. Flayed, skinned and all in a bubbling stew. Better let her bite the leather to silence her shrieking.

Eyes closed, her sphincter opening into a puckering crater, Edwina crushed her wet pussy into the pillows. The maid delayed the strokes. The mistress began to beg.

Strachayle Castle woke to a sharp frost. Lady Alice chivvied her guests to the kirk and back along the glittering lanes. After lunch in the draughty dining room, the women heard the men departing for more rough shooting. The Godolphin girls declined the invitation to sew samplers and retired to their respective rooms.

Edwina, claiming a headache, locked her door. She assured Lady Alice that all she required was a little rest. Listening to the retreating footsteps of her hostess, she started to loosen her bustle. Before the full-length looking glass, she raised her crinoline and petticoat and tucked them up at her waist. Slowly peeling down her cami-knickers, she thrust her bottom pertly towards the glass. Over her shoulder, she glimpsed the angry weals. The red stripes where the tawse had kissed her so savagely were still vividly imprinted across her rounded cheeks. Staggering across to the bed – hampered by her partial state of undress – she buried her face into the pillow which had captured the soak of her wet heat the night before. Moaning softly as her fingers scrabbled at her pussy, she sniffed the white pillow case, then kissed it devotedly.

Fuelled by the delicious memory of the tawse across her upturned cheeks, Edwina arrowed her arms down to the base of her belly. Just as Heather the maid had shown her, she nipped her little pink love-thorn between her thumb-tips. Moments later, Edwina bit the pillow, tearing it open with her clenched white teeth.

'Lady Alice wondered if there was anything you required, ma'am.'

Charlotte, bored and discontented, did not even bother to turn her gaze away from the window. Ignoring the maid, she shook her head.

'Sure, ma'am?'

'Nothing,' Charlotte snapped.

Heather hesitated, reluctant to depart.

'One moment, girl.'

'Ma'am?'

'Have all the men gone to the shoot?'

'Yes, ma'am. Lady Alice insists that all the guns go out.'

'Even young Hugh Lambton?'

'The poet, ma'am? Most reluctant, he was, but Lady Alice was firm.'

Charlotte received and accepted the disappointment in silence, but the maid, perceptive and shrewd, suddenly understood. What else would a stern young beauty like Miss Charlotte want with a poor stick like that long-haired poet Hugh Lambton if not for an afternoon of games – games in which the rules were strict and the penalties severe?

Heather was anxious that Lady Alice did not discover this green-eyed young vixen entertaining her young poet after dark. Somehow, she would have to amuse the cruel blonde here and now.

'Nothing I can do, ma'am? I'm here to serve.'

To serve. Charlotte whispered the words softly. 'Tidy up my dressing table,' she commanded.

Heather busied herself at the task, her mind less than half on her duties. Her knuckles swept a glass bottle on to its side. The room was instantly heavy with spilled perfume.

'Be careful,' Charlotte rasped, springing up and rushing to the dressing table. 'Just look what you've done. I've a good mind –'

'To punish me, ma'am?'

Silence, as suffocating as the sudden scent, filled the air. Heather bowed her head down and drew her hands together at her apron like a penitent schoolgirl before an angry Dame. Charlotte drew her left hand up to the pearl choker at her throat. Impossible possibilities flashed behind her green eyes. Could she punish this pert little minx? Bare her bottom and spank her hard? The desire to do so fluttered in her tightened throat.

'Just be careful,' she snapped, turning on her heel. 'Get my green gown out for dinner this evening. You can help me dress.'

In the silence of the late afternoon, with two lamps lit against the gathering gloom, the obedient maid knelt and slowly removed the last vestiges of silk and satin. Charlotte, her fluffy blonde bush sparkling in the lamplight, stood naked above her kneeling maid, naked and imperious, with her head tossed back and her hands planted firmly upon her hips.

Heather gazed up, seeking permission from the hard, green eyes. The nude inclined her head and stared dominantly down at the servant shivering at her feet.

'The perfume you spilt –'

'I'm sorry, ma'am, please –'

'Be quiet. I am thinking of a fitting punishment.'

Heather closed her eyes and bowed her head. It was brought up instantly by Charlotte's taloning hand. Heather's face was drawn closer to the gleaming pubic mound.

'Kiss me,' Charlotte murmured. 'Kiss me for not whipping you as I should.'

The maid's eager little tongue licked at the curved inner thighs, rapidly working its way towards the golden pubic fern. With a soft crackle and a wet rustle, the tongue lapped the length of the pouting labial fleshfolds, then probed their salty interior. Charlotte snarled her pleasure and, gripping the maid's hair with both fists, forced the upturned face into her aching heat. Heather whimpered, her protest smothered by the hot pussy filling her mouth, but submitted to the desires of her mistress.

'Kiss,' Charlotte commanded. 'Do not lick or suck.'

Cradling the maid's head against her flesh, Charlotte spread her legs wide, ready to accept the sweet kisses. Heather defied the stern instructions, and sucked and bit the slippery fleshfolds with savage tenderness. Moments later, Charlotte buckled and collapsed, screaming softly as she rode the upturned face between her quivering thighs.

As she staggered forwards and stumbled, Charlotte forced Heather down on to the carpet beneath her. Her hips jerking now in the sweet frenzy of her gathering climax, the naked mistress straddled then squatted on the maid's face. Wriggling and burning her bottom on the carpet, Heather twisted her face to avoid the hot juices. The movement ravished the nude above. In her ecstasy, Charlotte squeezed her thighs, punishing the face below. In a spirited rebellion, Heather poked her short, thick tongue up in defiance, piercing the bitter sphincter. Choking on her lust, Charlotte savoured the ultimate submission and rose like a rocketing game bird into an explosion of delight.

* * *

'Impudence. Such wicked impudence. How dare you use me so? I'll show you who is the mistress –'

'Oh, no, ma'am, please don't –'

So far, both had played their parts to perfection: the outraged young aristocrat and the snivelling maid. But there was a touch of raw severity in Charlotte's tone, and a trace of real fear in Heather's pleading.

'How dare you put your tongue there?'

'I'm sorry, ma'am, please don't –'

'Silence. You must be taught a lesson, girl. A very painful lesson.'

Across the bed, her bottom bared – it had been soundly spanked – and her hands tied tightly together, the maid shivered beneath the menace of her mistress above.

'Keep absolutely still or I'll use the slipper on you.'

Heather whimpered. The wooden finger, smooth, straight and polished, approached her bottom an inch at a time. It grazed the curve of her left buttock. Heather spasmed, flinching as the finger briefly dimpled the soft swell.

'Be still.' Charlotte steadied the pearwood glove-stretcher then guided it directly into the shadowed cleft. Heather swayed her hips and, moaning softly, wriggled evasively.

'If you struggle you will suffer.'

'No, ma'am, don't. I didn't mean to –'

'I told you to kiss me, not feed upon my flesh as if it were a breast of boiled fowl.'

'But I thought –'

'Thought?' Charlotte echoed sardonically. 'Don't trouble your pretty little head with thoughts, girl. Just listen and obey.'

Heather squealed as the smooth finger nuzzled her wet anus. Her bound hands writhed helplessly as the glove-stretcher slid in between the soft mounds of her spanked cheeks.

Relishing her absolute dominance, Charlotte pinched her nipples and let her fingertips fall down to her prickling pussy. Stepping back from the bed, she grasped Heather's small, naked foot and brought the soft instep up against the wet flesh between her thighs. The maid cried out in shame and outrage at this usage, sensing where her tiny foot had been placed and hating the notion. Staring down at the tightened cheeks clenching the wooden finger between them, Charlotte ground the soft instep into her pussy, and came loudly. On the bed, helpless and humiliated, Heather sobbed.

Thrilling to the maid's sorrow-sobs – and the writhing bare bottom – Charlotte picked up the second glove-stretcher. Leaving the ivory kid leather glove impaled on the wooden finger, she knelt once more upon the bed and rested the tip in the hollow of the maid's knee.

'No –' begged the sobbing maid. 'Please. Not there –'

'The greatest impudence of all,' Charlotte purred, her green eyes dilated then sharply narrowed with lust, 'was your attempt to humour me. Don't deny it, girl. You dared to come to me and indulge my little whims.'

'I only meant –'

'You know what happens to a clever little maid who gets too big for her boots? Hm?'

On her bed, Heather sobbed brokenly.

'She's brought to heel, girl. Brought to heel.'

The little wet foot, sticky with Charlotte's wet heat, curled up in a reflex of fear.

Charlotte stroked the stretched finger of the glove down along the naked leg. At the wet ankle, she tapped the straightened finger upon the shining flesh. 'Brought to heel.'

'Please, ma'am, I've learned my lesson –'

'Not quite, girl,' Charlotte whispered, inching the tip of the erect finger up the leg towards the maid's wet pussy.

A week after the guests had departed from the rough shoot, Lady Alice sat at her desk in the estate office. The accounts books and green ledgers lay closed and set aside. She had more pressing business to attend to. Her right hand fiddled with a length of bamboo cane. It rattled on the polished surface of the desk.

'A very gushing letter from Lady Edwina, with no less than five pounds sterling enclosed. A similar note from her sister, with a curious gift. A tiny pair of gloves fashioned in beaten gold. Explain this largesse to me, girl, if you will.'

Standing before the desk, Heather blushed but sought refuge in silence.

'Speak up, girl, or my cane will soon quicken your tongue.'

'I can't say, ma'am, I'm sure.'

'Cannot, or dare not? Don't be pert with me, girl.'

Heather remained silent.

'I can only conclude that you conspired with the wretched girls and procured for them forbidden assignations. What Lady Godolphin will say upon the matter of her daughters' violation, I shudder to think. I'll need the names of the men, of course.'

'But it isn't so, ma'am.'

'These letters and generous gifts tell me otherwise. Across that chair. Bare-bottomed.'

'But ma'am –'

'This instant.' Lady Alice rose from behind her desk, cane in hand. Striding across to the chair, she tap-tapped the seat impatiently with the tip of her quivering bamboo. 'I am going to whip you until you confess all.'

Across the chair, her bare buttocks trembling beneath the hovering cane, the maid softly cursed her own willingness to serve.

GISELLE

Jean Aveline

Jean Aveline has written three novels for Nexus; in our opinion some of the finest SM novels written to date. The first two – *Sisters of Severcy* and *Exposing Louisa*, are original, highly arousing and strikingly well written. Her third, *Giselle*, continues that tradition. In this extract, Giselle is taken to the island for her sexual initiation.

As soon as Giselle was inside the old Land Rover, Thierry slipped his hand inside her shirt. She was in the back this time – another girl sat next to Xavier. Giscard watched from the corner of his eye as Giselle let Thierry explore her breasts. Any thought of protest was snuffed out by Xavier's eyes in the driver's mirror. It felt as if Thierry was the agent of his desires and, before they had travelled a kilometre, she was wet beneath her skirt.

The girl in the front seat turned to watch as they entered the pine woods. Her jet-black eyes sparkled.

'I'm Joan,' she said, holding out her hand. Giselle shook it self-consciously. The girl laughed when Thierry refused to let go of Giselle's breasts.

'Are you his?' she asked.

'No,' replied Giselle quickly. The word was half strangled as Thierry ran his fingers in quick circles around her nipples.

'He likes you, though,' said the girl with a giggle, watching the hand beneath the shirt. With that, she turned in her seat again and whispered something in Xavier's ear.

'What is she saying?' demanded Thierry.

'She thinks that Giselle can't be a virgin. She gets turned on too easily.'

Giselle blushed, partly because they must have been talking about her earlier, and partly because it embarrassed her how quickly Thierry – a boy that she hardly knew – could arouse her so. She glanced guiltily at Giscard. He shook his head in disapproval, but smiled.

'Kiss me,' she said, wanting still to be his.

He leaned across and she closed her eyes as his lips opened and pressed about hers.

When she opened her eyes, the Land Rover was slowing as it slid down the white beach to the lake. There was already a car parked on the sloping sand and the boat was half-full of people. Thierry undid the buttons of the shirt completely as Xavier parked. Her breasts were free as Thierry pulled her out of the door and led her down to the water's edge. Billy and Paige waved from the boat. There were two other boys, boys that Giselle had never seen before. They looked at her with unconcealed interest.

Xavier and Giscard hauled some provisions out of the car in large cardboard boxes and carried them to the boat. It sank lower and lower as boxes and people filled it.

'We'll have to throw you out if we start to sink,' Jean told her.

The others thought that he was joking but Giselle wasn't so sure.

As soon as they reached the island, Paige slipped off her clothes. The boys whistled and she waved her naked behind at them. Giselle envied her naturalness. She left her shirt undone but didn't have the courage to remove the little skirt of shiny silk. A boy would have to do that – if any boy wanted to when Paige was so beautiful and so easy.

They spent the afternoon swimming and sunbathing. Giscard fished from the rocks at the edge of the bay and caught a carp. He refused to gut it and Jean was forced to, calling him a baby and throwing the intestines at him once it had been done.

Giselle helped Paige to prepare a barbecue. Fires were lit as the sun began to sink.

Night was the great transformer; night and fire. Thierry took Joan into the shadows and they heard her groaning. They heard his grunts as he came. Giselle was handing out plates of charcoal-grilled chicken when the girl came

138

back on her own, naked but carrying her clothes. Giselle saw the languor in the girl's tread and the brightness of her eyes.

Xavier had spent the afternoon reading, talking to no one. Now he was drinking from a bottle of cheap wine with Paige on his lap. He took the food from Giselle without even looking at her. It stung. She wanted to be noticed.

It was only later, after they had all eaten, that he called for her. Paige smiled from his lap as Giselle came to stand in front of them.

'So, what do we have to enjoy from Giselle tonight?' he asked.

Giscard looked up as if the question had been directed at him, but Xavier's eyes were locked into Giselle's. She shrugged self-consciously. Thierry appeared behind her, entering the light of the fire for the first time since he had taken Joan into the shadows. She caught the scent of girl mucus as his hand slipped inside her open shirt. His fingers twisted one of her nipples sharply and she jumped, but didn't struggle. The feeling was too good to escape, the sharpness like cold water on a hot night.

'Let's see her,' said Joan from her place by the fire.

Thierry slipped the shirt from Giselle's shoulders. He licked the side of her neck obscenely, and she giggled. Now all that she wore was the short silk skirt – hardly a scrap about her waist. If Thierry had undone the little zip at the side it would have fallen to her feet.

'Still a virgin?' Xavier asked.

She nodded. Joan laughed, but Xavier silenced her with a quick glance.

'Don't you want Giscard?'

She couldn't reply. She couldn't say, 'It's you that I want,' not with so many eyes on her. Perhaps he would read it in her face. She wanted him to see her desire. She wished that Thierry would undo the little zip and let the dress fall. It would make her seem less childish. It would make Xavier want her more.

Xavier pushed Paige from his lap. The girl rose with good grace as Thierry delivered Giselle into Xavier's hands. Paige didn't go far. As Giselle sank into Xavier's lap, Paige sank down beside him on the fallen tree.

Xavier's closeness, and Paige's eyes, pinned her firmly to the fabric of the night. She was a butterfly laid out on a black field. They could do as they liked with her. She wanted to say that; she tried to show it in the meekness of her gaze. Her belly was already on fire. She wanted them to lead her into temptation and to deliver her unto evil. Still a virgin – it embarrassed her. Giscard's cowardice, his respect for her protestations of innocence, was costing her too much. No flesh was innocent. This was her education. Xavier was her priest, and she wanted him to take confession with the hard penis that she felt pressed into her behind. Her penance would be the other boys, satisfying them – even her brother, who watched her every move.

Xavier's hand was on her breast. He had already sucked out her soul, now he explored the void. Soon he would feel the wetness that was seeping from between her legs, down to the sex that it desired.

'Giscard,' he called, and he motioned to the boy. She watched from her dream as a figure came out of the shadows and stood before her.

'She will whore for you if you want it,' Xavier said. 'Can't you see that, can't you read it in her face?'

Giselle looked up and saw Giscard's troubled eyes.

'Don't you want a whore of your own?'

Giscard seemed upset by the words. Giselle knew that she should be upset as well. But she wasn't. She knew that Xavier was right. Her unused belly needed to be filled.

'Undo his shorts,' Xavier said.

She was being addressed but it took a moment for the fact to register. It took even longer to understand what had been said.

Xavier picked up her hand and rested it against Giscard's belly. With thick, heavy fingers, as if she were drugged, she began to pick at the buckle of his belt. Amazingly it opened. The buttons too. Each opened, one by one.

'Pull them down,' Xavier told her.

She had never seen a boy's sex before. Not close to. Not a grown boy's sex. With both hands, she eased the shorts and the underpants beneath them down. The tube of flesh sprang free, bounding upwards, frightening her for a moment, then fascinating her. The head was rounded and smooth, the eye, a moist slit. It was so close that she felt the heat of it on her cheek.

'What do you want to do?' Xavier asked.

'Touch it?' asked Giselle, not really knowing. Looking would have been enough, familiarising herself with the strange, ugly, beautiful thing that pulsed so close to her lips.

Her fingers were tentative, her expression reverent, as she ran the tips of her fingers slowly from head to base. Further down was a tight sac of skin covered with curls of blond hair. She wondered if she could touch these too, but was too shy to ask.

'How else could you touch it?' Xavier asked.

She glanced from Giscard to Xavier and back again. Giscard's face seemed to shiver as she stroked his sex. Her fingers made a loop around the girth of the tube and drew slowly downwards. His eyes widened. There was sweat on his forehead, a film that made him shine in the firelight.

'Kiss it,' Paige told her. She was leaning forward, close enough for her knees to touch Giselle's thighs.

When Giselle did nothing, Paige darted her head to the exposed flesh and her tongue emerged wet and pink. The tip was pointed and flew like an arrow to the head of Giscard's sex. It swept quickly across the moist eye and circled beneath the bulging head. The boy groaned as Paige enveloped him with her lips and Giselle felt him stiffen beneath her enfolding fingers. Looking up, she saw from his face that he liked her lips. He had never asked for this from her. It would have been a pleasure; she wanted that pleasure. When Paige removed her mouth, Giselle gave hers. The flesh was hot. Her tongue was nervous as it teased its way across the tight skin.

Giscard pulled away suddenly. She didn't understand. He had wanted Paige. She looked at him, the hurt showing. He had wanted Paige's mouth – she had seen that in his eyes. Why didn't he want hers? If he thought that he was sparing her in some way, he was wrong. Didn't he realise that to be spared this was to be deprived of Xavier? If she took his sex, Xavier's would follow. And her mouth was made for Xavier – every instinct and nerve told her that.

Xavier moved abruptly, his hand as quick as a snake. He seized Giscard's balls and pulled him back to where he had been. Giscard's fists clenched and Giselle sensed that he would fight. Rapidly, she took his sex again and moved her head in quick circles, wanting, in her unskilled way, to make it as good as she could. She felt his relaxation and knew that he had accepted her gift. Her eyes closed and she lost herself in the pleasure of sucking. It was awkward leaning forward – her dress was restricting her. She pulled the hem upwards until her legs could move freely and so that Giscard could see her sex and know that she was showing it to everyone. Now she was like the other girls and she would belong. They wouldn't send her out into the night so that Paige could dance for them. Giscard groaned as she opened her legs wide and crouched closer to him, driving his sex deeper, to the frontier of her throat and the promise of the tightness beyond.

She gave herself as fully as she was able. Fingers came to caress her lips. She felt them work over Giscard's shaft too. Paige's, she thought as they began to masturbate Giscard in long, easy strokes. When she opened her eyes though, she saw blue tattoos on the wrist that owned the fingers and sat back in surprise. There was something demonic in Xavier's eyes. Giscard looked beaten, humiliated. But his erection didn't fade. There seemed to be a guilty pleasure in being caressed by a boy.

The hand moved more quickly. Paige ran her fingers up the back of Giscard's legs. She grinned as the fingers made a spear and jabbed upwards. Giselle couldn't see what was happening but Giscard suddenly sighed and groaned.

'Be ready for him,' Xavier whispered.

She watched as Giscard swayed and his belly filled with deep, successively quicker breaths. He was panting and she knew that soon he would come. She had heard how it happened, how a white fluid spurted from the tip of a boy's penis. Some of the girls in her class regularly performed this service for their boyfriends, used hands and mouth, and were drenched in the fluid that would have made a child in their wombs.

Xavier took her chin with his free hand and tipped her head back.

'Open,' he told her.

Feeling foolish, but also unbearably aroused, she waited with open mouth while Xavier pumped harder and harder.

'Look at her, Giscard. Look at the virgin at your feet.'

Giscard looked and came. Thick ropes of milky liquid sprayed across Giselle's face and fell into her mouth. Xavier pulled them together, mated sex and mouth, so that she felt the final pulses coating her tongue.

As soon as the last drop had issued and Xavier had released him, Giscard tore himself away. She tried to smile but all she saw in his face was hurt and a sense of betrayal. He stumbled away, pulling up his shorts. At the edge of the firelight, he paused to look at her in a sort of horror, then he ran into the night. Bewildered, she turned to Xavier, hoping that he would understand, hoping that he would explain what had happened.

'Find him,' he said. 'Make it all right.'

She rose, picked up her shirt and hurried in the direction that Giscard had taken. In the pitch darkness, outside the circle of firelight, she stumbled as she called out his name. She passed the fishing hut and climbed the slope to the cliffs, buttoning her shirt as she went. Some instinct told her that he wouldn't want to see her unclothed.

Gradually, her eyes adjusted to the night and the moon lit her way. She called again as she passed under the trees but there was no reply. Then, as she reached the place where the rope hung, she saw a figure slouched on one of

143

the rocks looking out over the lake. She went to him tentatively.

'Giscard,' she said softly.

His face was pale in the moonlight when he turned to her.

'Go away.'

She hesitated. 'Please, I don't understand. Don't send me away.'

He looked at her again. She saw the evidence of tears in his eyes.

'He shouldn't have done that,' he stated flatly. 'I'm not . . . I don't . . . He shouldn't have touched me like that.'

She understood. It was the excitement of being touched by Xavier. Another boy had made him climax. Her mouth was secondary, just a receptacle.

'Is it so very bad?' she asked, remembering the pleasure of being kissed by Paige.

'I know what people will think.'

'Xavier has a power,' Giselle began. 'I think that the other boys will understand that. Perhaps they would want the same thing.'

He shook his head, but seemed calmed by these words.

'Now they will all want you to suck them.'

She was silent as he looked at her. She couldn't say that she wanted that. She didn't know if she did. The thought that Xavier would enter her mouth was overwhelming; that she did want. But the other boys, her brother amongst them? She didn't know.

'Is that why you never tried to make me do it before?'

'Everything that you do for me you have to do for them!' he said in a burst of anger. 'I want you for myself.'

'Then we should leave the island and never come back,' she said without conviction.

He looked at her derisively. 'Neither of us want that.'

She drew nearer to him. 'When we are away from here, I will be yours alone.'

'A whore of my own!' he said, spitting out the words as if they were poison.

'Someone who won't say no.'

She saw his eyes flare.

'If that is what you want, I'll take you back naked and open your mouth for each and every boy. I'll come for you every night and bring my friends!'

His rage shocked her and she stepped back.

'Will you say no to that?' he asked.

A tear eased from the corner of her eye.

'If you hate me so much, I'll go, and you can forget me.'

'I don't hate you. Don't you understand? I love you. That is why I don't want to see you on your knees in front of anyone who wants you!'

She sighed.

'It's all gone too far.'

'Tell me that you don't want Xavier and we'll leave.'

She looked at him steadily, unable to lie.

'Tell me!' he said again.

'You wanted him,' she said softly. She saw shock in his eyes, then rage. He jumped to his feet and she backed away, but not quickly enough to avoid a slap across the face. It was her turn to be shocked. Seizing her, he pulled the shirt from her shoulders and tore the skirt downwards, tearing the waistband. When he stepped back, her naked body was quaking and the tears were coursing down her face.

'Then it will be me who gives you to him.'

He took her hand and pulled her roughly down the slope. Twice she fell. Branches struck at her nakedness, the pine needles stung and made her cry out. Giscard was beyond pity; all sweetness was gone. He seemed mad to her and she was frightened. As they drew closer there was the sound of raised voices and laughter. She saw Joan chasing Thierry around the fire. She saw him dodging and laughing as the girl tried to hit him. They froze as Giscard dragged Giselle into the light of the fire. All eyes were on her as she was thrown at Xavier's feet.

'Tell him what you want.'

Giselle looked from Giscard to Xavier. She was gasping for breath and half-blinded by tears.

'Tell him!'

She shook her head, and began to curl into a ball.

Giscard fell to his knees and took hold of her ankles, pulling them wide. When she struggled, he slapped her across the face. It was harder than the first slap, even more shocking because it was calculated, cold-blooded. She lost the will to defend herself and became rigid. He spat on his hand and smeared the wetness between her legs, then began to undo his shorts. It felt as if she had fallen into a nightmare. The boy who pulled his erect sex into the light of the fire had the appearance of Giscard, but Giscard was never like this, never so cruel, never so full of hatred. He took her wrists and pinned her hands above her head. His mouth took her breasts and bit as his sex nudged between her legs. She struggled, and he bit harder.

'You want this. It can be easy or hard,' he hissed in her ear.

His sex lodged in the wet slit, the head nudged forward and found the beginning of the virgin passageway. This quietened her, like a knife at the throat. Fear and disbelief staked her out like a blood sacrifice.

'Now say it!' he shouted. 'Say that you want them all.'

His sex was pressing hard at the membrane which had sealed her innocence since birth. His eyes blazed. It shouldn't be like this. It had always been soft in her imagination. The boy would be tender. There would be intimacy and trust. But then she turned her head and looked at Xavier. He watched like a statue from the vantage of the fallen tree. She had his attention now. She had everyone's attention.

'I want it,' she said with a sudden surge of strength and, before Giscard could move, she jammed her pelvis upwards, hard, impaling herself. The membrane tore and she screamed but her eyes never left Xavier. She heard Giscard call her a bitch and then felt him pull out. He struggled to his feet and she looked up in fear as he towered over her with clenched fists. The hatred in his eyes had become contempt. She knew that he would never forgive her. She had robbed him of the chance of taking her virginity. She had given it instead to Xavier. She had

146

given it with her eyes – Giscard's rapidly shrinking sex had merely been the tool, his rage the mechanism.

'She's your whore,' Giscard told Xavier savagely. 'Take her.'

She lay open-legged in the light of the fire. Her hands were still and quiet behind her head. Her newly opened sex gaped wide. There was absolute silence. For a terrible moment she thought that Xavier would refuse her. A sudden movement from the other side of the fire caught her attention. It was Jean, standing up, undoing the buckle of his belt.

'If you don't want her, I do,' he said, through clenched teeth.

She wanted to say no, tried to say it in her face when she turned back to Xavier.

'Oh, I want her,' Xavier replied, 'but you will be next.'

He pulled his shirt over his head, revealing the tight, tanned muscles of chest and abdomen. There was a tattoo that she had never seen before, a pair of crossed torches in the centre of his chest, blazing as if they were the fire of his heart. He stood and pulled his trousers down. His sex was hard, curving upwards like a scimitar. A golden snake had been engraved on the tall column and seemed to dance in the light of the fire. When he knelt between her legs she was aware that every part of him was hard. The beauty of taut muscles and stretched sinews made her feel weak. His hands, as they ran along the insides of her thighs, were like polished steel. They dug beneath her behind and lifted her easily so that only her shoulders were pressed to the sand and her sex was an open wound for him to explore.

She groaned as his tongue entered and arousal flared in her belly like the torches on his chest. Savage words formed in her throat. The night had her now; she was its creature, dark and lost, willing and easy. She was aware of faces around her, coming closer, of expressions of envy and desire. The soil of the island abraded her shoulders as Xavier's tongue explored her wounded belly. There were murmurs from the watchers, a joke and low laughter as she strained upwards to open herself more fully. Xavier was crouched over her like a wolf gorging itself at a kill. When he released her, his mouth was covered in virgin blood. The faces moved back a little as he stood, respectfully giving him room. Giselle, looking up through half-closed eyes, was aware only of his hardness. He loomed over her like an executioner's sword, ready to slice away all remaining innocence.

The murmurs rose in pitch, became more excited. This wasn't just Xavier and her. It was all of them, and the island too. If the cliffs had shouldered their way forward, parted the group around the fire and stood waiting for her with erections of jagged rock, she would have felt it as right. She was the island's bride, sworn to honour and obey the desires of sky and earth. More than that – she was a receptacle for all desires, and for all those who needed her.

There was a flush of pleasure as Paige knelt by her side. The softness of the girl seduced her and Giselle's mood changed. Now she was on the other shore of that vast lake of desire. Here were all things feminine; petal-soft kisses, moist heats, enveloping mists of care. Paige kissed her with a tenderness that made Giselle want to weep, made her want to be an infant in her mother's arms again. The rapacity of men, the hardness of rock, which had seemed so desirable a moment before, was suddenly a sharp threat. Xavier, as he took his sex and worked it around the entrance to her belly was rapist and assassin. Giselle reached out and took Paige's face. She had never felt such a desire to belong. She would be a votaress of the goddess's order, a worshipper of the goodness in Paige's smile.

Then Xavier brushed the head of his sex over her clitoris. There was a spasm in her belly, sharper than the stones that desired her, more compelling than the soft kisses of Paige. The conflicting desires bisected her. She was suspended over the dark lake, torn between the desire for a woman's tenderness and a lust for the penetration that would break her to pleasure.

Xavier let her down to the ground slowly. Her body fell open as she settled to the soil. Paige fastened soft lips on her breasts. Jean knelt on the other side and ran his fingers down her cheek. He was naked and erect. Paige whispered for her to look, to see her brother's desire. Giselle looked, and wanted him – wanted them all. She wanted to be enough for any who came to her. Her hand went to Jean's lap and lightly brushed the hard flesh – the caress of waterweed across smooth stone. She saw him tense, saw the involuntary tightening of his abdomen and the upwards thrust of his sex. She smiled, letting him know that she would welcome him as more than a brother. Xavier slipped his sex home, but lodged only the head. She turned to him with the same smile, letting him know that she was also his. He asked her if she wanted it, and she nodded. He buried himself with a quick thrust and she twisted like a fish as the pleasure stabbed through her. Her groan was the groan of someone who has waited too long, the groan of the believer when their god finally answers them. She wrapped her legs around his behind and held him strongly, so that he would never quit her. Jean pressed his lips to hers. Her mouth was penetrated as swiftly as her sex. Her brother's tongue writhed and stabbed. Paige bit into her breasts making her doubt the kindness of women.

Xavier began a slow rhythmic movement and her groans became a steady, unbroken keening. Jean released her mouth and the sounds spilled out into the night. He knelt up and, touching Paige's cheek, brought her mouth to his sex. Giselle watched enviously as the girl sucked her brother. Her neglected breasts, imprinted with Paige's teeth marks languished and Giselle was obliged to caress herself, to squeeze hard and pinch cruelly at her own nipples. Then Jean swung a leg across her chest and his sex came to her mouth. Paige lifted Giselle's head so that Jean could fuck her more easily. He fucked her as she wanted Xavier to fuck her, hard and fast, jamming into her throat. Then, abruptly, he withdrew and Paige used her fingers to milk him. Gelatinous semen rained on to

Giselle's face as he arched his back and cried out. The stream seemed endless and Paige – pumping the brother with one hand, cradling the sister with the other – directed the flow to cover Giselle's face completely.

'The perfect baptism,' she murmured as Jean gave one final cry and slumped to the ground. He watched with sleepy, hooded eyes as Paige husbanded the semen into Giselle's mouth, using tongue and fingers. There were soft words and girlish giggles as they shared in the liquid feast.

Then Xavier began to move more quickly, torturing Giselle with the pleasure that he refused to bring to completion. As Jean rested his hand on Giselle's chest, she fought for air to fuel her gasps and sobs.

'You will kill her,' Paige told Xavier. It was Paige's pity, her fingers at Giselle's sex, that brought the relief of orgasm. The lightest of grazes across Giselle's clitoris was enough. She screamed and Xavier fucked her hard, pounding her behind into the soil as if he would first kill her, then bury her.

He didn't come. He fucked her until she was too exhausted to respond, then pulled out and took his place on the tree. Sweat glistened on his body but his expression was the same as ever. He had changed her for ever but had been untouched himself.

Giselle closed her eyes as Jean lay his head on her chest. She felt Paige curl around her and the girl's cheek settling on her belly. For a moment there was absolute peace and Giselle felt that at last she belonged. She could have stayed as she was for ever, but others wanted her. Paige's head was pushed aside and a boy's sex was hurriedly buried within her belly. The first was Billy. He was quick from the beginning, almost frantic. She lay her hand on his back and stroked him with the patience of a mother as he pistoned his desire. He came in a rapid series of spasms and she rained kisses on his neck and cheeks as he yelped out the pleasure.

Before Billy had completely finished, Thierry appeared, lifting the smaller boy by the shoulders and pushing him aside. Thierry's sex was long and thin. He was clumsy but

150

strong, and she came again. He laughed crazily as she writhed with pleasure but it wasn't cruel or mocking. There was exhilaration and joy in his voice. His rough energy pushed her to further madnesses. She took Jean's hand and sucked his fingers as she came, revelling in letting them see her greed. Thierry came in a disjointed cataclysm of thrusting pelvis and shouted obscenities.

'I'll take her now,' Xavier said as Thierry finally rolled aside. They had all had her but, from Xavier's tone, Giselle guessed that it was only the beginning. There were other places to go, new rites to perform.

Xavier stood and fetched one of the torches that always lay ready in the shadows. He thrust it into the flames and the sudden flare of ignition highlighted the muscles of his chest and abdomen. He took Giselle's hand gravely and, pulling her to unsteady feet, led her out of the circle and into the night. She was shaking from head to toe and her thoughts swam as if her head had filled with treacle.

They followed a path that she hadn't noticed before; one that led them into the centre of the island. The flickering light of the torch on their naked bodies made them seem like spirits, as ephemeral as fireflies. The path became tortuous; they had to squeeze between rocks and scramble up steep inclines using the roots of trees as hand- and footholds. Xavier helped her, but said nothing. Finally, they reached a clearing and paused to recover themselves. As her breathing eased, Giselle became aware of a profound silence and absolute stillness. The water of the lake was gone; its perpetual movement was lost. This was the island's sanctuary, a respite from things fluid and changing. Xavier allowed her to experience this for a few moments, then drove the torch through the covering of pine needles, deep into the soil. Once it stood safely, he led her to a place beneath a tall, broad fir tree. Symbols had been carved into the rough bark, indistinct in the half-light. She could make out birds and fishes, signs of the zodiac and men and women crudely sexualised. Tatters of fabric hung from the overarching branches. Attached to them were dolls roughly made of straw. At the base of the tree, the carpet of pine needles had been cleared and there was compacted soil, as if the place was used regularly.

It felt as if they had slipped somehow, passed into another world. The dolls, as they turned in the light breeze, chilled her. The images of men with erect phalli and the women with inflated breasts and bellies were shocking – not because they were sexual but because they were keys and signposts to something archaic. He was leading her somewhere, taking her further from her known world. She wondered if these were the gates to a place that the priests called hell. Xavier would qualify as guide and demifiend to that place. The torches on his chest lit passageways that sense and fear occluded. There was also moonlight, pushing its fingers into the clearing and turning their naked flesh a silver blue. He told her to squat and then knelt between her opened thighs. He kissed her and told her to pee.

It wasn't easy. She was self-conscious. Her belly hung between her open legs like a hard, unripe fruit refusing to yield its juice. He stroked her face reassuringly. So many fluids had issued from her that evening, but this was the hardest. Finally, with a great sigh, she relaxed and the sphincter eased.

The fluid issued in a steady stream, hot and strong. He mixed it into the soil with his fingers where it fell. Once the self-consciousness had gone, it was strangely erotic to urinate with a stranger watching her. It was even more erotic when he slipped the fingers of his left hand inside her belly so that the stream played over his hand and ran back along the inside of her thighs. The liquid caressed her like a tongue, found her most sensitive places, seethed in hot swirls across the pouting lips of her anus.

The fingers of his left hand were still inside her as the fingers of his right made the sign of benediction. He took in lips, breasts and forehead as before, but this time her sex as well. At the extremity of each sweeping pass, his fingers pressed into her flesh, leaving a dark mark, an amalgam of the island's soil and her own fluids.

152

Anointed thus, he led her to the other end of the clearing, plucking up the torch as they went. Half-hidden behind a bush was a dark, narrow opening. Xavier squeezed through first. When Giselle followed she found herself in a low passageway. They had to crouch and edge forward like crabs. Narrow spaces had always made her nervous. When the torch brushed the roof, stones fell, bringing a feeling close to panic. There was a sharp turn to the right.

Suddenly they were in a large, high-ceilinged chamber, lit not just by the torch but by a column of light in the centre. As Xavier moved forward the column became brighter and she realised that it was pure rock crystal sparkling in the light of the lamp. The crystals were large and well formed, their geometry striking amongst the rough-hewn walls of the chamber. Xavier walked around the column slowly and Giselle followed. She remembered the rock crystal at the summit of the island and wondered if the mineral vein ran clear through the island, from base to summit. Peering within the transparent pillar she could see refracted images of Xavier and reflections of her own awed eyes.

They walked twice around the pillar, then Xavier knelt and gestured for Giselle to do the same. The feelings that she had had as a girl in the Church of Saint Saviour filled her breast. Then, she had knelt and gazed in awe at the statue of the Virgin Mary. The pillar had the same power and was a greater mystery – a natural column that pierced mother earth like a phallus.

Xavier reached out and touched the column, his fingertips tracing the edges of the crystals, testing the sharp edges, encompassing the octagonal sections. There was reverence, and surprise, in his eyes though he must have seen them many times before. This unselfconscious absorption was so different to his usual coolness.

'In daytime there is a snake that dances in this column,' he told her. 'The energy of the sun is drawn downwards, concentrated, metamorphosed. Sometimes, too, on nights such as this, when the moon is full . . .'

He snatched up the torch and buried the head in the soft soil. Abruptly, they were in darkness. Giselle's feeling of claustrophobia returned. She had to wrestle with the feelings of panic, push them into the corners of her mind.

They remained silent as their eyes adjusted. Then, Xavier grasped her hand suddenly, making her jump.

'Look! There.'

He ran her hand across the column but, at first, she saw nothing. All was blackness. Then, as she looked more closely, she was aware of movement. In the midst of the column there was a faint blue light, a snake that coiled and uncoiled before her astonished eyes. It was one of the most beautiful things that she had ever seen, as mesmerising and seductive as the gaze of a lover.

'It is the moon,' Xavier breathed.

'How?'

Even as she spoke, she remembered the crystal at the tip of the island and realised that the column really must be continuous. Somehow, the light of the moon had been captured and transmitted through the column, down through the island itself, passing beyond them to depths that she could only imagine. She remembered the tattoo on Xavier's sex, the gold and blue snake that writhed as he came to erection. It was a symbol of power, but not corporeal, not the power of flesh. The essence before her was spirit, a natural magic whose power was wonder.

The memory of his sex fired baser feelings; there was a jolt in her belly as if she had been touched deep inside. The knowledge of their nakedness, an awareness of the hard body beside her, produced a need to be filled. In the darkness and isolation she felt weak, and that weakness amplified her desires.

Perhaps it was her hand squeezing his that transmitted those feelings, perhaps he heard her breathing snag, then quicken. It seemed that something prompted him to push her to the ground and enter her. His hardness in her belly was a revelation, as if the darkness had parted to reveal the gardens of Elysium. The arousal she had felt when he had taken her beside the fire was a mere taste, a foreshadowing of the arousal that swept through her body there in the bowels of the earth.

All sense of who she was disappeared. His flesh was an envelope. He was her air and earth; the feelings in her belly were fire and water. The thing inside her moved slowly. The teeth at her neck bit deep. There were words and groans as if overheard. Perhaps it was her cries that filled her ears, perhaps it was the creatures of the island. In the darkness, her eyes made their own images. Snakes of blue and gold danced. Crossed torches blazed. Beautiful boys touched and tore at her. In the centre of all this was the pleasure – high and fine like a stretched piano wire. He struck chord after chord from her womb and the chamber reverberated to a mighty symphony. His sex was a hardness that burned and her belly was consumed in its flames. When he withdrew, her screams were suddenly real. She lay in the darkness, alone, not knowing who or what she was, and the sense of loss was complete. It was as if she had woken from sleep in deep space, without even the comfort of the stars.

Then there was a flare of light and she saw Xavier holding a match to the torch. It blazed with a sudden golden light. The pillar gleamed and she quietened herself.

When he knelt and looked down at her heaving chest and disarranged limbs she had the sense of being read. Without the strength to resist, she let him thumb through her as if she were a text written in blood and sweat. It felt good to be so known. She was grateful that an inventory was being taken. If she ever forgot herself completely, he could reinstate her, make her who she was again.

'You will be mistreated,' he told her softly. His expression was regretful, as if the decision was beyond his power, as if external agencies had made the decision. 'You will not be Paige to be doted on, or Joan to be tolerated and indulged.'

She looked at him in surprise. He talked for a long time and it felt as if she was being instructed in inescapable facts, as if he were helping her to accept a fate that couldn't be altered.

155

'Your innocence and beauty fit you perfectly to the path of suffering,' he said at the end, after he had spoken for what seemed hours, but could only have been minutes.

Reality returned with a sudden chill feeling in her stomach. She remembered Giscard as he had dragged her into the circle of the fire and thrown her at Xavier's feet. She remembered the slaps – how they had shocked her, but also quietened her. Would there be more of that? Worse? She wanted to ask him exactly what would be expected. Instead, she responded like an automaton as his hand pushed her head to his groin. She sucked him as he described what would be done. His language was blunt and crude. Each obscenity was like a stab to her sex, cruel and arousing. A tingling began in her stomach as he said that she would be tied. A wetness bred in her sex when he said that she would be beaten.

She was lost again.

He turned her over and slapped the inside of her thighs. She looked up at him, mildly. The pain was a long way away; only the echoes of it touched her. Afterwards, he might have penetrated her. Or he might have licked the tears from her eyes. She seemed to remember both things. The pleasure of being treated softly after she had been hurt was intense. She didn't protest when he told her they would use more than their hands.

She would be a toy for the boys who came to the island. She would be a sink for their most perverse desires. She would bring all evils to the surface, she would cleanse them with her suffering. She would never condemn. Her lips would bless their cruelties. She would seek out the secrets of their hearts – their darkness would be her light. She would ask if they wanted more. She would win their trust.

The great storehouses of sin would be opened and she would enter in. Her innocence would survive. She would transform all things, be the philosophers' stone transmuting base metals to gold, remaining pure and unchanged in herself. Silver would be her colour, the moon her planet. Lacking light in herself she would be like rock crystal, lit by the lights of others. She would hold all of their images. The souls of the boys would refract through her. The impurity of the ages would flow through her and issue as golden light. The Bacchae would collect her tears in adamantine jars. Her pain would be a healing unguent, her excitement the elixir of the ancients.

His voice changed as he spoke. There seemed to be many voices in the small chamber; as many voices as there were lights. She gazed up at him, meekly accepting the metamorphoses. She saw her priest and her teacher. Her father glowered from dark eyes. He was Paige and Joan, soft but demanding. The shifting light of the torch on the rough walls allowed her to see all creatures: foxes and bats, swans and magpies. Many of the apparitions were too transitory to be named. Wild boars frightened her but her fears were contained. The chamber around her was warm like a womb. An antelope drank from a silver pool. The man touched her forehead and smiled – Xavier again. The shades that she had seen now vanished. The walls were blood red and warm.

He enunciated his words with gravity and passion, as a priest speaks. It was a voice that used a mortal frame but had no earthly origin. It seemed that the crystal spoke through him, and the island through the crystal.

She was drunk with his sex. The places that he had anointed burned. She wanted to feast on his seed, to consume his essence. She seemed to be only a mouth – formed to swallow, bred to need, blessed with the grace of giving and taking. Her throat opened as she drove down on his sex. It was effortless to take him all. A relief for the void to be filled.

The thought that she would be beaten seized her and she groaned, rubbing her sex into the beaten soil. Her legs opened to their fullest and her belly pressed down of its own accord. When she asked, he told her how she would be beaten – those parts of her body that would be spared, those that would not. At each word she grovelled more deeply, impaled her throat more fully on his sex. There was a lust for the rivers of impurity that he promised. She

157

wanted to be used, to transform all that is bad into the goodness of pure light. Her spirit would be crystal, her body the island. The boys would climb her, tear at her roots, bury their treasures in her, take her fruits, cast their seed and empty their wastes into her uncomplaining soil. She would be a Mary to them and a Magdalen; a whore, a sweetheart and a mother. As this madness washed through her, Xavier sat back on his heels, raising his pelvis and arching his back. The semen began to flow. She was greedy for it but he seized her hair and pulled her head away. The first pulses of white coated her lips and cheeks.

'Agree!' he told her. 'Agree now and never renounce me!'

She nodded, gazing into his eyes with the devotion of a pilgrim. He released her hair and she immediately buried his sex deep in her mouth, catching the last pulses of semen on a worshipful tongue. There was a gratitude that came from beneath conscious feeling – from her muscles and bones; deeper still, from cell and membrane, enzyme and protoplasm.

It was a long time before he ceased shuddering.

He filled her mouth many times but seemed always to remain hard. Perhaps there were quiet times. She had a memory afterwards of being held, but it was indistinct, like a dream. Only his hardness as he filled her mouth and the taste of him was clear – and the words that outlined her fate: his insistence, though she made no argument, and his hardness when she was as soft as love.

THE BLACK GARTER

Lisette Ashton

Lisette Ashton is one of the most talented new authors of erotic fiction in the field. Her novels always have unusual and contemporary settings: one is set on the Amazon (*Amazon Slave*), while another (*Fairground Attractions*) is set – you've guessed it – in a fairground. Her characters are always credible, and they demonstrate her enthusiasm for the perverse world of domination and submission.

The following extract is taken from Lisette's third Nexus novel. Here, Debbie is worried that the members of the Black Garter know that she's been selling stories about them to the local paper. Here's a full list of Lisette's novels:

Debbie replaced the telephone receiver, her heart beating fast. She did not like having to use the public telephone in the common room but her mobile was charging back in her dorm and she had needed to make the call quickly. The fear of being overheard had stayed with her as she talked and it was only when she finally severed the connection that she allowed herself to breathe easily again.

'Chalmers. I want a word with you.' A hand fell on her shoulder and the gentle tinkle of golden charms, rattling softly on a heavy bracelet, left Debbie in no doubt as to who had caught her.

She whirled around, startled to hear Hera's voice so close to her. She swallowed nervously when she saw that Hera was not alone. Standing on either side of her, arms folded and impatient scowls twisting their lips, were Melanie and Grace. The two women glared menacingly at Debbie.

'Hera?' Debbie said, her heart beating like a military tattoo. 'What do you want?'

Hera smiled. 'I think you know what I want,' she said coolly. 'It will be best if you and I talk in private.'

Debbie glanced around the empty common room, wishing there was someone she could turn to for help. The idea was ludicrous as she had few friends at the Kilgrimol and, even if she had been adored by everyone, Debbie knew that she would still have been alone in a confrontation with Hera. 'I have a class,' she stammered nervously, snatching at the first excuse her frightened mind could think of.

Hera shook her head. 'All your classes have been cancelled for today.'

Debbie glanced from Hera to Melanie and Grace. She knew she had no choice other than to do as Hera commanded. The prospect of what might lie ahead left her cold.

'We'll talk in your room,' Hera said, turning her back on Debbie. 'Anna's going to be out for most of the evening so we should be afforded some privacy.'

Debbie watched the woman walking away and when she noticed Melanie and Grace still staring impassively at her, she knew she had to follow. As she fell into step behind Hera, the two women walked on either side of Debbie. Sullenly, she realised she had no hope of escape. Whatever Hera had in mind, there was no chance of avoiding it.

They walked along the empty corridors of the Kilgrimol's long halls, heading towards the east wing where the dormitories were situated. The sun had already fallen from these corridors and the building was held in the thrall of a still, grey light. Debbie glanced at the baize-covered cork-boards they passed with unseeing eyes. She was dreading whatever lay ahead and she knew she had every reason.

'I was a trifle hard on you the other evening,' Hera said quietly. She was still walking purposefully forward, the words thrown casually over her shoulder as she marched towards the dormitories.

Debbie frowned, not sure she had heard the woman correctly. 'When?' she asked.

Hera stopped and turned to face her. Her features were contorted into a dark mask of anger and Debbie wanted to cower away from them. 'The other evening when I had you tied to a bed and I was dripping candle wax on your cunt lips,' Hera hissed sharply. She pressed her face close to Debbie's and said, 'Do you remember that, or do you need a reminder?'.

162

Debbie's cheeks coloured darkly. She remembered the evening so vividly that when she closed her eyes, she could still feel the burning spatter of wax against her bare flesh.

Like the majority of girls at the Kilgrimol, Debbie had embraced the dream of becoming a Black Garter girl. The panache and flair of the women involved with the group was enviable and to be accepted by them would have meant she was part of an elite team.

The night had started with the usual air of menace and gloom that seemed to pervade all of Hera's ceremonies. The bedroom was dark save for the flickering glow of the candlelight; long, wavering shadows stretched along the walls of the bedroom. Naked, and frightened, Debbie had been tied to the bed. Before she had started to do anything, Hera had demanded Debbie remain silent throughout the initiation. It was the only condition she had insisted on. If Debbie managed to obey that condition, Hera explained that she would have earned her black garter.

Desperately wanting to join the group, Debbie had agreed to the condition. She had tried not to fidget restlessly as the woman undressed and she had tried to contain her rising panic when Hera had dripped molten candle wax across the taut buds of her bared nipples. She had stayed silent throughout the entire beauty of the punishing experience. The pleasure of submitting herself to such indignities was greater than she would have believed and she did not know if the promise of acceptance was the thing that excited her or if she had a submissive side that Hera had inadvertently discovered. Whatever the cause of her enjoyment, the fact was she had orgasmed twice whilst Hera punished her. The pleasure had been bitter and tinged with degrees of pain that should have made her scream. Aware that she was unable to make a sound, Debbie had stayed silent until the last moment. As Hera held the candle over the lips of her pussy, Debbie had thrilled to the exquisite sensation of having her labia waxed. The searing sensation inspired an explosion of delight to rush through her body and she had barely managed to hold back her scream of joy.

And then Hera had blown the candle out. She had placed the base firmly against the lips of Debbie's sex, and was about to push it inside her when Debbie had screamed for her to stop. The words had come out before she knew she was making them. The initiation had ended abruptly. And so had her chances to join the Black Garter. She had allowed herself to be subjected to Hera's initiation ceremony and before it was over, she had failed. The memory of what she had lost was more unsettling than the pain could ever have been.

'I don't need a reminder,' Debbie whispered softly.

Hera nodded. She turned away and started back towards the dormitories. 'I was a trifle hard on you then,' Hera repeated, 'and I suppose I owe you some sort of an apology.'

Debbie stared uncertainly at the woman's back. She had been expecting a punishment of some sort, or worse. Because Hera had caught her concluding the telephone call, Debbie had thought her secret had been exposed and waves of relief washed over her.

'An apology?' Debbie whispered.

'Not that I'm going to apologise,' Hera went on, turning a corner and starting up a flight of stairs. 'But to try and rectify the situation, I thought you'd appreciate a second chance to join us.'

Debbie felt her heart beginning to soar. She glanced from Melanie to Grace, her eyes wide with disbelieving happiness. A sudden thought struck her and she felt a heavy storm cloud pass over the sunshine of her hopes. Placing a hand on Hera's shoulder, she stopped the leader and placed her mouth to the woman's ear.

Hera frowned. 'Initiates have no place dictating what will or won't happen.' A smile softened her face and she added, 'But because you had the guts to say that, I'll bear it in mind.'

Debbie followed the woman into the dormitory with a grateful smile on her lips. Melanie closed the door and Grace sat herself on the dusty chair next to the cluttered desk. Anna was continually complaining about the untidy, dishevelled appearance of the dorm but Debbie was quite fond of its homely charm. She stared at Hera, standing amongst the clutter and disarray of the room.

Before the woman had a chance to say anything, Debbie uncoupled her mobile phone from the battery charger, annoyed that it had already replenished its battery. The realisation of how much she could have lost through using the public telephone still weighed heavily on her mind. Aware that Hera was frowning at her, Debbie placed the phone in a drawer.

'You didn't do very well the other evening,' Hera said crisply. 'Silence doesn't seem to be your strong suit.'

Debbie blushed, her cheeks not just reddening at the memory of blowing her first chance of acceptance with the Black Garter. But before she had a chance to dwell on the other matter, she realised Hera was still talking.

'In the light of what you've just told me, I suppose I can understand your stopping me. I realise now that I was right to give you a second chance but be warned, this is the last one. You won't be given a third chance to join us.'

Swallowing nervously, Debbie nodded.

'Strip her,' Hera commanded crisply.

Before Debbie had a chance to respond, she felt Melanie and Grace grab hold of her. The two women tugged at her clothes and began to briskly remove them from her body. Not daring to protest, Debbie allowed them to do as they wanted.

'Before we get down to business,' Hera said tersely, 'I think we need to talk about your abominable behaviour this morning.'

Debbie swallowed unhappily. 'Yes,' she said quickly, remembering her outburst in the canteen. 'I'm sorry about that. I –'

Hera cut her words off. 'Assume the position,' she commanded crisply.

Debbie opened her mouth, about to make a protest, then stopped herself. The delight she felt at being given a second chance to join the Black Garter was stronger than her fear of Hera's punishment. The woman had said this was a matter to be dealt with before her initiation and that meant she could look forward to being allowed the chance of joining after she had earned her forgiveness. She turned her back to Hera and bent over, pushing the cheeks of her arse out.

A pair of hands, Hera's she assumed, caressed the peach-like skin of her backside. The touch was soft, almost loving, and Debbie suppressed a tremor of excitement.

'Nice arse,' Hera murmured.

Debbie felt the woman's fingers brush daringly close to the cleft of her sex and, unable to stop herself, she drew a sharp breath of surprise. The intimacy of Hera's touch had aroused her more than she had anticipated and she struggled against the emotion that welled within her.

A hand slapped hard across one cheek. The blow was hard and unexpected and left a stinging redness in its wake that had her shivering. She released a small groan of surprise, not wanting to give her discomfort greater voice for fear of being thought unworthy.

A second blow, harder than the first, slapped the other cheek.

This time it was harder to bite back the squeal of surprise as the stinging handprint on her arse burnt dully.

From the corner of her eye, she saw Melanie and Grace move behind her. Their hands were suddenly holding her legs and she could feel their fingers close to the tops of her thighs. Without any care or tenderness, she felt the cheeks of her arse being spread wide apart.

She held her breath, not daring to think what Hera had in store for her. The woman's intentions already seemed obvious enough but Debbie dared not dwell on them for too long. She was afraid that her nervousness would make her do, or say, the wrong thing.

She felt another stinging blow of pain on her backside and she grunted unhappily. This time the bite had been harder and crueller. This had been no slap from Hera's open palm, she realised. The blow had been too stiff and impersonal for that. Recalling the untidy clutter of papers,

166

sweet wrappers and stationery on her desk, she wondered if Hera had taken something from there.

Her thoughts were confirmed a moment later when Hera asked softly, 'You don't mind my borrowing your ruler, do you?'

Debbie shook her head. Her thoughts were a turmoil of fear and excitement and she was dreading the sting of the ruler against her arse again. She dared not contemplate why Melanie and Grace were holding her in such a way as, although the proximity of the two women and the softness of their touch was exciting, Debbie still felt more apprehension than she was comfortable with.

Repeatedly, Hera slapped the ruler hard against Debbie's arse. The tip bit like acid into the hot flesh and it took every ounce of willpower she possessed to stop herself from shrieking. Each blow seemed to get closer and closer to the ultra-sensitive flesh of her sex and the effort of self-restraint became greater with each resounding thwack of the plastic against her exposed skin.

The hardest stroke, as she had feared it would, landed squarely against the puckered ring of her arsehole. In spite of all her efforts to contain her cries, Debbie heard herself shriek as a bolt of pain shot from her backside, filling her body with a tingling explosion. The sensation felt so close to pleasure she wondered briefly how she should be able to tell the difference.

A second blow, lighter but just as accurate, sparked a second eruption of fire throughout her. The ruler's tip felt suddenly sharp against her anus and instantly she could differentiate between these feelings and true pleasure. Pleasure, she could endure. The intolerable explosion that now inflamed her body was something she could not endure for a moment longer.

As though she had read Debbie's thoughts, Hera commanded her aides to let go and turn Debbie around. 'Do you consider yourself punished?' Hera asked crisply.

Blushing and unwilling to meet the woman's eyes, Debbie nodded.

Hera smiled softly. 'I suppose that will do for the moment,' she conceded. 'I'll allow you to speak during this initiation,' Hera went on magnanimously. 'You may say yes, or no. Just remember if you do say any other word, your last chance will be over. Do you understand?'

Debbie nodded. 'Yes,' she whispered.

'That's good.' She glanced around the untidy room and her eyes fell on a collection of sweets on the corner of Debbie's desk. Hera picked up an M & M and placed it in her mouth. As she teased the sweet with her tongue she appraised Debbie's large breasts. 'I love your tits,' she said in a matter-of-fact tone.

Debbie blushed. She was about to mumble a thank-you when she remembered the condition Hera had given – the words 'thank you' were neither a yes or a no. Smiling with embarrassment, she tried not to meet Hera's lascivious gaze. When she felt Hera's finger tracing softly against the dark brown flesh of her areola, she forced herself to stay still and endure the woman's touch.

'Do you like Debbie's tits?' Hera asked.

Debbie glanced up to see the question had been directed at Melanie. The mousy-blonde girl smiled and nodded. Without any encouragement, she placed her hand over one of Debbie's orbs and squeezed the mound fondly.

Debbie inhaled deeply.

Melanie's fingers stroked and caressed the bare flesh, her long manicured fingernails teasing the taut tip of Debbie's nipple and rolling the hard little bud between her finger and thumb.

Still fearing Hera's retribution, Debbie resisted the urge to sigh.

Hera was smiling at her. 'I want to test your obedience,' she explained carefully. 'Is that acceptable to you, Debbie?' As she asked the question, she slipped a second M & M into her mouth.

'Yes,' Debbie replied nervously. To get into the Black Garter she was prepared to do almost anything.

Hera made a show of enjoying the sweet and reached for a third. 'Do you like these sweeties, Debbie?'

Puzzled by the sudden distraction, Debbie frowned and nodded. Aware that she was able to respond properly, she said quickly, 'Yes.'

Hera placed the third sweet between her teeth and moved her mouth close to Debbie's. 'Take this one,' she commanded.

Debbie moved her mouth close to Hera's, all too aware of what she was being asked to do. Her lips touched Hera's and she reached for the small round sweet with a hesitant tongue. She felt the sweet fall into her mouth and before she could move her head away, she was being kissed. Hera's tongue plunged into her mouth, tasting her, exploring and exciting her.

The tight buds of her nipples, still enjoying the gentle caresses of Melanie's fingertips, stood harder than before and then a second pair of hands began to stroke her body and she realised that Grace was touching her as well. The multiple stimulation was delightfully unanticipated and a light film of excited sweat rose across her forehead.

Hera broke the kiss and grinned at Debbie who was still enjoying the attention of the two other women. She swallowed the untasted sweet whole and fixed Hera with an expectant expression.

'Did you enjoy that?' Hera asked coolly.

'Yes,' Debbie replied.

Hera grabbed the packet of sweets and passed one each to Melanie and Grace. They both seemed to know what was expected of them. Melanie placed an M & M between her teeth and placed her mouth mere inches away from Debbie's.

With a sigh of excitement, Debbie found herself kissing another woman within seconds of having kissed her first. On the night of her initiation, even though they had both been naked and Hera had been exciting and aroused her, there had been no real intimacy. Then, there had just been the flickering threat of the candle and the exquisite delight of the molten wax. Admittedly, she had climaxed and each orgasm had been a rich, satisfying experience but they had not been warmed by the pleasure of intimacy.

This was different and, although she felt just as frightened, not all of the excitement could properly have been called unpleasant. Her breasts were still being expertly fondled by Hera's colleagues and shivers of delight were erupting inside her body. When her kiss with Melanie had ended, she felt her head being twisted to meet Grace's mouth.

Grace virtually spat the sweet into Debbie's mouth before greedily pressing her lips against the blonde's. The fury of her animal passion was so intense it was frightening and Debbie felt overwhelmed by the woman's urgent command of her. Grace's tongue filled her mouth and, as she kissed, her fingers pressed mercilessly hard against the soft flesh of Debbie's eager breast.

When their kiss finally ended, Debbie dared to swallow the sweet. She glanced meekly at Hera to see if she was still meeting with the woman's approval.

Hera was smiling at her.

'You do like those sweets, don't you,' Hera observed lightly. 'I can't recall the last time I saw someone enjoying chocolate so much.'

Debbie grinned softly, not daring to look away.

'Perhaps you'd care to take another from me?' Hera suggested. She waited for Debbie to nod acceptance before reaching for the packet. Settling herself on the chair, Hera raised the hem of her short skirt and parted her legs so that the lips of her half-shaven pussy were on bold display. With elegant fingers, she placed the M & M against the lips of her labia and then moved them away. Smiling excitedly up at Debbie, she said quietly, 'Take your sweet.'

Debbie could feel her heart beating fast with excitement. The woman was breathtakingly beautiful and Debbie had always found herself drawn to her. She had not considered her feelings to be sexual before, but now that the chance was being offered she saw no reason to deny herself. She was already enjoying stimulation from Melanie's and Grace's caress and if her mind considered that to be acceptable, then she saw no reason not to take the sweet that Hera was offering.

She licked her lips as she moved her mouth close to the warmth of Hera's sex. The sight of Hera's black garter circumnavigating her leg reminded Debbie of the reward she would receive for going through with this. It was inspiration enough to make her move her mouth quickly downwards.

More than anything she wanted to join the Black Garter. If this was what she had to do to join then Debbie was more than willing. The thoughts of atonement and revenge were now gone from her mind. She knew she had wronged the group over the last few weeks but she believed she could end all of that whenever she wanted. No one knew what she had done and, if she had her way, no one was going to know. If Hera deigned to accept her into the Black Garter, then Debbie was prepared to work hard to make up for the wrong she had done the group. If it involved doing things like this, then she believed she could honestly look forward to making amends.

She placed her mouth gently against the soft folds of Hera's sex and licked the sweet away from her. Without thinking, even after she had swallowed the confectionery, Debbie traced her tongue against the flesh a second, then a third time. The heady taste of Hera's musky pussy juice filled her nostrils. The fragrance was so rich and erotic, she could feel her own excitement mounting quickly.

Melanie and Grace had followed her to the floor as she knelt before the group's leader. Relentlessly, they still teased and caressed her. Grace nibbled playfully at her ear, exciting the sensitive flesh of her lobe, whilst Melanie had daringly moved her mouth over one of Debbie's nipples and was rubbing the tip with her tongue. Sparks of pure delight erupted from the sensitive tips of her breasts. Exhilarating waves of delicious pleasure had begun to rush over her, filling her with warmth. Debbie tried to ignore the distractions they were giving her. Both women were exciting and glamorous creatures and whilst neither of them compared to Hera she would still have been happy to entertain their individual attention. Having them both touch and caress her was so exquisite it was almost intolerable.

'Eat my cunt,' Hera whispered softly.

Debbie held her breath, not daring to believe what she had heard Hera command. Her nose was a kiss away from the lips of Hera's sex and, although she had already brushed the woman's labia with her tongue, the thought of being commanded to perform oral sex still unnerved her. She gazed at Hera's nether lips, trying to inhale the intoxicating fragrance of pussy honey that glistened against the darkly flushed folds of flesh.

'Prove your obedience and eat my cunt,' Hera whispered.

Debbie glanced up from her silent appraisal of Hera's cleft and realised the woman was staring at her darkly. A smile twisted her lips but there was a subtle air of menace lighting her eyes and Debbie feared the retribution that lurked at the back of them. Without delay she pushed her tongue into Hera's depths. Her mouth and nostrils were suddenly filled with the heady scent of the woman's desire. The delicate pink lips of her sex seemed to kiss Debbie's mouth as she rubbed her tongue deep inside and the musky bouquet and the rich flavour of her arousal seemed to envelop and possess her.

Aware of the pleasure she was deriving from the act, Debbie stopped, realising she was on the brink of an orgasm. She was baffled. She knew that Melanie and Grace were stimulating her sexually and she could not deny that they were highly skilled, but they could not have inspired this magnitude of arousal; their touch was so soft and subtle her body was simply enjoying it, not revelling in it. The climactic thrill that filled her was far greater than anything either of those two could arouse. Smiling up at Hera, Debbie realised what the source of her excitement was.

Considering her great beauty and magnificent charms, Debbie knew that Hera was the one who was affecting her this way and, when she saw the smile being returned, Debbie moved her mouth back to the cleft between Hera's legs. She plunged her tongue deep inside Hera, guzzling pussy juices that filled her mouth and made her feel dizzy with the delight of being allowed such a

172

privilege. Then she flicked the tip of her tongue against the hardening swell of Hera's clitoris, surprised to see the nub pulse beneath the slick touch of her tongue.

Hera's fingers brushed through her hair, tugging softly at the blonde tresses and urging her to lift, then lower her face. For a moment Debbie felt as though she were a machine that Hera was using just to perform cunnilingus. It was not unpleasant and Debbie realised distantly she did not mind being used in such a way. She could have lapped at Hera's pussy for the rest of the evening.

'Enough,' Hera snapped abruptly. She spoke as though she had read Debbie's thoughts and knew she was enjoying her initiation too much. Pulling Debbie's hair sharply, Hera moved herself away from the deft ministrations of the blonde's eager tongue. 'I want to see how obedient you are,' Hera reminded her, standing.

Debbie nodded, trying to hide her disappointment at not being allowed to continue using her tongue. She realised Hera was studying the untidy clutter of her desk and she saw the frown of disapproval crease her forehead before she spoke.

'This place is a fucking dump,' she murmured softly. 'No wonder Anna despises this place and calls it a hovel.'

Debbie drew breath as though she had been slapped. She needed Hera's praise and encouragement; the woman's reassurance and support were like a drug that she suddenly craved. Words like this hurt worse than the fiercest blow she had received from the ruler.

'You'll tidy your act up if you're allowed into the Black Garter, do you understand?' Hera growled, running her fingertips through the scattered papers.

Debbie nodded earnestly. 'Yes,' she whispered. The word was not simply an agreement. It was a pledge.

Hera nodded, seemingly satisfied. Her fingers found something on the desk and she picked it up. Dangling between her finger and thumb, she held a long chain of paper clips high. She grinned happily at them as though an idea had just occurred to her. A cruel smile thinned her lips and she stared at Melanie and Grace.

173

'Take the seat, Mel,' Hera commanded generously. 'Let Debbie have another sweetie while you sit there.'

Melanie reached beneath the hem of her short skirt and pulled her panties off in one lithe, well-practised motion. She settled herself in the chair that Hera had vacated, smiling gratefully at the leader, then slowly turned her attention to Debbie. She raised the hem of her skirt to reveal the thick swatch of dark curly hairs that covered her sex and took two M & Ms. She placed one against the lips of her vagina then licked the second one, wetting the crisp sugar shell so that it was slightly sticky. With a careful finger, she touched the sweet against her anus. She held it with a fingernail for a moment, then moved her hand away. The M & M remained against her arsehole, waiting for Debbie to remove it with her mouth.

Hera grinned when she saw this. 'Eat your sweeties, Debbie,' she insisted gently.

Swallowing nervously, wishing the thought of what she had to do was not so disturbingly arousing, Debbie placed her mouth between Melanie's legs. She licked the first sweet easily, her tongue tracing lightly against Melanie's pouting labia. Before she even dared to contemplate the second one, she moved her mouth away and tried to pluck up the necessary courage. The sweet rested against the forbidden flesh of Melanie's anus and Debbie knew that if she wanted to join the Black Garter, she had to take it from there. The scent of Melanie's sex was drawn into her with each nervous inhalation. Perhaps the woman's fragrance was not as intoxicating or as divine as Hera's, but Debbie found she was still excited by the subtle aroma. The pulse of her desire was beating a strong, urgent staccato. As she moved closer, her eyes seemed to close involuntarily. She felt her nose brush against the folds of skin. The tip was suddenly wet with the glistening dew of Melanie's honey and her nostrils were plunged into the warm, moist haven of her sex.

Daringly, holding her breath with excited anticipation, Debbie flicked her tongue out and touched the M & M. The hard, pill-like sweet stayed where it was, and Debbie realised it was not simply going to jump into her mouth. She opened her eyes and stared at it, poignantly aware of Melanie's nearness. She realised that to get the sweet in her mouth, she had to put her lips against the flesh of Melanie's arsehole. The realisation brought with it a shiver of nervousness that was not wholly unpleasant.

Placing her tongue below Melanie's backside, Debbie gently drew the tip upwards, keeping it placed against the hot flesh. She felt herself touching the sweet, then it fell into her mouth. In that instant, she realised she had her tongue pressed firmly against the tight ring of Melanie's anus. The sensations of excitement and sheer humiliation were so thrilling she wondered if she was going to orgasm merely from licking someone. She swallowed the sweet and with a bold thrust of her tongue, she entered Melanie's backside. The woman's squeals of delight from above were encouragement enough for Debbie to continue and she prodded her tongue as far into the dark canal as she possibly could.

'You're enjoying that too much,' Hera barked suddenly.

Debbie felt Melanie flinch away from her. In the same instant she heard a slap and wondered what had happened. When she glanced up she saw Melanie holding a bruised cheek and staring miserably at Hera. The scene explained itself. She stared warily at Hera, wondering if she too was due for another bout of punishment. The thought brought mixed feelings of excitement and trepidation.

'You're not here to cream your fucking knickers,' Hera growled in Melanie's ear. 'You're here to help me with an initiation.'

Melanie mumbled an apology, still rubbing her face. From the corner of her eye, Debbie saw that Grace was staring at Hera with a certain degree of wariness and she sympathised with the emotion. She barely knew Hera and although she revered the woman, she still regarded her with a great amount of caution.

'Do you make these chains?' Hera asked, holding up the string of paper clips.

Debbie nodded quickly.

Hera grinned and allowed the string of clips to dangle purposefully between her fingers. She placed her hands on either side of the centre and tugged hard. The central paper clip gave and bounced against a wall with a gentle clink. Hera held the two freshly made lengths of chain in her hands and grinned down at Debbie. 'Stand up,' she commanded.

Debbie hurried from the floor, eager to do everything Hera commanded. She watched as Hera took one of the chains and moved towards her breast. The thin sliver of metal glinted dully between her fingers and, as she reached for her nipple, Debbie saw exactly what the woman had in mind.

Words of protest rushed to her lips but she had promised to obey the rule of silence and maintained control despite the fear of what Hera was planning.

'Relax,' Hera snapped coldly. 'You'll only make it hurt more. Melanie could tell you that much.' A wicked glimmer illuminated her face and she smiled at the sullen Melanie. 'Let me show Debbie what I mean.' Her hands moved towards Melanie. Debbie heaved a soft sigh of relief. She knew the moment's reprieve was bound to be short-lived but she was prepared to enjoy any diversion that did not cause her too much discomfort.

Reluctantly, Melanie stood up. On Hera's command she removed the top she was wearing and stood there meek but defiant with her pert breasts exposed to the room.

Debbie snatched a quick look at the small, softly rounded orbs and tried not to stare. In the hedonism of the afternoon's events she felt as though she had lost all sense of decency and proportion. A voice at the back of her mind still insisted that what she was doing was wrong and that she was immoral for enjoying the embarrassment and humiliation of this initiation but, as she gazed at the perfect splendour of Melanie's naked breasts, Debbie could not find it in herself to listen to that voice. The throbbing pulse of her own arousal was too strong to allow her to listen.

As she watched, Hera took the end of the paper-clip chain and fastened one piece of wire against the tip of Melanie's exposed nipple. The metal pressed cruelly hard against the sensitive flesh, making the nub stand awkwardly.

A pained expression flitted across Melanie's face, quickly replaced by a smile of surprised excitement. Melanie drew a deep breath and stared curiously down at the source of this new-found pleasure and her grin broadening, she glanced up at Hera.

Debbie could see the slap coming before it hit Melanie. The mousy-blonde released a soft growl of annoyance but there was no hint of retaliation in her voice or her manner. She met the challenge of Hera's gaze with sultry defiance.

'Stop creaming yourself,' Hera repeated sharply. 'Next time, I won't tell you in such a nice way,' she added menacingly.

Melanie nodded.

Watching, Debbie realised Melanie was manfully resisting the urge to stare at her own nipple. She admired the woman's composure and if she had not been suffering the brunt of Hera's wrath, Debbie knew she would have envied her.

'Doesn't that look good?' Hera murmured, stroking her fingertip softly against the rose-tinted flesh of Melanie's tightly clipped areola.

Debbie nodded and whispered her agreement.

Hera reached artlessly for Debbie's breast and grasped the nipple between her finger and thumb. She rolled the pliant flesh gently, stimulating her with the subtle pressure of her touch. Debbie could feel a groan of delight welling inside her but she suppressed the sound, aware that Hera was likely to punish her for it. She held the woman's gaze, hoping that she was doing exactly what was expected of her.

With deft fingers, Hera slipped the cruel wire of the paper clip over the tip of Debbie's teat. The metal pressed hard against the flesh and Debbie wondered how the biting pain could feel so exquisite. She coughed back a groan of joy and fixed her eye determinedly on Hera, awaiting her next instruction.

Nodding, Hera smiled silent approval.

Debbie could see that her nipple was on the end of the same chain that was attached to Melanie. The length of ineffectual links bowed into a U between them. When Hera accidentally caught the chain with her fingertips, its gentle sway caused delicate waves of delight to ripple through Debbie's breast. Her eyes opened wide as the unexpected pleasure took over her body and filled her with joy. Unconsciously, she realised she was staring at Melanie who seemed to be feeling the same excitement.

Hera took the second length of chain and with quick fingers, she fastened one end to Melanie's other breast. Melanie closed her eyes. Her lips were pressed tight together in a silent grimace that did not look totally pained.

Hera snatched at Debbie's nipple and again rolled the nub between her thumb and forefinger. She seemed to be watching Debbie, as though she was waiting for hesitancy or reluctance. Debbie met her gaze coolly. The expression was rewarded with a smile.

This time, when Hera had fastened the clip against her nipple, she pressed the metal hard against the sensitive flesh. Debbie drew a slow breath, not sure if she was struggling against a moan of despair or a cry of delight.

'And there we have you both,' Hera observed. 'The pair of you are linked.' Her smile tightened cruelly and she moved her mouth close to Debbie's ear. 'Take a step back,' she whispered.

Without any hesitancy, Debbie did as she was instructed. She could see the chain pulling against her nipples but that did not stop her from obeying. Melanie released a soft growl of surprise, her breasts being tugged sharply by Debbie's movement.

A furious passion stole over Debbie and this time she could not suppress the sigh of excitement from escaping. Prickles of pleasure erupted inside her breasts, igniting explosions of delight that seemed to traverse her entire body.

'Kneel down,' Hera commanded.

When she saw the expression of horror that filled Melanie's face her grin broadened. 'I did mean both of you,' Hera explained patiently. She turned her attention to Grace and spoke softly into the woman's ear.

With a reluctant expression and a nervous glance in Melanie's direction, Grace nodded assent to Hera's whispered command. She helped her friend into a kneeling position as Debbie lowered herself to the floor. They both managed to make the movement without experiencing any great measure of discomfort from the chains that linked them.

Hera stepped between them, her legs straddling the chain easily. She smiled down at Debbie and raised her skirt. 'This is your last test of obedience,' she explained quietly. 'All you have to do is lick my cunt, and keep those clips on your tits.'

Debbie nodded her acceptance. She saw Grace move behind Hera and realised that Melanie was going to have to do the same thing for her. The chain between their breasts was already stretched taut. With the two women between them, the links felt as though they were being stretched to biting point and Debbie could feel her breasts being gently pulled and tugged by the merciless clip that bit into her nipple.

Trying not to think of the discomfort or the pleasure it aroused, Debbie raised her head to Hera's sex. She pushed her tongue into the moist hole and licked greedily at the slick wetness that waited for her. The pain in her nipples was already thrilling her beyond belief and with the added excitement of drinking Hera's pussy honey she could feel herself hurtling madly towards a powerful orgasm. Her body ached with the pounding pulse of her joy and as she lapped furiously at the delicate folds of Hera's sex, she could feel the euphoria of divine bliss sweeping over her like an all-encompassing blanket. Her entire body seemed to have been filled with the delight of orgasm and she wondered distantly if such an act was permissible in the middle of an initiation. She was unable

179

to see Hera's face from her position below her but she was determined to stall her climax until she felt sure it was allowed.

Gradually, as the biting in her breasts seemed to increase in intensity, she realised she was being pushed backwards. She could just make out the delicious mounds of Grace's backside and noted the woman had moved slightly away from Hera. With a soft smile of realisation, Debbie saw that the two women were deliberately forcing her and Melanie backwards. Each careful step was placing more and more pressure on the links of the chain that connected them.

Hera's hand, pulling her hair sharply, yanked Debbie's head back into the proper position. She knew she should not have needed reminding about the task at hand and eagerly plunged her tongue back against the warm, succulent flesh of Hera's sex.

A soft growl escaped the leader. Debbie felt the noise rather than heard it but she could not stop herself from smiling when she realised she had been the instigator of the woman's pleasure. Her smile disappeared when Hera stepped forward, thrusting the lips of her demanding pussy into Debbie's face.

Pushed backwards, Debbie felt the pressure on her nipples reach an unbearable pitch. The delicate pleasure they had given her at first was now replaced by a constant pulse that was almost an ache. Her body was screaming for the release of an orgasm and she did not know if she could contain the explosion of delight much longer.

Grace and Melanie were making sounds of enjoyment and she tried not to think of the things they might be doing to one another. Instead, she tried to channel her thoughts away from her own enjoyment and into the task of pleasing Hera. Her concentration was focused on Hera's pussy. Both the scent and the taste were totally exhilarating.

'Yes,' Hera growled, her voice rich with triumphant elation. Her fingers still rested on Debbie's hair and she tugged hard as she enjoyed the explosion of her orgasm.

Debbie could feel her face being pressed into the dark swatch of pubic curls and a fine spray of pussy juice spattered against her cheeks and nose, exciting her with their warmth and intimacy. Too late, she realised the excitement of Hera's climax had proved too much. As the leader orgasmed, she had bucked her hips forward with the force of the pleasure and the pressure on the paper clips had finally grown too strong. Her breasts were suddenly aflame with the exquisite joy of such torturous punishment when the clips delivered their final bite before departing.

She screamed happily as a powerful climax overwhelmed her. Unable to stop herself, she toppled backwards, away from Hera. She fell heavily to the floor, too lost in the rapture of her delight to note the bruises she sustained to her forearm and elbow. The waves of bliss that swept over her were so great she did not even realise Hera had tugged a handful of hairs from her head as she fell.

When her mind finally cleared and she was ready to face reality after the thrill of her climax, she opened her eyes to see Hera smiling benignly down at her.

Behind her, Grace was helping Melanie to dress. The two women seemed to share an intimacy that went beyond their membership of the Black Garter and in her mood of sublime satisfaction, Debbie found herself wishing them well.

'Congratulations,' Hera said, kneeling on the floor next to Debbie. She leant forward and placed a soft kiss on Debbie's lips. Moving back slightly, she reached for Debbie's ankle and moved her hands over it.

Debbie's heart was beating with excitement as she realised what Hera was doing. An inane grin split her lips and she smiled giddily at the woman.

Hera fastened the garter at the top of Debbie's leg and, after sliding her hands from beneath it, she allowed her fingertips to tickle gently against the subsiding pulse of Debbie's labia. 'Welcome to the Black Garter,' Hera whispered.

Debbie wished she could find words that summed up her gratitude properly.

'I wish we could stay and talk,' Hera said, stretching herself as she moved from the floor. 'But I still have a lot to do. I'll want to talk with you in the next couple of days though,' she went on. 'So, I trust you'll make yourself available to me.'

Eagerly, Debbie nodded. She heard the muted ring of her telephone from its drawer. Hesitantly, she glanced at Hera, wondering if she had to ask permission before she could use it.

Hera nodded. 'Take your call,' she told her, 'we're leaving now.'

Debbie watched the three of them leave before going for the telephone. She was warmed by their parting words of farewell and touched by the new look of respect they graced her with. Smiling, she realised it was not truly respect, they were simply looking at her now as though she was an equal.

The telephone continued to ring. Taking it into the bedroom, Debbie lay wearily on the bed and pressed the receive button.

'Bunny? Is that you?'

Debbie recognised Steven's voice straight away.

'Yes, it's me,' she replied quickly. A sudden wave of horror stole over her as she realised how close she had come to destroying her chance of joining the Black Garter. The stories she had told Steven, the information she had given him, it could all have worked so badly against her.

As she held the phone in one hand, she teased the fabric of her new black garter with the other. The sense of accomplishment and belonging that the black garter embodied made her tremble.

'Did you leave a message on my voice-mail?' Steven asked sharply. 'I don't know if my PC's playing up, or if I've had someone snooping through my records.'

Debbie frowned. 'Yes, I left a message,' she assured him. She repeated the words she had left on the recording, though the prickle of her conscience weighted the words with regret as she spoke.

'Where are they meeting, Bunny?'

182

Debbie hesitated. 'I'm not sure.' It suddenly seemed so wrong to be betraying the Black Garter that she found it difficult to talk to Steven. 'Listen, perhaps I've been wrong to go telling tales on these girls,' she suggested suddenly.

Even over the telephone she could sense the iron in Steven's voice. 'You'll go on telling me about them if you know what's good for you.'

Debbie caught a frightened breath. 'Are you threatening me?'

'That's as good a word as any,' he agreed boldly. 'Now speak, Bunny. I want to know about these two girls tonight, and I want those three yearbooks you promised me. You'll tell me what I want to know, or I'll make your life at that school a living hell.'

Unhappily, Debbie realised he was in just the right position to make good with the threat. Closing her eyes, and hating herself as she did it, Debbie told him about Anna and Cassie's planned night out.

'But just that and the yearbooks,' she said abruptly.

His sinister laugh was chilling.

'I mean it,' Debbie insisted, unable to keep the rising panic from her voice. 'I've given you enough already. You should be happy with what you've had.'

'Just carry on making me happy and neither of us will have a problem, Bunny,' he said easily. 'Do you follow my meaning?'

Miserably, Debbie realised that she did.

BLACK TIDE

Aishling Morgan

Aishling Morgan's tales evoke a world of bold and wanton strumpets, gorging rakes, sex-crazed goblins and girls with tiger fur and fangs. And with domination and submission – together with all kinds of bizarre sex – weaving themselves throughout her plots, this is fantasy fiction in more ways than one. Her Nexus books are as follows:

Black Tide, however, is a stand-alone story you won't find in print anywhere else.

'Josepina is a wanton, Brother Florian, no more than a wanton.'

'Indeed, Brother Siward, yet we must persevere.'

'Just so, Brother Florian. Doubtless her obstinacy is sent to try us. Her sin?'

'In essence, gross moral turpitude. Do you wish the particulars?'

'Name them to her face. Who knows but she might feel shame and thus begin to repent.'

'As it is willed.'

Florian struck a gong, admitting a girl, slight, dark-haired, freckled, gently rounded at haunch and chest. Her expression, initially of trepidation, altered to sullen defiance, her snub nose turned deliberately up.

'You have erred, child,' Brother Siward addressed her. Josepina remained immobile.

'Possibly when confronted with your sins you will show less impudence,' the Brother continued.

'To whit,' Brother Florian stated, 'a series of acts so base as to seem animal, yet distinguished by an intricate sensuality that discounts all possibility of your pleading blind lust. Self-abuse, on occasions too frequent to numerate. The sucking of members, three times at the least. The taking of seed in your mouth. Enjoining the shippen-men to spill their seed across your face, with offering to share the pallet of he who could perform this revolting act in the least time. Bedding with Grey Simon. The wilful surrender of your cunt without intent to procreate, much less within the sanctity of marriage. Urinating in the boiling-vat. Sodomy.'

Josepina made no response, save to shift her weight from one foot to the other.

'Revolting child,' Brother Siward added. 'Do you have no plea? Will you not say you were forced to these uncouth acts?'

Again Josepina stayed quiet.

'Dishonesty, at least, cannot be numbered among your vices. Will you at the least show remorse?'

The girl shook her head, the tiniest of movements.

'So be it. Fifty strokes. Bare yourself.'

Without a word Josepina turned her back to the men. Bending, she flicked her long dress on to her back, revealing culottes of coarse linen, loose around the thighs, tight at the waist and across her buttocks. Her hand went to the drawstring with a motion indifferent, almost contemptuous, tugging the bow out to allow the garment to drop to the level of her ankles. Naked, her bottom formed two chubby hemispheres of girl-flesh, firm, yet heavy, each marked with a scattering of freckles. Between them, her sex showed clearly, a soft mound richly covered with black hair, the pout of her lips and the knot of pink flesh between them conveying not shame and misery, but insolence.

Tugging the waistband of her dress high, she let her breasts swing loose, two plump handfuls of dangling meat marked with the same freckles that decorated her face and bottom. Each nipple was stiff, a dark bud that gave the same message as the single bead of white fluid that had formed at the mouth of her vagina. Resting her hands on her knees, she composed herself for punishment, serene and to all appearances indifferent both to her nudity and the coming pain.

'Incorrigible,' Brother Siward sighed as he rose to his feet.

'Take heart,' Brother Florian answered. 'I have a cut of blackthorn fresh from the vinegar barrel. Perhaps it will have some effect where lesser instruments have failed.'

Brother Siward nodded, his eyes never leaving the girl's exposed body. Brother Florian moved to one side, opening a chest to take up a length of black wood, thin and pliable, its surface reflecting dull gleams in the sunlight. Josepina watched from the corner of her eye, her expression betraying nothing of the responses of her body. Making a polite inclination of his head, Florian passed the whip to Siward.

'Beat her well, Brother,' he intoned. 'Who knows, she may yet be moved to repentance.'

Josepina's flesh tightened as the wicked instrument of punishment was raised, her bottom cheeks tensing to part and hint at the dark pucker of her anus. Her eyes closed as the whip lashed down. It hit, making the flesh of her bottom bounce and quiver and her lips peel back from her teeth, briefly. A line of white sprang up across the smooth globes of her bottom, quickly turning to a fresh pink bordered in red.

'Make comparison,' Brother Florian addressed her, 'as you are beaten. Your habit against that of your sisters, in particular Epiphany. At the quiet hours she prays; you perform lewd acts with menials. Commands she follows with placid obedience; you respond with poor grace, if at all. Her answer to the ribald calls of the churls is a shy blush and a turn of her head; you give back ripostes that bring colour to the cheeks of your tormentors.'

Three more cuts had landed across Josepina's naked rear as he spoke, and three times her bottom had bounced under the impacts, the flesh deforming briefly before returning to its natural, female shape. Each time her teeth had drawn briefly back, but not so much as a grunt had escaped her lips.

Brother Siward continued with the beating, aiming hard cuts to make the girl's buttocks jump and jiggle, one after another until her bottom was a mass of purple welts and double, scarlet tracks. All the while Brother Florian lectured, commenting on Josepina's depravity and comparing her with the virtuous Epiphany. At last, red-faced and puffing, Brother Siward threw down the blackthorn whip.

189

His colleague took the stick up, measured his aim across Josepina's quivering bottom and brought it down with all his force across both nates. Brother Siward, his breath recovered, began in turn to berate the girl, remarking on the vulgarity of her exposure.

'Do you not feel shame?' he demanded. 'Bent, with your cunt flaunted for all to see? Have you no modesty? Does revealing your breasts and buttocks mean nothing to you?'

Josepina said nothing, gritting her teeth in response to Brother Florian's now frantic belabouring of her buttocks and thighs.

'Wanton trull!' Siward contined. 'We have made you strip! We have thrashed you! The hole of your cunt is showing, the hole from which you evacuate also, all that you should hold most secret! You respond with not so much as a flush to your cheeks!'

Still Josepina declined to answer, her sole response to the savage punishment being the quickening of her breath and the gradual juicing and swelling of her sex. Her whole bottom was a mass of welts, nothing left uninjured save the depths of her cleft. Some small change in her poise had left her buttocks flared, pushing both vulva and anus into prominence, blatant and wet with her sweat and the fluid from her sex.

Teeth set, eyes staring in furious determination, Brother Florian continued to thrash her, well beyond the designated fifty strokes, until at last the blackthorn whip snapped across her rear. As the end flew clear to skip briefly across the stone flags of the floor and come to rest against the far wall, Josepina allowed the lightest of sighs to escape her lips. Florian stepped back and she held her pose, moving only to pull her back further in and make her sexual display yet more flagrant.

'She has the hide of an ox!' Florian declared, wiping sweat from his brow.

'So many beatings,' Siward answered. 'Yet most learn quickly that to howl and jump brings mercy.'

They paused, both men considering the beaten girl, Josepina looking back, her large dark eyes fully open, her expression unreadable.

'I confess to a degree of tumescence,' Brother Florian stated.

'I also,' Brother Siward answered.

'Blind lust must be answered, the Lord forgive us our frailty.'

'We are human, Brother, no more. To refuse to answer to our base needs would seem to be an act of hubris.'

'Just so.'

As one the men pulled up their robes, tucking the hems into their belts. Both revealed large bellies resting on spindly legs, pale skin, thick growths of pubic hair from the centres of which sprouted penes already close to erection. Brother Siward, the fatter of the two, stepped forward, took Josepina firmly by the hair and pressed his cock to her lips. Her mouth opened and she took him in, sucking the man who had just beaten her without hesitancy or resentment.

Brother Florian watched the girl suck, tugging at his cock as he moved behind her. Lifting his belly, he laid it on her well-whipped buttocks, prodding at her vagina with his erection. It went in, finding the wet hole and slipping inside until his balls found the thick tangle of her pubic hair.

Together they used her, one in each end, mouth and cunt, never once meeting the other's eyes as they shared her body. Her reaction was indifferent, and showed nothing of guilt. Siward's balls were soon in her hand, stroked and rubbed as she sucked on his erection. Her own breasts came next, cajoled as they swung to the motions of Florian's pushes, caught up, weighed, the nipples teased and gently pinched. At last, with both men beginning to grunt and puff, she put her hand to her sex, rubbing at the swollen clitoris even as Florian's heavy belly slapped against her bruised buttocks.

Siward came, his face puce and his teeth gritted hard as he emptied his semen into Josepina's throat. With the cock held deep in her gullet she began to gag, the spasms of her throat milking his sperm even as her own orgasm started. She came with her face red and her cheeks blown out, her eyes shut tight and the muscles of her bottom locking over and over against Florian's gut. With that Brother Florian also came, jerking his erection free of Josepina's hole at the last instant to spray thick, cream-white fluid across her beaten, upturned buttocks.

Both men moved back quickly, dropping their robes and mumbling prayers. Josepina stood, stretched, reached back to wipe the come from her bottom. Running her fingers over the bruised surface of a nate, she scooped what she could into her palm, put her hand to her mouth and ate the semen. She swallowed and licked a last blob from her lip before her expression returned to its earlier serenity, showing not one trace of the sorrow, misery or contrition expected in a beaten girl.

'Slattern! Trull!' Brother Florian exclaimed. 'Are you not in the least repentant?'

'Are you a she-devil, a succubus, to remain so indifferent to your sins?' Brother Siward demanded. 'Have you no sense of rectitude, no compunction?'

Josepina said nothing but hauled up her culottes to cover her welted bottom and let her dress drop back into place.

'This will cease!' Brother Florian snapped. 'This sour disobedience, this vile behaviour! In future you will model your conduct not on Lilith, as you seem to do, but on Epiphany. Be meek! Be virtuous! Follow her example in every way!'

Briefly Josepina's mouth curved into the smallest of smiles.

As Josepina walked from the room in which she had been beaten, Epiphany sat in the chapel, her eyes closed, her hands folded in prayer. Sunlight struck through the high windows to her side, dust motes dancing in light that showed the first trace of dusk. An irregular diamond of rich blue, cast through the window, moved slowly on the pale locks of her hair as she knelt. For an hour she had barely moved, even her lips still as her mind dwelt on matters far removed from the mundane.

Only when the bells in the tower high above her began to chime did she move, rising and walking from the chapel, hands clasped in her lap, head bowed. As she moved across the busy court each person she passed was greeted with the same, barely audible blessing, as if her soul were too delicate to bear such brute contact. Never once did she raise her eyes. At the gate she mumbled a meek request to the doorman, who answered with a grunt.

Beyond the gate she followed the line of the high wall, moving with yet greater timidity, her hood pulled tight about her face. All about her was bustle, brothers answering the call of the bell, boys hurrying on errands or in simple mischief, the fishermen, moving down towards the quay and boasting of the octopus they would take on the high-tide that evening.

Many gave Epiphany admiring stares, watching the way her breasts and buttocks moved beneath the light material of her dress. A few made ribald remarks, commenting on the way the sun revealed the contours of her body, even offering money for sexual favours or demanding she lift her dress. To all of this Epiphany responded with the shy aversion of her eyes, never angry, never hurried, blushing faintly and occasionally murmuring forgiveness for the more outrageous comments.

At the quay she stopped, looking out across the sea and then down into the still waters of the harbour. The smaller octopuses had already started to come in, darting among the weeds in water tinged dark with their ink. A few children stood, knee deep in the rising water, tridents poised in a vain attempt to catch the creatures. Older fishermen ignored the water, indifferent to such small quarry, intent on the preparation of their nets and tridents for when the black tide was high and the giants came in from the sea. All spared a glance for Epiphany, the old men in brief admiration before returning to their work, the young in speculation, each urging the others to make an approach. None tried, every one aware of her purity and unwilling to suffer certain rebuff.

Presently she turned and began to walk, south, along the shore, with the sun falling slowly towards the sea in the west. Only when she reached the headland did she look back, pushing her hood from her eyes to scan the beach and dunes, alert for any who might have followed. Content that she was alone, she moved on, faster, now, her eyes fixed to the grey-green bulk of the next headland.

She reached it as the sun touched the horizon, skipping quickly through the gentle waves as the water lapped at the base of the low cliff. Beyond, a bay opened, the cliffs rising above a shore strewn with great boulders of yellow stone and a beach of pale sand. Choosing a rock at the centre of the cove, she climbed to its smooth upper surface and composed herself, arms hugging her knees to her chest.

The tide rose fast, cutting her off as the last red glimmer of the sun faded into the sea. Water, black with octopus ink, washed close to the base of her rock, the brilliant moon throwing reflected silver from the waves. Epiphany remained still, listening to the murmur of the waves, her eyes fixed to the water, watching.

Shapes began to rise, black humps among the waves, as smooth as the water, yet moving with a power of their own. Eyes appeared, broad ovals reflecting dull silver in the moonlight, the size of coins, the size of apples, the size of saucers. Epiphany shivered, her teeth chattering despite the warmth of the night as she watched the great, black octopus pull themselves up into the shallows.

With the press of fat, gleaming bodies pushing against the base of her rock she stood, her trembling hands going to the clasp of her dress. A soft click and it fell away, the linen garment dropping around her feet. Her culottes followed, pushed quickly down, her boots last, to leave her standing, naked in the moonlight, her skin ghost-pale, her hair like silver.

Her mouth came open as she stepped down from the rock, her lower lip trembling hard. Cool water touched her foot, and the muscular firmness of a tentacle. A wave splashed on to her leg, breaking to wet her thighs and the soft, yellow down of her underbelly. The body of an octopus squeezed against her leg, soft yet resilient, pressing itself between her calves and on into the calm shallows among the boulders.

Epiphany stepped forward, feeling the water rise until it reached her knees, then kneeling, submerging herself to the level of her chest to leave the waves lapping at her breasts. To all sides she could feel the bodies of the creatures, smooth, rubbery tentacles sliding against her skin, suckers using her flesh for grip as they pulled themselves inshore. One, its bulbous body the size of a marrow, nudged between her thighs, pressing to her sex and sliding beneath her, one tentacle tracing a slow line along the groove of her bottom as it passed. Epiphany let out a quiet whimper at the sensation, spreading her knees wider to the black tide.

Around her the octopus had begun to mate, the males reaching out distended sperm-arms to the females, caressing and sucking, seeking the apertures to the mantles and egg clusters within. Many touched her, arms moving in exploration, unsure of her taste, unsure of her texture. Her vulva was open, swollen and wet, leaking her femininity to the sea. Again and again tentacles found her flesh, drawn in by the taste of her sex only to reject her as alien. Others used her body as an anchor, coiling their arms around her, sucking at the flesh.

With fat, resilient bodies pressing in on every side, she let herself sink lower into the water, submerging her breasts. More tentacles immediately found her, gripping both breasts, curling around her back, squeezing her waist and belly. She began to sigh, and to rock, her breath coming slow and deep as she moved her body back and forth in her cage of rubbery arms and swollen bodies.

A tentacle gripped between her legs, lying from pubic mound to anus, tiny suckers clamping to her sex lips and clitoris. She groaned, feeling the suction on the sensitive bud at the heart of her vulva. Another, large cup closed on one nipple, drawing the bud out, stiff and sensitive. Beneath her two beasts began to squirm, their bodies writhing against the sensitive flesh of her bottom in their ecstasy of copulation.

A wave splashed her face, and as it cleared she found herself looking into two huge eyes, as large and pale as the cut halves of a melon. A moan escaped her lips as thick arms took her about the waist and curled beneath her bottom, brushing the smaller creatures aside. A sperm arm as thick as her wrist brushed her thigh and she knew the newcomer was a male.

Reaching down into the water with a new urgency, she caught hold of an octopus, her fingers busily checking the arms for the tell-tale groove that would reveal its sex. None existed, marking it as female, and she quickly pulled it between her thighs, her fingers sliding gently beneath the mantle, opening the cavity and pressing it to her sex.

As she rubbed the female octopus against herself the big male pulled her closer, his thick arms powerful beyond her strength. She released the female, sinking her slime-covered fingers into her vagina as the full bulk of the male squeezed between her open thighs. With a deep groan Epiphany threw back her head, abandoning herself to the fate she had worked for, leaning back and pushing her sex out to the now eager male.

Eight arms took her, holding her, pulling her in. Two were behind her back, two around her waist. The fifth cupped her bottom, much as a human lover might have held her to mount her body on his. The sixth and seventh held her thighs, spreading them to the point of pain, opening her for exploration and fertilisation. The last, the elongated sperm arm, had already begun its work, caressing her, stimulating her to the point when she became receptive.

Epiphany writhed in the arms of the octopus, sobbing and whimpering with reaction, her whole body engulfed in an ecstasy far beyond anything else she knew, the horrid thrill of the black tide, with her body locked helpless as the slime-covered sperm arm stroked her naked flesh. With her nipples aching beneath suckers, her vagina gaping as it leaked the taste of the female into the water, she could only lie back, moaning and sobbing, crying in her ecstasy, heedless of the waves breaking over her body.

196

A tentacle tip had found her anus, working inside to fill her rectum with cold, rubbery flesh. Helpless to stop it, she let the pleasure come, feeling her bowels bloat and fill with the arm reaching up, coiling and uncoiling deeper into her gut. Her arms went around the body of the big male, hugging it to her, her warm embrace against his cold, bulbous mass. His sperm arm was at her belly, moving lower, drawn in by her taste, rubbing between the lips of her sex, squirming against her clitoris . . .

She came, crying aloud as the pressure of the sperm arm squeezed down past her clitoris, pressing against it. He found her hole as her climax peaked, making her scream as her vagina filled with tentacle. With his sperm arm inside her he pulled her close, crushing her to him. The tentacle in her anus pushed deeper up, anchoring in her bowels and stretching her ring until she felt she would burst. More sperm arm squeezed into her vagina, filling her until her front hole felt as bloated as the back.

Lost on a plateau of exalted, obscene bliss, she let herself be taken, feeling her body fill with bulbous tentacle, squirming her breasts against his body, kissing and licking at his dome, crying in-between, calling herself names that would have had Josepina blushing in confusion.

The second orgasm came as the sperm started to flood her vagina. She could feel it, running sticky into her body, bloating out her cavity and spilling from the mouth to the rhythm of her contractions. Part of an arm was pressed to her clitoris, rough yet soft, and with a frantic wiggling of her hips she brought herself off, bumping her bud over the ridges and papillae of the beast's skin and coming with a long, drawn-out scream.

With her cunt brimming with octopus sperm she began to buck wildly in his arms, everything forgotten but the pleasure of being mated. Her orgasm held, every muscle in her body locked tight, anus pulsing on the thick, intruding arm, mouth agape in one, long scream, arms tight around his resilient bulk. Still the sperm came, filling her and flooding out into the water around her, washing over her face with the waves so that she could taste it. Driven to an unbearable peak of lust, her senses began to slip, her mind riding on bliss so high, so sublime that nothing whatever mattered beyond her act . . .

Epiphany came to her senses as her open mouth filled with water. Gagging and choking, she quickly pulled herself back up on her lover's tentacles, bringing her head clear of the water. He was spent, and pulling back, the tentacle in her anus working out in slow waves, the suckers moving across her back, buttocks and legs. Her vagina was still contracting and she felt the end of the sperm arm pull free. She leant forward, giving him a parting kiss between his great pale eyes before pulling herself back and standing, only to sink down once more to her haunches, exhausted.

Staring out across the moonlit sea with vacant eyes, she allowed the spent tip of his sperm arm to slide from her vagina. Her body arched, her anus smarting and pulsing, her vagina dribbling octopus sperm into the water. She knew she would be covered in sucker marks, bruises and tiny cuts, yet all would be covered by her long dress and the demure hood she always wore.

Only when the sea had begun to retreat did she rise. Washing the last of her lover's sperm from her body in a rock pool, she set her face to the village, walking the moonlit sand, her expression meek, timid, and above all, innocent.

DISCIPLINE OF THE
PRIVATE HOUSE

Esme Ombreux

Esme Ombreux has a remarkable reputation when one considers that she has written only four books for Nexus. These aren't just any four books, though: the first; *One Week in the Private House*, sold out within weeks of first publication and has been reprinted twice; and the sequel, *Amanda in the Private House*, more than lived up to expectations, as did the third and fourth, *Discipline of the Private House* (extracted here) and *An Education in the Private House*. Esme followed these with *Captives of the Private House* and *Pet-Training in the Private House*.

She also edited the first two *New Erotica* books, and used to write *Letters from Esme* in the back of a number of Nexus novels – all in all, a true devotee of erotica.

In the following extract from *Discipline . . .*, Jem, Mistress of the Private House, is due to be put through her paces by the Chatelaine's depraved minions.

As Jem and Robert made their way from the dungeons to the north range of the Chateau, Robert's right hand roamed continuously over the curves of Jem's bottom. She was naked but for her collar, matching leather cuffs around her wrists, the chains, and a tightly fitting leather helmet within which her hair was contained. From time to time Robert would pull on the leash and laugh when Jem stumbled. With the movement of her arms restricted by the chains, on occasion she almost fell; each time this happened Robert grabbed her roughly, pinching her nipples hard as he righted her, and gave her six lashes for being clumsy.

As he led her through the lamplit corridors he maintained a steady stream of muttered invective: 'Not so high and mighty now, are you, little whore?' he said, over and over again. 'My Mistress has got you, and she'll never let you go. She'll keep this pretty little arse so sore you'll never want to sit down again. And if she ever takes pity on you, you can be sure I won't.'

Jem succeeded in maintaining a subversive cheerfulness as she dutifully thanked Robert for his consideration, but she could not help feeling apprehensive. It was clear that Robert had an ordeal prepared for her in the Chateau's kitchens, and that he expected her to be unable to remain subservient throughout it.

They had reached the wide passage that ran down the spine of the north range of rooms and separated the dining hall, with its tall, south-facing windows, from the cryptlike kitchens, sculleries and storerooms of the Château. This was one of the oldest parts of the building: the ceiling vaults rose from semicircular arches that were supported by thick, round, age-pitted pillars, and the flagstones had been worn by centuries of feet scurrying from hall to kitchen and back again.

Robert led Jem past the pair of vast swinging doors which led directly into the main kitchen. He stopped instead a little further down the corridor, in front of a single, plain door. Jem thought that behind the door was one of the smaller rooms devoted to food preparation: the bakery, perhaps. The main kitchen, of course, was so cavernous that the blackened ceiling was difficult to discern; the bakery, buttery and sculleries were therefore small only by comparison – each was much larger, for instance, than the spacious cell that Jem had shared with Olena the previous night.

Jem thought she could hear raised voices and laughter from behind the door. When Robert pushed the door open, the sound of voices abruptly ceased. The silence seemed ominous.

Robert propelled Jem through the doorway. She found herself standing indeed in the bakery, a large, square room of yellowed stone, its ceiling supported on squat pillars. The air smelled organic: yeast and hot bread, carried on currents of warm air. All the oven doors were open, the ovens were empty, and in the vast fireplace only a small pyramid of logs was burning. Nonetheless, the room seemed hot to Jem.

It also seemed crowded. Lounging on and around a sturdy wooden table were half a dozen kitchen slaves; all men, all young, and all staring at Jem with unconcealed interest.

Jem almost allowed her amusement to show on her face. Six strong, libidinous lads: was this supposed to be the ordeal that would break her will? She lowered her head and did her best to look demure; it would not do, she decided, to let Robert catch her eyeing the bulges at the fronts of the aprons that were the only garments the male kitchen slaves wore. She concentrated on absorbing the masculine atmosphere of the room: the heat; the earthy, arousing aromas; the penetrating gazes of hard-working, hard-bodied young men.

'Here she is, lads,' Robert announced. He unclipped the chains from her collar and cuffs, but left the leather helmet clasped around her head. 'She's all yours. The head chef's expecting her for lunch, and you'll be in trouble if he's kept waiting. But how you prepare the dish and cook her is up to you. Just remember a few things.' Robert hooked a finger through the metal ring at the top of her helmet and pulled her up on to her toes. 'This promiscuous little slut will do anything you tell her to. And she'll enjoy it. So don't be gentle with her. You like rough games, don't you, slut?'

'Yes, sir,' Jem said. She couldn't honestly deny it.

She felt Robert's free hand cup and squeeze her left breast and then thrust itself into the gap at the top of her thighs. 'She's already wet,' Robert said, 'and she doesn't know yet what you have planned for her.' He removed his hand and wiped a line of clear fluid on to Jem's stomach. 'Tell them the things you like, slut. You know what to say.'

'Yes, sir,' Jem said. She had a fairly clear idea of the words Robert wanted to hear her say. 'I like young men's cocks,' she said, shaking her head free from Robert's grasp. 'I like to touch cocks, and to lick them.'

The men had moved to form a semicircle in front of Jem. Several of them had their hands under their aprons. They passed sidelong comments to each other: 'Look at those tits,' 'She's a real whore,' 'I can't wait to get started.' Jem knew she was supposed to feel threatened, but instead she was excited, and anxious for the fun to begin. It occurred to her that perhaps, despite her efforts subtly to disseminate the tales throughout the Private House organisation, Robert hadn't heard the rumours about the excesses of the Supreme Mistress. It was said, for instance, that during one night she had drained the energies of an entire fifteen-man sports team that had been brought to the House specifically for her purposes.

And Jem had taken care to ensure that the rumours were always less remarkable than the real occurrences on which they were based.

'I like to take cocks in my mouth,' Jem went on, warming to her subject. 'And in my cunt. And in my arsehole. All at the same time,' she added, with a coquettish smile that drew a growl from the surrounding men.

'Tell them about the whip, slave,' Robert said.

Jem snatched a strap from his belt. She drew its tongue across the tops of her breasts. 'You can punish me, if you like,' she whispered. 'I'm your slave. You can do anything to me. You can whip me here. Or here.' She turned round, took one end of the strap in each hand, leaned forwards, and swung her bottom from side to side against the strip of leather. Then, as the young men roared their approval, she parted her legs, bent further forwards, and held the strap by its handle so that the tongue slapped between her buttocks and up against her sex.

'You lads just make sure she gets a thorough lashing,' Robert said, with a note of exasperation in his voice. Jem pirouetted and with a bow proffered the strap. He snatched it from her hand, raised it as if to strike her, and then, scowling, turned and left the room. 'Don't forget to have her ready for Chef's lunch,' he shouted as the door closed behind him.

The room was suddenly still and silent. Jem looked enquiringly along the line of lust-flushed faces surrounding her.

'We'd best make a start on preparing this little bird for cooking,' one of the young men eventually said.

'First step is to truss her,' another said. 'Hold her still while I fetch the rope.'

Two of the men stepped forwards and grasped her arms with hands that had been strengthened by months of kneading dough. Jem felt suddenly vulnerable, and began to struggle even though she knew it was futile.

She felt a line of fire across her right buttock, and then another on her left. A man carrying loops of a rope, and swinging the loose end of it, emerged from behind her.

'Master Robert said you'd let us do anything,' he said. 'No struggling, no complaining. Said we've to tell him if you disobey, or even if you're just a bit unwilling. You're not unwilling, are you, you pretty cock-lover?'

Jem took a deep breath, and relaxed. 'I'd love to be tied up,' she said. 'Bondage is always a delight. Just make sure to tie me nice and tightly.'

She noted, with a managerial satisfaction that she realised was entirely inappropriate in her circumstances, that the men were using the correct type of rope. She had decreed that throughout the Private House, when rope was to be used for tight bondage it should be made of braided cotton. This material was soft to the touch, and of a light weight, and yet was quite strong enough to withstand any one person's attempts to break free.

The men had planned precisely how to bind her, and worked in silence. One stood on each side of her, holding her arms away from her sides. A third and fourth stood in front of her and behind her, passing the rope back and forth as they wound it around her.

A long loop was passed round the back of her neck. The two hanging ends were then pulled beneath her arms and crossed behind her back. The man in front of her pulled the two ends to the front, crossed them at the centre of her ribcage, and pulled them tight so that her breasts were resting on the rope. He then tied a knot, and left the long ends hanging to the floor.

'You'll need to work on her tits,' suggested one of the two men watching the operation.

'I know,' the man in front of Jem said. He placed his hand under her chin and lifted her head so that she was looking up into his eyes. 'Move your legs further apart, slut,' he said.

'Yes, sir,' Jem replied. The man had large hazel eyes and curly brown hair. His expression was carefully stern, as if he were concentrating on maintaining his masterly demeanour. Jem thought he looked lovely.

'Ask us to play with your tits,' he said. Jem widened her eyes and pretended to be shocked. 'And with your arsehole, too,' he added.

Jem understood the reasons behind the instruction. If her breasts were massaged, particularly while she was aroused, they would swell, and would look and feel heavier and larger. Once tightly bound with rope, they would remain enlarged, and would both look more prominent and feel more sensitive. She knew exactly what was required.

'Please play with my breasts, sir,' she said. 'And please don't be gentle. Pinch my nipples hard. And if one of you could insert a finger into my anus at the same time, that would be wonderful.'

She leaned forwards, and the man behind her slapped her bottom for a few moments before cupping his hand against her vulva. She felt his fingers press upwards, and couldn't prevent herself wriggling happily against the pressure.

'The little whore's got a cunt as hot as an oven,' the man behind her said. 'And she's sopping wet.'

He twirled a finger inside her vagina, and Jem, still holding the gaze of the brown-eyed man, smiled contentedly as she felt ripples of pleasure begin to expand within her.

The finger was withdrawn, and with a final smile Jem bent forwards a little more, so that her anus was exposed to the man behind her and her breasts were just swinging freely.

The brown-eyed man took one of her breasts in his left hand and began methodically to smack it with his right. At the same time Jem felt a finger, lubricated with her juices, begin to press against the tight ring of her anal sphincter. She relaxed the muscle, pushed back against the pressure, and gasped as she felt the familiar, yet always pleasurable sensations of intrusion and fullness. The finger began, very slowly but insistently, to creep into her; her breast was released, and the other was grasped and smacked. Jem surrendered to the sensations. She was in heaven.

As the brown-eyed man began to pinch her breasts, using the callused tips of his strong fingers and concentrating on her areolae and nipples, Jem was only dimly aware of tossing her head and moaning. Each shock of pain seemed to arc directly to her clitoris; she realised, vaguely, that if the two men continued to play with her she would start to rise towards a climax – and she had not been given permission to do so. She tried hard to clear her mind, but the feelings engendered by the men's persistent fingers could not be banished. A small part of her consciousness began to panic as she felt the pulsing of her climax gather pace: she was about to lose her wager with the Chatelaine.

'I think that'll do,' the man in front of her said. He gave her nipples a final pinch and twist, and took a pace back to look at her.

The finger was pulled from her anus, and with a gasp of mingled disappointment and relief Jem straightened her body. Her breasts felt hot and heavy, and they tingled all over and deep inside.

The man's brown eyes were fixed on the reddened, quivering cones of manhandled flesh. He seemed pleased, and Jem felt a strange sense of pride. His work on her breasts had clearly excited him: his member was so stiff that his apron was being held out in front of his stomach.

'Thank you, sir,' Jem said. On a whim she shook herself free of the men holding her arms, dropped to her knees, looked up at him and added, 'May I show my gratitude by kissing you?' She stared longingly at the front of his apron.

The men around her laughed and made lewd comments. The brown-eyed man stepped forwards and pulled on the ring at the top of her helmet. 'You really *are* a whore, aren't you?' he said.

'Yes, sir,' Jem said, and smiled up at him. She was happy to agree to the description. She wanted his cock in her mouth.

He released her hair, lifted his apron and draped it over her head and shoulders. Jem found herself in a tent that smelled of warm bread and male sex. His erect manhood was standing almost vertically, and almost touching her face. She pressed her lips to the veined base of the shaft and inhaled the musky odour of his testicles. She cupped her swollen breasts in her hands, and sighed with pleasure as she started to lick the wrinkled sac.

She heard a voice say, 'Show us your arse, slave,' and she obliged, making her back concave and thrusting her bottom up and back. She felt hands on her buttocks and between her thighs, and resulting tremors of delight, but they seemed distant: her world had been reduced to the dim, flour-powdery canopy beneath which she was lovingly licking her way towards the head of the proud member before her.

At last she reached the tip and, after tonguing with delicate flicks the slit of the urethra, she moved her head up and engulfed the entire helmet. It filled her mouth. It was warm, and as smooth as a polished plum. It pulsed against her tongue. The moment of taking a man's erection into her mouth never failed to give Jem a frisson of pleasure, and she let out an exclamation of distress when the velvet hardness was pulled suddenly from her mouth.

'That's enough,' the man's voice said from above her head. 'On your feet, slut. We've got to get you trussed up for cooking.'

He pulled his apron from Jem's head, and she blinked in the sudden light, even though the bakery was illuminated only by lamps hanging from the vaulted ceiling. She stood, and the men beside her grasped her arms once again in their unforgiving hands.

Once the brown-eyed man had assured himself that Jem's breasts were still engorged and sensitive, the business of tying them proceeded. He picked up the trailing ends of the rope and tied them together in a knot that was less than a finger's length from the one he had already made, thus creating a small loop. With the second knot resting above the first in the valley between Jem's breasts, the ends of the rope were passed beneath her arms, and the man behind her pulled the ends tight and knotted them together in the middle of her back. The ends, still long, hung to the floor. Each breast was now roped on three sides, although there was as yet no constriction.

'Cross her arms,' the brown-eyed man said to the man behind Jem. She put up no resistance as her arms were crossed behind her back. She glanced sideways and saw that two new lengths of rope were to be employed: each had one end tied to one of the cuffs that she had around her wrists.

The two ropes from Jem's wrists were passed to the brown-eyed man, who pulled tightly on them to ensure that Jem's crossed arms were pressed into her back, and that each of her hands was pulled up to tuck under the opposing upper arm. He passed the loose ends of both ropes through the loop between the knots that separated Jem's breasts, and then passed the ends over Jem's shoulders to the man behind her. He pulled them tight, so that the two knots were pulled upwards and the rope running beneath Jem's breasts embedded itself in the crease there; he tied the ropes together behind Jem's neck.

Still Jem's breasts were relatively unfettered. The man with brown eyes called for another length of rope, and carefully found its halfway point before tying the middle of it to the lower of the two knots nestling between Jem's breasts. There were now two long ends of rope hanging down the front of Jem's body, and two hanging at the back, from where the ends of the first length had been tied together.

'Legs wide apart, slave,' the man behind Jem said.

Jem obeyed. The man with brown eyes held the two ropes in front of her, one in each of his big hands. She assumed the man behind her was holding the two ropes there. The men who had been holding her arms were still at her sides, and all four of the men now worked together to bind Jem's body tightly with the ropes.

The ropes from her back were passed to the front, where they were slipped under the front ropes and then passed to the back again; both pairs of ropes were pulled against each other to create a tension that held the rope taut as it followed the contours of Jem's body. This procedure was followed once more, creating a rope lattice around Jem's torso, back and stomach.

Then, as Jem had expected, a pair of ropes was passed from her belly between her legs. It was quite usual in this school of bondage, Jem knew, for a pair of ropes to run between the labia and buttocks; often such ropes were tied particularly tightly, so that the bound woman was very aware of her bondage, and often large knots were tied in the ropes to put pressure on the clitoris or the anus. On this occasion, however, Jem noted with a slight pang of disappointment that the ropes were drawn into the creases at the tops of the insides of her thighs, so that her vulva was framed between them. The ropes came together between her buttocks and, once pulled very tight, were tied together to the lowest crossing-point of the ropes that zigzagged down her back.

The men stood back briefly to admire their handiwork. They tested the knots, and pulled on the ropes to ensure that all were tight. Now that Jem was attractively but very securely bound, with her arms tied behind her back, the men seemed more confident about touching her. Their hands strayed from the ropes to her breasts and bottom; within a few moments Jem found that all six of the men, jostling for space around her, had their hands on her. At least one man's fingers were puddling in the wetness of her vagina; other fingers were trying to infiltrate her anus; both of her breasts were being squeezed and pinched; fingers were inserted into her mouth; and at least one hand was slapping her buttocks. With her arms bound up Jem would have toppled over had it not been for the press of nearly naked strong young male bodies about her.

The brown-eyed man at last called his comrades to order. 'Let's get on,' he said. 'Chef won't be pleased if we're late. Let's tie her tits now.'

The knot behind Jem's neck was untied, and the loose ends were crossed and were passed back over her shoulders; at the front they were brought together and put through the loop between the two knots that separated her breasts. This loop, now anchored to the rope lattice around Jem's lower body, moved upwards hardly at all when the loose ends were pulled tightly up and to the left and right. They were passed under the ropes that ran from Jem's neck to under her arms, turned back over these ropes and pulled downwards, to the outer sides of Jem's breasts. Here they were looped under the ropes that ran under the breasts, and pulled upwards; the brown-eyed man used his big hands to adjust the tightness of the ropes and to prod and pull the flesh of Jem's breasts, so that they were entirely contained within the tightening network of bonds.

Jem's breasts were now constricted from underneath and from both sides, and were beginning to feel very swollen and tender. The two ends of rope went back up to and over the ropes lying diagonally across the upper part of Jem's chest, across to the central knot, and then, with a tug that Jem thought would snap the ropes, underneath Jem's arms to be tied at her back. Jem's breasts were now encircled with taut rope, and were held more tightly than by any corset or harness Jem had ever worn. Distended and almost spherical, their skin shining with tension, they jutted from her chest. Her nipples stood out as large and hard as thimbles.

Jem was impressed. She had rarely been tied up as thoroughly. 'Thank you for binding me, sirs,' she said. 'I hope I'm adequately trussed now.'

'You'll do,' the brown-eyed man said, and rubbed his hands across her breasts. 'What's the next stage, lads? What do we do next before we cook our bird?'

'Tenderise her, tenderise her,' the other young men chanted. This made Jem apprehensive, and her fears were realised when one of the men went to a cupboard and produced various instruments of correction: four long, thin wooden dowels, and two leather straps.

Without further words, the men took one instrument each and arranged themselves in a formation that took up the entire length of the bakery. The two men swinging the leather straps stood facing each other at opposite ends of the room; between them, the four men with wooden switches stood at intervals.

It was clear to Jem that she was to run a gauntlet from one side of the room of the other. She had played games of this sort before, although she usually preferred watching to participating. At least, she thought, I'm not wearing high heels, and my legs and feet aren't tied.

'Come here, slave,' shouted one of the men holding a strap. 'Stand here in front of me, and turn to face the others. That's the way.'

Jem waited patiently for further instructions. She felt nervously excited, but she no longer believed that she was in danger of losing her wager with the Chatelaine – at least not here, this morning, in the bakery. All she had to do was to submit and show no resistance; in bondage, with her arms pinioned, and surrounded by six strong men, she would have little opportunity to rebel. They would carry out whatever plans they had made for her, and she would endure them. So far, she confessed to herself, it had been more a matter of enjoying than enduring.

'When I give you a smack, like this,' the man behind her said, whacking her bottom with the strap so hard that she almost fell forwards, 'you run straight ahead as fast as you can. Stop when you reach the other side of the bakery, turn round, and wait for another smack before you set off again. Understand, slave?'

'Yes, sir,' Jem said, looking over her shoulder and giving a smile to the serious-faced young man. 'And thank you for smacking me.'

The leather strap had been wielded with enthusiasm, and Jem's bottom felt afire.

'Get set, then,' the man said. 'Stick your arse out again.'

Jem did so, and was rewarded with another blazing stripe. She set off, running awkwardly because her arms were tied behind her back. As she passed the four men along her route she tried to duck and weave to avoid the hissing switches. Her breasts, held tight and prominent within their rope bindings, seemed alarmingly vulnerable, and most of the men tried to strike her bosom as she ran towards them. They missed their target, but laughed as she bobbed and swerved, and shouted when one of them managed to imprint a glowing line on her right buttock as she raced past him.

She stopped in front of the other strap-wielding man, and drew in lungfuls of air. It was the young fellow with the hazel eyes, and she smiled at him as she tried to catch her breath.

'Turn around, you slut,' he said. 'You'll get no rest until we've finished this. We've got to make up time. Come on, turn round and stick your arse out.'

Jem had no sooner leaned forwards than the strap landed forcefully on her left buttock, making her gasp and propelling her at a run towards the men waiting with big grins on their faces and their switches raised. This time none of them aimed for her breasts; copying the example of the one who had succeeded in lashing her during her first run, they all waited until she had run past before swinging their thin wooden rods at her backside.

Jem's buttocks had four fresh stripes by the time she reached the end of the room.

'Turn!' the man shouted at her. 'Bend! Run!'

With a breathless sob, Jem started on her third run. The men wielding the switches had now learned the technique of swinging them in Jem's wake, adding a flick of the wrist to catch one or other of Jem's buttocks as she raced past. Jem could do nothing to avoid the blows except to try to outrun them. A rational part of her mind kept trying to remind her that the men would whip her as much or as little as they pleased, whether she ran through the gauntlet or strolled; the stinging lashes and the shouted instructions impelled her to run, however – and, in any case, she would lose her wager if she failed to obey the men's commands.

And so Jem ignored the voice of reason, and the jeering laughter, and the throbbing of her bound breasts, and the tightness of the ropes around her body and between her legs, and the increasing temperature of her bottom; she simply ran up and down the room, as fast as she could, until her legs felt weak and she was gasping for breath.

'Turn,' ordered the brown-eyed man as she staggered towards him for what, she thought, must have been the fifth or sixth time.

Panting, and proceeding at little more than a walking pace, she lifted her head and stared at him with what she hoped was her most winsome, wide-eyed expression of helplessness.

There was not a hint of pity in his face. 'Turn around, slut,' he shouted, 'and be quick about it.'

Sobbing with breathlessness and indignation, Jem presented her bottom to him. His leather strap swung upwards and landed with a loud report on the lower inside curves of both of Jem's buttocks; the tip went between her legs and caught her vulva. With a gasping cry, Jem set off again towards the other end of the room.

She could no longer sprint. Tears of frustration blinded her as, with her chest heaving, she trotted towards the line of young men with the wooden dowels. They were cheering her ironically, calling her vile names and making loud claims about which parts of her body they intended to aim for.

This time they concentrated on her breasts. Bound, distended and sensitised, the constricted bulbs of flesh were irresistible targets. With her arms tied behind her back, Jem could do nothing to protect them except to swing her torso from side to side, which seemed to make the young men even more excited.

The wooden dowels were very thin and smooth, and circular in section: they had no rough or sharp edges, and were obviously light and difficult to wield with much force. Nonetheless, each of the three that landed on one or other of Jem's breasts wrung a little shriek of pain from her, much to the amusement of the young men.

The fourth lash caught her stingingly on the right buttock, and then she was through the gauntlet and approaching the end of the room. She slowed to a walk, and veered from side to side as though she was having difficulty staying on her feet. If she exaggerated her exhaustion, she thought, the men might lose interest and move on to the next stage of this culinary ordeal.

At the last moment Jem stumbled, and fell against the man standing with his back to the wall. Her tight, sore breasts were pressed against his naked chest. She looked up at him imploringly.

He grinned. 'Turn around, slave,' he said. 'You're not ready for cooking yet. Turn and bend, my little chicken.'

The lash against her bottom was almost gentle this time, and Jem jogged forwards. As she approached the waiting line of men a voice behind her called out, 'Stop!', and she came to a halt in the centre of the room.

Grinning and joking, the four men with switches converged on her, surrounded her, and allowed her a moment to recover her breath before they began to whip her.

As she writhed and twisted within the circle of swishing laths, Jem felt stinging lines all over her body, catching her in such quick succession that she had no time to register them as individual stripes. She knew only that her buttocks, thighs and breasts were becoming incandescent. Her breasts, in particular, had never felt so hot and sore. Worse than the punishment was the sense of helplessness; she could not run away, she could not protect the vulnerable and tender parts of her body. The only way to escape from the torment was, she knew, to protest: to stand still, gather the tattered remnants of her dignity, and demand that they stop. And if she were to do that, the Chatelaine would have won.

As the switches continued to hiss and sting, and she found herself gasping with each lash so rapidly that, as the men laughingly commented, she sounded as if she was reaching a climax, she decided that she could bear it no longer. She would call a halt to this, and admit defeat. But then the whipping ceased.

It was the man with brown eyes who inspected her. He ran his hands over her breasts, and then her buttocks. He put a hand between her thighs, and pushed upwards so that Jem was lifted on to the tips of her toes.

'She'll do, I reckon,' he announced. 'Breasts and haunches feel nice and tender. And I tell you what, lads,' he added, 'she's still as wet as a lake down here. I think she enjoyed being tenderised. Did you, you little whore?'

Jem couldn't deny that she was aroused. Her whole body felt raw but alive, and the man's rough hand pressing into her vulva had shocked her by causing an almost climactic spasm of desire.

'Yes, thank you, sir,' she said, trying to control her panting voice. 'It was very exciting.'

The man laughed. 'We'd better hurry,' he said. 'Give me a hand to get her oiled.' With his hand still between her legs he lifted her from the ground, and with enthusiastic cries all of the other young men crowded around him, trying to grab Jem and to help carry her towards a corner of the room.

Jem had hardly had time to realise that she was being held aloft by six pairs of strong and intrusive hands before she was lowered into a shallow copper dish as wide as a bath. The vessel had a flat bottom, and apart from Jem contained only a few fingers' depth of warm cooking oil. She had been placed on her back, which she found uncomfortable because her arms were tied behind her. When she tried to sit up, however, she succeeded only in sliding across the floor of the pan: her bottom skidded sideways, and she toppled slowly on to her side.

'Let's turn her a few times,' the brown-eyed man said, 'and make sure she's coated all over.'

The young men formed a circle around the copper vessel. Some of them pushed Jem with their feet; others flicked her with the long switches. She wriggled and squirmed to avoid the stinging lashes, and was soon rolling over and over in the oil.

She was grateful, now, for the tightly fitting helmet, which was protecting her hair from becoming drenched in the viscous fluid. She presumed, as she tossed and writhed in the slippery vessel, that the helmet had been provided for precisely this reason. Rolling over and over in oil was, she decided, a pleasant interlude: her sore breasts and bottom, in particular, felt soothed by the emollient sweet-smelling oil.

216

The hissing switches fell silent, and the men stooped towards her. 'Get the oil worked well in,' she heard one of the men say, and suddenly hands were all over her body.

She was turned on to her back; her legs were lifted into the air; and two of the men started to massage oil into her bound breasts. Others began work between her raised legs, pushing oily fingers again and again into her vagina and anus. A rhythm started to develop, and Jem found herself gasping with pleasure as the insistent rubbing and pushing started to ignite sparks within her. She gave herself up to the sensations, and was disappointed when the brown-eyed man said, 'That's enough. She's ready. Let's get her on to the spit.'

With difficulty, slithering and ribald laughter the men took hold of her and pulled her from the copper dish. As they carried her towards the fireplace Jem began to worry that the conceit of preparing her as a bird is prepared for roasting was becoming too realistic; did they really intend to impale her on a spit and cook her on an open fire? She would have no choice but to object; the Chatelaine would have won; and she would have endured for nothing her rough treatment by the six young kitchen-slaves.

When she saw the cunningly wrought metal frame that was suspended between the two fire irons, however, she felt a wave of relief. The long, black structure, while it looked sinister and uncomfortable, was obviously not designed for cookery.

It was, she supposed, something like a spit, in that it was long, its core was a black iron rod, each end of which was resting on a soot-darkened support, and it was situated in front of a fire – although not close enough for roasting.

Welded on to the central rod, however, were a number of ornate curlicues of wrought iron, some of them padded with cushions of black leather. Hanging from the structure at various points along its length were leather straps. Jem recognised it as a framework to which a person could be secured, and she was in no doubt that she was destined imminently to be bound to it.

Jem's body was still slippery with oil, and the young men took great care as they lowered her on to the spit. Her hips, stomach and ribcage rested in a shaped, upholstered cradle that was fixed horizontally and lengthways atop the central pole. Jem found it comfortable enough, although the men did nothing to loosen her bondage or to ease the strain in her shoulders caused by the tying of her arms behind her back. In fact, Jem soon found herself tied even more tightly: a broad strap was placed across the small of her back and tightened, to keep her in place in the cradle.

Like the arms of an armchair, two leather-upholstered spurs projected forwards and slightly upwards from the main part of the cradle to provide support for Jem's shoulders, and then curved towards each other to create a padded rest for her breastbone. Jem's tightly constricted breasts, still stinging and aching and feeling more sensitive than ever, hung unencumbered below her with the central bar of the spit running between them. When she lifted her head Jem found herself looking down the length of the spit to where one end was supported on a fire iron.

At first Jem had been allowed to keep her feet on the floor and bend forwards on to the padded leather in order to have her body secured to the spit. She had noted, however, that the cradle held her hips tilted up at the back, and that attached to the spit behind her were projections from which hung stirrups and straps; she knew that soon her legs and feet would be arranged in a much more revealing and uncomfortable position.

As soon as the strap was fastened across her back, the men turned their attention to her legs. Grasping the slippery limbs in many hands, they lifted her feet from the floor and bent her knees as they parted her thighs. They placed her feet in stirrups, which they then moved upwards and outwards, so that Jem's knees were lifted to the level of her torso. With her hips uplifted by the cradle, Jem's private parts were now exhibited for all to see, and her rounded buttocks were raised high.

Jem knew that her bottom must by now be cherry red and covered in stripes; her anus, she knew well, was

218

delicately formed and its crinkled skin was dark pink; her shaven outer labia were prettily plump, while her inner labia, which she was sure must also be visible, were exquisite fronds over which several of her lovers had enthused. Headman, she recalled, had liked to whip her there because it was, he said, the prettiest part of his prettiest woman. With every part of her glistening with oil, Jem decided with satisfaction that from the rear she must be a most delectable sight.

Jem knew that she was positioned well for either penetration or more punishment, and she wondered which it would be: the sudden sting of a whip laid across her buttocks, or the thrilling insertion of a phallus.

The next words she heard, however, were, 'Let's get the skewers into her,' which filled her with dread. Were they going to pierce her flesh?

She was slightly reassured when she saw two of the men attaching something to the spit in front of her. They slid the contraption towards her along the metal bar, and fixed it in place in front of her face.

Suddenly she felt her head being tugged back, and she realised that one of the men had pulled her helmet. The tugging ceased, but she found she could no longer lower her head: it was being held up, presumably by a chain from the top of her helmet to a ring on the strap across her back, so that she was obliged to look straight ahead and could not lower her face.

The two men in front of her were once more at work on the complicated bracket they had fixed to the spit. They moved it back a little and adjusted its height, and then began turning a crank. Slowly, and pointing directly at Jem's mouth, a torpedo-shaped cylinder began to emerge. It was a carved phallus, and it was clear to Jem that she would have no choice but to take it into her mouth. She opened her lips and tried to remain calm as the cold, solid cylinder filled her mouth. At last it stopped, before it reached the back of her throat and could make her gag. She could not close her jaws, however, or move her head, and she reflected that she had indeed been very effectively skewered.

The men had referred to more than one skewer, and so Jem was not at all surprised to feel the rounded nose of something hard and cold insinuating itself between the delicate membranes of her inner labia. She assumed that a second device had been fixed to the spit behind her, between her splayed thighs. The phallus felt huge – much larger than the one in her mouth – but she felt no discomfort: even if she had not been aroused by the morning's events, the oil that had been massaged into her would on its own have eased the entrance of the giant cylinder.

'She's well skewered,' one of the kitchen-slaves said. 'Can we baste her now?'

'Just a moment,' another replied. 'Chef likes his rump-meat good and tender. Maybe we'd better just give her arse one more turn.'

'You're right,' a third said. 'And in that position, the little whore's just asking for it, I'd say.'

Jem could not have argued that her bottom was other than perfectly exposed for a flogging. And she was in no position to prevent the young men from inflicting one on her. As the switches hissed once more through the air, and a new network of thin lines was laid over the marks that had begun to fade on her taut and reddened buttocks, Jem clenched her teeth against the phallus in her mouth and consoled herself with two thoughts: the men were using the switches, which stung wickedly but only briefly and could not leave lasting marks; and in her current position, unable to move or speak, there was no danger that she might renounce her vow of submission.

Jem's bottom had become no more than a source of throbbing heat, and she was not immediately aware that the whipping had ended. It was only when something warm nudged her cheek that she realised that most of the kitchen-slaves had gathered around her head.

'Let's baste the bird,' one of the young men said. Jem heard another snigger. She could not turn her head but from the corners of her eyes she saw that four of the men were standing around her, and each of them had lifted aside his apron and was grasping in one or two hands his erect manhood. They began sliding their hands, still slick with oil from her body, up and down their shafts. They began to count the strokes; they masturbated in unison; the movements grew faster, the strokes shorter.

Jem heard their voices, and their increasingly loud cries of anticipation; she caught glimpses of pumping hands and glistening cock-heads. But she could do nothing except wait for the inevitable sticky climax.

With shouts and groans, they came. First one: Jem felt a splash of hot fluid on her forehead, and another next to her eye. Then another three reached their climaxes simultaneously, and Jem's face was deluged with spurts of hot, viscous semen. The musky smell was in her nostrils; the salty taste trickled over her lips and into her mouth, around the circumference of the phallus. She felt the cooling suspension begin to drip and slide down her face.

A moment later Jem heard more cries of ecstasy, and the two remaining kitchen-slaves shot their spurts of seed on to the pulsing, tender skin of Jem's buttocks. The hot fluid was soothing, and Jem was grateful when the two men used their hands to smear their semen all over the reddened, rounded surfaces.

Jem was confident that, when it came to tests of sexual endurance, she had as much stamina as anyone. But by now even she was beginning to feel tired, sore, used and uncomfortable. She was finding it difficult to keep at bay fantasies about hot baths full of scented bubbles. However, she reasoned, all six of the young men had now had their climaxes, and she knew that they would no longer be as diligent in their testing of her. Perhaps, she allowed herself to hope, she would shortly be released, and would be allowed a brief respite before she was obliged to submit herself to the next of the Chatelaine's ordeals.

She heard a door being flung open. A loud male voice filled the extensive space of the bakery.

'Is my bird ready, lads? Can I have her now?'

There were shouts of 'Yes, Chef,' and 'Here she is, Chef,' before the voice of one of the kitchen-slaves emerged from the concatenation. 'She's trussed and tenderised, Chef,' said the brown-eyed kitchen-slave, 'and oiled, and skewered on the spit, and basted. Just the way you said you wanted her. All she needs now is the stuffing.'

'Sauces and stuffings, those are my specialities,' the Chef said. 'That's a nicely done rump,' he added, and the shock of pain as a heavy hand landed on her backside revealed to Jem that the Chef had come to stand behind her. She felt strong but nimble fingers tracing the lattice of lines on her buttocks, and exploring the folds of her vulva under the stretched membranes of her penetrated vagina.

'This one's good and juicy, too,' the Chef commented. His fingers moved to Jem's anus, into which, thanks to the oil, he was very easily able to insert two fingers. 'She's ready for stuffing,' he announced, and without further ado he withdrew his fingers and instead presented to Jem's prettily and pinkly crinkled arsehole the head of his manhood.

As he buggered her he stroked her burning buttocks with one hand and used the other to vibrate the shaft of the phallus in Jem's vagina. As a result, Jem soon forgot her discomfort and was about to reach a deep and slow-building climax of her own when the Chef shouted, and jetted hot lava into Jem's bowels.

'A very tasty morsel,' the Chef commented as he withdrew his shrinking penis. Jem groaned with frustration. Around her, the kitchen-slaves began to untie her bonds.

THREE BEASTS

Penny Birch

Penny Birch is a naughty little minx. Not only does she shamelessly reveal her love of the bizarre world of pony-girl carting in her first novel for Nexus, *Penny in Harness*, she also reveals dark secrets about her best friend in *A Taste of Amber* and tells us everything we ever wanted to know about her cheeky activities in *Bad Penny*. Fans of Penny's enthusiastic writing and encyclopaedic knowledge of perversion will know that these books really are treats to look forward to. Penny is, moreover, a founding member of one of the UK's first pony-girl carting clubs, so everything you are likely to read is based on real experiences.

The following story is not published elsewhere. However, her previous Nexus books are as follows:

Ariolimax columbianus

W endy and I were still racing the Banana Slugs when the Minister entered the department. They had arrived that morning, flown in direct from Seattle, six fat yellow monsters nestled in a moss-packed box. One was a real whopper, brilliant banana yellow and as long as my hand even when limp and sleepy. We put him on a wet bench top and sprinkled him with water to get him going, and discovered he measured an impressive twenty-seven centimetres when fully extended. Wendy wanted to call him Grandpa, but I didn't think that was fair because it felt wrong to give a hermaphrodite a male name. Wendy giggled and said a male name was perfectly suitable because he looked like a huge cock. Huge was right, over ten inches and nearly as thick as my wrist, although I've never seen a bright yellow cock. I called Wendy a dirty-minded trollop and pointed out that Grandpa was still an unsuitable name because the slug was speeding away down the bench while we argued and anything but decrepit.

That was what started the slug racing. The others were getting frisky and one was already out of the box. It was an orangey yellow, rather like Wendy's hair. I pointed this out and earned myself a slap on the bottom, but she immediately adopted the slug and christened her Clementine, then bet me ten pounds that Clementine could beat Grandpa over a measured course. My bottom was tingling from the slap, so I took the bet and added a spanking for the loser, panties down, to be delivered as soon as it was safe.

I was confident in Grandpa. While Wendy and I had been arguing he had crawled a good metre, and more importantly, done it in a straight line. Slugs aren't like horses and dogs, you can't teach them to race along a course. You can't force them to race at all, in fact, they do as they please, but Grandpa seemed game. Wendy was convinced Clementine was even more active.

We marked off a metre and let them go. Wendy was right, Clementine went at a hell of a pace, for a slug. Unfortunately she went in the wrong direction and was halfway up a window when Grandpa crossed the finishing line. I was cheering by then, and laughing at the prospect of getting Wendy's panties down and turning her wobbling bottom a nice rich shade of pink. I was even more confident too and offered double or quits, adding the humiliation of stripping nude for her spanking if she lost.

She accepted and we set the slugs up again, only for Clementine to win by half a length. That meant quits, which was boring, so we agreed on a third race, with a naked spanking for the loser and six of the cane for good measure. We retrieved our champions and put them on the starting line once more, only for the door to open before they had travelled much over an inch.

I heard the catch go and turned to find Professor South pushing the door wide with his face set in the obsequious smile he reserves for visiting dignitaries. The next person who came in was obviously the Minister, although I had completely forgotten he was coming to inspect the department. After him came various sidekicks and several reporters, while I gave a smile every bit as unctuous as the Professor's and tried desperately to remember what the visit was supposed to be about. If I was right he was the new Minister for Genetic Research, a department or sub-department or something created to calm public fears about genetic engineering.

He was a small man, very formally dressed and precise, straight out of the 'fifties, and just the sort of MP you could imagine going on about permissiveness and the moral decay of society. What he was doing overseeing genetic research when he probably hadn't been in a science lab since he was at school I couldn't imagine, but Professor South had made it very clear that our continued funding depended on his good will.

Wendy and I came to attention, greeting the Minister politely while the flunkies hovered around and the reporters photographed our apparatus. We'd been setting up a practical for the first years, and the lab looked like something out of a Frankenstein movie, although it had nothing whatever to do with our work. It kept the reporters happy anyway, while the Minister surveyed the arrangement of retorts, tubes and burettes with every evidence of suspicion.

'Dr Birch and Dr Smith are currently working on a gene sequencing project,' Professor South explained, making a sweeping gesture to include the whole lab.

'Ah, indeed?' the Minister asked. 'And what, exactly, does that involve?'

'We are mapping the DNA of various species of gastropod,' I answered. '*Limacidae* and *Arionidae* at present, slugs that is.'

'Slugs?' he queried. 'And how will that be of benefit?'

'Essentially we are learning to map DNA more efficiently,' I answered quickly. 'We in fact use genetic material from slugs' eggs, thus avoiding contentious issues of experimentation on living animals. Besides, if all our slugs are released by animal liberationists at least we'll be able to catch up with them.'

He didn't even crack a smile, but tugged at his chin and turned to examine a burette stand as if it was a piece of medieval torture equipment. Professor South began to explain our anti-vivisection policy in more serious terms, and at that moment I felt a wet, sucking sensation on my leg. I knew what it was at once, and a quick glance below the level of the bench confirmed it. Grandpa was crawling up my leg.

It would have taken a second to remove him, but I didn't dare move. Because I was wearing short boots he was already a good way up my calf, and under the hem of my lab coat. No less than six cameramen had their lenses trained on us, and I knew that if I picked him off every paper in the city would soon have a photo of me removing a ten-inch banana slug from under my coat.

I stayed still, trying to look calm and attentive and wishing the Minister would go away and take his entourage with him. He didn't but kept talking, asking inane question after inane question while Grandpa crawled slowly up my leg. He tickled, making me want to wriggle in the same way as when I badly need to pee, but I didn't dare move at all. I wished I'd worn jeans instead of a skirt, and then he began to spiral slowly around my knee cap and I really wished I'd worn jeans.

It was agony, desperately trying to stay still as his fat, sticky body traced a line under my skirt and up the inside of my thigh, along the groove between my tightly closed legs and into the V where thighs meet panty crotch. My pulse began to hammer as he reached my panties and the water started to well in my eyes . . .

He stopped, his long, turgid body lying from well down my closed thighs to half way up the tight white cotton that covered my pussy. I swallowed, near to panic, and then I felt a strange scraping, itching feeling right between my sex lips and I knew that he had begun to eat my panties.

Slugs like cellulose, they're about the only animals that can eat it, and cotton panties were obviously no exception. I hate nylon panties, but I was wishing I'd worn some as I felt his radula scrape away the only barrier between my naked pussy flesh and Grandpa's fat, slug body. I actually felt it when the threads broke, I'm sure I did, a sudden, tiny release of tension as the thin cotton gave in. Then I was helpless, bare to him as he began to enlarge the hole, moving his head slowly from side to side as I held myself stock still in front of those awful camera lenses and writhed and squirmed inside.

I was struggling to hold back my tears, tears of awful frustration as well as in reaction to the feel of Grandpa eating slowly away at my panties. My only hope was that he would finish his meal and crawl back down, but I knew it was vain. Slugs climb, and it wasn't just cotton he was enjoying, but cotton with a spicy tang of pussy juice. I knew I was turned on from all the talk about spanking between Wendy and me, and that my pussy was sodden. In fact it could even have been that which drew him up my leg in the first place.

Now he was well into it, squeezing his head through the hole in my panties, right against my pussy, prodding at me like a cock searching for the hole, bumping on my clitoris, then between my lips. I suppressed a groan of despair as he began to ease his fat body through the hole in my panties, squirming and twisting inside, pushing into the tight gap between pussy and cotton. Slugs move by sending waves of muscular contraction down the length of their bodies, and as Grandpa forced his way into my panties each wave was rubbed right against my sex, between the lips and on my clitoris. He got himself right in, his whole, fat, slimy, ten-inch body, packed into the tight chamber between my pussy and my panties. I could imagine the way it would make the front bulge out obscenely, with his body moving under the cotton.

It was right on my clitty, his body rubbing on me, each muscular wave pressing tight, until my heart was hammering and my pelvic muscles had begun to contract. I knew I was going to come, I just couldn't help it. My vision was going, with red spots in front of my eyes. My body felt weak and my nipples were straining against the material of my blouse. It was happening and I couldn't stop it. I was coming with a slug down my panties, coming in front of a dozen people, all staring pop-eyed as my arousal became impossible to hide and my mouth came open in a long, groan of helpless, despairing ecstasy as my thighs and bottom cheeks clenched tight and my pussy began to pulse.

Grandpa's tail found my cunt and slipped inside. The full, fleshy width of his foot settled on my clitoris and squeezed, sucking the little bud against his body. I choked back a scream as the camera flashes exploded and then I was going to my knees, sobbing and gasping as I came and came and came.

I never did it, I never pulled up my skirt and showed it all off, panties and slug and cunt and everything, all in a filthy, slimy mess. Despite everything I held from that, just coming over and over as Grandpa's fat body squirmed in my panties and they all looked on in shock and disgust and amazement. All except Wendy, my darling, wonderful Wendy, who pulled me up under my armpits and helped me from the room, all the time reeling off a frantic explanation about stomach cramps, period pains, appendicitis . . . anything except Banana Slugs.

Gigantopithecus grandipedis

It started as a student prank, and a pretty trivial one at that. I had left the order form for the Banana Slugs on my desk and, because it was addressed to Rocky Mountain Biological Supply, some joker had added on a request for a Big Foot Sasquatch. When I came back I didn't bother to change it. After all, it was obviously a joke, and a harmless one. Besides, I couldn't be bothered to fill out a new form.

The people at RMBS obviously found it funny anyway, because when the invoice for the Banana Slugs arrived it contained a note apologising for being out of stock of Sasquatch and promising to send one as soon as possible. Wendy and I replied with a request for delivery at their earliest convenience and an added note that for preference the Sasquatch should be male, not too old and in good condition. In return we got a note saying that they did now have a Sasquatch, but an elderly female with only one leg. We asked if she was available at a discount and they refused, citing the rarity of the species, and so it went, getting ever more ridiculous. Finally we accused them of giving preferential treatment to US universities and threatened to sue if we were not immediately supplied with an eight-foot male Sasquatch in prime condition.

The phone call came at one o'clock in the morning. I awoke with a surge of adrenalin at the thought of some tragedy, only to find that it was the airport customs, saying that they had a large, angry Sasquatch for the university and that I was to come immediately.

I knew it was some stupid prank by RMBS, but I still had to go. When you regularly bring in things like Banana Slugs and shrunken heads it pays to be on the right side of Customs and Excise. I didn't even argue, but threw on a tracksuit and trainers over my panties and set off. All the way I was wondering what RMBS had done, but when I finally arrived I really began to wonder. It had come in on a 747, a massive wooden crate with air holes and large 'This Side Up' stickers. They had forklifted it to the quarantine bay, where it stood inside an enclosure used for zoo animals. I signed several forms, each listing my consignment as 'Sasquatch, large, male, one'. With the formalities over I was allowed into the enclosure, while the customs officers, a dozen airport officials, several reporters and two policewomen looked on in fascination.

There was something in the crate, something big, and I could only imagine they had sent me a bear. It was one hell of a joke, but there it was. I peered through an air hole, standing on tiptoe to get high enough. There was a bar inside, clearly part of a cage and obstructing my view, so I moved to another. The interior was dim, illuminated solely by the faint rays of light striking in through the air holes. For a moment I could see nothing but dust motes dancing in the dull light, and then it moved, something hairy and a deep red-brown. So they had sent me a bear, and a big grizzly too by the look of things. It was a stupid thing to do, and I was pretty angry as I undid the catches that held shut the front of the crate, also sorry for the poor animal. The hatch swung down and I stepped aside to let it fall, then stepped up on it to get a better look at the grizzly.

It was the arms I saw first, great, long things totally unlike the forelegs of a bear. Then he turned and I saw his face and I could only stand and stare. It was an ape that was looking at me, a huge, heavy-browed ape, with the protruding muzzle and heavy jowls of an orang-utan and a fringe of dark orange hair. It was the eyes that had me fixed to the spot. You can see the intelligence in an orang's eyes, but these were different, these were human. I just stood, staring transfixed as he unfolded himself to his full height and my last hopes that he might have been a big male orang vanished. He was a Sasquatch, and he was huge, well over seven foot, and built more like a man than an ape, despite the massive, splayed feet, the knuckling, simian hands and the mass of hair that covered all but his face, his great swollen belly . . . and his genitals.

He was a male, there was no doubt about that. His cock had the dimensions of a cucumber, a great, ponderous thing, dark brown in colour and hanging over two balls the size of oranges, big oranges. It wasn't completely limp either, and as I stared at it the foreskin began to peel back to expose a head the size of my fist and a rich scarlet in colour. He growled and took his cock in his hand, looking right at me and jerking at it. The great bulbous head came right out, pointed straight at me with obvious interest. I heard a nervous, female giggle from behind me and I found myself blushing furiously. With a few more jerks he came erect, his penis a truly monstrous thing, some two feet of shiny brown cock meat with the head a bloated red-purple globe and a dribble of Cowper's fluid at the tip.

The Sasquatch came forward, hunched down in the cage, took hold of the bars and thrust his belly forward, jamming his straining erection out between them. He gave a grunt and pointed to his cock, a demand all too obvious: he wanted it attended to, maybe wanked off, maybe sucked. I backed away, damned sure that whatever I did I wasn't sucking a Sasquatch off in front of twenty or so people. He gave another grunt, angrier, more demanding. My back nudged the door of the enclosure and I heard the latch click into place. I turned, intending to let myself out, scrabbling the key into the lock, only to feel a touch at my waist.

He had reached out, all the way from the cage, his massive arm just reaching me. His fingers curled into the waistband of my tracksuit and I was being pulled back, inexorably, by a strength far, far beyond anything I could resist. I tried to cling on to the door but my fingers slipped away. I called out but they just stared at me, watching as he drew me in. I kicked and wriggled and beat my fists against his arm, but to no avail whatever, and then my bum had bumped against the bars of the cage and his cock was nudged up against my back.

I was held like that, wriggling helpless with one massive arm pinning me around my waist and his erection rubbing against my back. I was panicking, kicking and writhing against him, but it only seemed to stimulate him more. I was calling out too, my own voice sounding pathetic in my ears, but not one person moved to help me. They just watched, watched as he jerked my tracksuit top up over my braless breasts, watched as they were fondled and tweaked in huge, leathery fingers, watched as my nipples went hard and my legs kicked against the cage. The keys dropped from my nerveless fingers and he snatched them from the air. I heard the grate of metal on metal as he tried one key after another, and a click as the lock sprang open. The cage door swung open, still with me clutched to it.

Then he had me, raped me maybe, I don't know, because I couldn't resist, not physically, not mentally. First I was stripped, my tracksuit trousers wrenched down, then off as he held me around the waist with one hand and worked on my clothes with the other. Next came my top, jerked off over my head. My panties came last, wrenched down and then torn away to leave me naked except for my trainers.

Next I was pushed down and made to suck, my head taken by the hair and pulled hard against his erection until I opened my mouth and let it in. He jammed it deep down my throat, making me gag as he fucked my head. I was really choking, with the thick meat of his cock blocking my airway and the taste and smell of it filling my head.

Trying desperately to pull away I thrashed my head from side to side. He wouldn't stop, but just kept on pumping, forcing his erection further down my windpipe with each push, until my throat was full of it and his huge balls were nudged up against my chin. My neck had been forced up, like a sword swallower's, only it wasn't steel in my throat but a hard, two-foot bar of Sasquatch cock, slowly pumping, fucking my head to a lazy rhythm. Lights began to explode around me and I thought I was suffocating, only to realise that the reporters in the crowd had at last recovered their senses and were taking pictures of my mouth being used by the Sasquatch.

My throat was squeezing over and over on his cock as I gagged, and I know what that does to a man's cock. The Sasquatch was no different, grunting happily at the feel of my helpless contractions and then giving a deep groan and ejaculating down my throat. I felt the hot sperm flood my windpipe, masses of it, straining my gullet and filling my stomach, then bursting out of my nose and filling my cheeks as he mercifully pulled back. Then it was out, only for him to take his erection in hand and splash another massive wad of come full in my face. It went in my eyes and in my hair, down my neck and over my breasts, spurt after sticky, viscous spurt, but I didn't care, I could breathe again, and that was all I could think of as I panted and puffed on the enclosure floor.

I sat back, still gasping for breath with Sasquatch sperm oozing from my mouth and running slowly down over my face. My stomach was a hard, round ball, bloated with his sperm, while the taste and smell of it was making me as dizzy as the lack of air. I thought he would stop, having come, and immediately felt a pang of regret, followed by a yet sharper pang of shame for thinking such a thing. I was wrong though, he hadn't finished with me, not by a long way.

Vast, leathery hands took me by the shoulders and pushed me back, gently, but with a power far beyond my ability to resist. I let him do it, knowing what was coming and spreading my thighs because it would have been futile to try and keep them closed. His cock was still hard, and as it nudged my pussy I resigned myself to being fucked by an eight-foot Sasquatch.

RMBS must have been showing him American porno movies, because he wasn't just content with fucking me on my back. I got the full treatment, put through my paces in position after position, with my vagina vacated each time only to be stuffed full once more. First it was missionary, with me on my back and him over me with his huge cock in my pussy as he humped me. I'll say this for him, he took his weight on his elbows, like a gentleman, but I was still squashed helpless under his great round belly. My pussy was really bursting, with perhaps half his monstrous cock inside and the mouth stretched so wide I began to wonder if it felt similar to having a baby. Somehow it went though, and it didn't even hurt, just filled me and stretched me until my whole body felt bloated with penis.

He fucked and fucked, no, we fucked, because my hips had begun to move to the rhythm of his pushes, and it wasn't against my will any more. I began to squirm under him in sheer joy, laughing and rubbing my nipples in his long chest hair, revelling in the overwhelming sensations he was giving me despite myself. Shame burnt in the back of my mind, but it didn't matter, I couldn't stop anyway, but only submit to his use, over and over as his cock moved in me and his sperm ran down over my head and chest.

After missionary he rolled my legs up to my chest and fucked me like that, supported on the full length of his arms. Then it was doggie, with me rolled over and humped from the rear with his long hair tickling my bum and making me giggle in between gasps and pants. He made me suck him after that, then it was back in my pussy, with me pressed to the enclosure fence and one leg cocked high so the audience could get a prime view of his erection working in my hole. We stayed like that for ages, really playing to the crowd while they photographed me being used, well, no, not being used, thoroughly enjoying a really good fuck, a fuck far beyond anything any human male could achieve.

He had me on my side next, then on my back again with him kneeling up and watching his cock slide in and out of my open, gaping pussy. I had given in completely by then, and was playing with my tits, rubbing the thick, slimy sperm over them and tweaking my hard nipples over and over. After that he rolled over and stuck me on his cock, letting me control the fucking while I fondled my breasts and the rounded bulge of my sperm-swollen tummy. I began to masturbate then, rubbing my clitty and feeling the hard bulk of his cock through the front of my body.

I nearly came, only to be suddenly lifted off and put back on my knees, then once more filled with cock from the rear. Soon I was gasping and rubbing myself, determined to come with my bum in the air and my pussy straining around his lovely cock. They kept photographing me, but I didn't mind, I wanted them to, to show everyone how I'd been fucked and how much I'd enjoyed my supposed rape. He let me, but not in the way I'd expected.

His finale was to bugger me, spreading my bum wide and forcing his penis into my sperm-slick anus. I was sure I couldn't take it, that I would split, but in it went, my ring stretching to capacity as I gasped and sobbed on to the floor, struggling to accommodate his cock in my rectum and all at once ashamed and thankful that I'd been buggered often enough to loosen my muscle. Up it went, inch after inch of huge cock crammed into my backside until I was pop-eyed and gasping for breath, only for yet another section of arm-thick cock shaft to be jammed past my protesting ring. He put it right in, all two foot of monstrous Sasquatch cock, rammed to the hilt up my poor little bottom until his huge balls came to rest against my empty pussy.

I was taken by the hips, his hands so big they held the full spread of a buttock under each thumb and the fingers still met around my tummy. He buggered me in earnest, squeezing me as he pushed in again and again, knocking the breath from my body over and over until I was fighting for air and clutching at my pussy in my desperation to get at my clitoris.

He made it first, his sperm erupting up my bottom, masses of it, until it was gurgling and bubbling in my gut and I felt fit to explode. Still it went on, more and more pumping into me with my anus a ring of fire and my clitty a hot nubbin of flesh under my fingers. The camera flashes were bursting in a sea of light as he came up my bottom and I squealed and yelled, begging for more, for deeper, harder penetration, to be buggered until I screamed, to be buggered until I passed out.

It wouldn't work though. He was jerking me about like a doll as his spunk filled me and I was slippery with it anyway and could just get the purchase I needed on my clitty. The frustration was appalling and I had begun to scream to be let come when he suddenly stopped. I was still, and the monstrous cock was being pulled from my body, making me feel as if I was being pulled inside out as my poor, aching anus everted. I was still rubbing though, riding my ecstasy over the pain until the fat penis head popped from my bumhole and it closed with a long, sonorous fart.

With that I came, and as I came about a gallon of Sasquatch sperm burst from my anus, spraying him, the floor, the reporters, the police, the customs officers, the airport staff, the quarantine room, the whole airport, as my world dissolved in unbearable ecstasy and I woke up, screaming, drenched in sweat, twisted into my bedclothes and with one hand down the front of my panties.

Formica rufa

Term was over, Christmas approaching, the students gone, the labs and lecture theatres empty. I had stayed on, unable to abandon my research, tending the Banana Slugs and helping the few remaining staff with various scientific chores. Not that I had much to do, in terms of actually filling my time, yet my experiments had to be checked every six hours, without fail. That meant being in the lab late, often the only person in the huge building, which made me feel melancholy and introspective.

Sex is really the best way to break that sort of mood, and the first two nights I masturbated, sat naked in my chair with the door locked against accidental intrusion, my legs cocked wide over the arms and my mind running with dirty fantasies. The first night I came over a simple spanking fantasy, imagining myself turned over Dr South's knee to have my bare bottom smacked in front of a class of students. The second it was my Sasquatch dream and the pain and humiliation of my imaginary ordeal. Both orgasms were good, but a little spoilt by being over unreal things, while I knew I would only upset myself if I fantasised over Amber or end up on a nostalgia trip if it was over something I'd really done.

On the third night I was feeling distinctly dissatisfied with myself. I was feeling rude and wanted to do it again, but I needed something more concrete than the products of my own imagination. I wanted feelings of helplessness and panic, much like those the dream had given me, so my first thought was to give myself an enema in my room, pull up my panties and try to make the loo. If I made it the sense of rudeness over what I'd done and relief at letting go would be enough to leave me in a frenzy of masturbation. If I failed I would fill my panties, which would be even better.

Unfortunately it was just too risky. Even with just two janitors responsible for the entire science block there was a chance one or the other might choose to wander into Genetics at the wrong moment. It was a nice thought anyway, and had me more excited than ever when the time came to take my six-hourly readings and adjust the apparatus. That distracted me for a while, but afterwards I was worse than ever.

I went to check on the animals, watching the Banana Slugs feed and remembering how it had felt to have the largest of them squirming in my panties. It was even tempting to do it again, disgustingly dirty but tempting. Fortunately watching their radulae scrape at the algae-encrusted glass put me off. They do, after all, eat meat as well. I had to do something though, and I knew that if I didn't decide soon it would be the Banana Slugs.

If I hadn't been so worked up I'd never have done it, but my pussy was aching and my head full of thoughts of sexual pain and filthy behaviour. Next to the Banana Slugs was an ant colony, used for first-year behaviour practicals. They weren't *Lasius* either, but *Formica rufa*, wood ants, big, fox-red, biting wood ants. A silly thought came into my head, something the boys used to say to tease us, about a girl taking down her pants to let out the ants. It had always humiliated me, with my overactive imagination sending the blood to my cheeks as I imagined being tickled and bitten until I at last gave in and took my panties down in front of everyone.

I had to do it. It would hurt, but I didn't care. Working with trembling fingers I went to a fume cupboard and took a disposable face mask from the drawer. Pulling it up under my skirt, I settled it in place, my panties holding it snug to my pussy, the elastic strap pulled tight around my hips. It was perfect, cupping my pussy to make a chamber over my vulva, a chamber for my own personal torture.

Even hurting an ant is against my principles, especially for my sexual thrills, so I was careful, opening their tank and allowing them to crawl into a beaker until I had enough. With my hands trembling hard I hitched up my skirt, revealing the soft bulge of the mask beneath my panties. I felt naughty and scared, foolish yet incredibly aroused as I opened the front of my panties, revealing my thick pubic hair. Taking up the beaker, I held it over the opening, hesitating, almost backing out, then tipping it suddenly, sliding the ants into my pussy chamber.

They were furious and bit immediately, the burn of methanoic acid making me gasp even as my skirt fell back into place. It hurt, really hurt, a furious stinging as they vented their anger on the flesh of my pussy, first my pubic mound, then lower, on my lips and in my vulva, leaving me with my head thrown back and my teeth gritted in pain. I could feel my flesh swelling and I wanted to scream, but I held on, wriggling my toes and dancing on my feet as my pussy became a ball of agonised fire.

I had meant to wait until I could stand no more, take the pussy chamber off and replace the ants, then come under my fingers. As it was I knew the sensation alone would make me come, if I could only hold on long enough. They were tickling as well as biting, making my flesh writhe and jump, not just my pussy but my bum cheeks too. I was shaking my head, whimpering and sobbing in my pain, but my pussy felt so hot, so swollen that I couldn't bring myself to stop.

Then it happened. I swear I felt one clutch on to my clit, her legs clamping to my sensitive flesh, her mandibles closing on my tiny, excited bud, the acid squirting on to my helpless, tender skin. It hurt, hurt so much I screamed aloud, but I was coming too, arching my back, shrieking in agony but also ecstasy, my swollen, burning pussy the centre of everything, my head full of the extremity of what I'd done. My panties were full of ants, my cunt swollen and burning, fat with acid, tortured to orgasm . . .

Looking back, the climax was superb, one of the best, lasting for what seemed an age, my body totally out of control, pure bliss. At the time I was crying out in pain, lost to everything but the feel of my sex and the rudeness of what I'd done: filling my panties with biting ants to deliberately torture myself to orgasm.

It hurt dreadfully afterwards, as I pulled my panties down with desperate urgency and returned the ants one by one to the tank. My whole pubic mound was red and swollen, my flesh marked with dozens of bites. I found some antihistamine and rubbed it in to dull the pain, and ended up masturbating in it to a second climax. Still, it's not a technique I'd recommend to anyone else. If you get ants in your pants, take them off, fast, and never mind who's looking!

DOLLY DEAREST

Jennifer Jane Pope

Jennifer Jane Pope's first Nexus novel, *Slave Genesis*, is a story of pony-girl training in a remote Scottish institution. However, genetically re-engineered and with a higher-than-normal threshold for pain, these are girls with a difference. Her second, *Slave Exodus*, continues the events of the first, with new and imaginative twists, as do the third and fourth — *Slave Revelations* and *Slave Acts*.

Meanwhile, here is a delightfully strange new story from Jennifer . . .

I am making this tape in the hope that one day someone will find it and write down my story, something I would dearly like to be able to do myself and cannot, for reasons which will soon become only too awfully obvious to you.

Once upon a time I hoped that someone would find me and take me back into the real world, but that I now know is a hopeless dream. Even Maudie, the new 'maid' who has managed to get this tape machine to me and operate the controls, cannot now go beyond the boundary fence which girdles the estate outside the window of the nursery in which I sit, day and night, waiting the whims and pleasures of my owner's daughter, the unspeakably horrid Dorothea.

I am therefore resigned to this so-called life, at least for the foreseeable future and, as time continues to pass – and largely to pass me by – I fear that if the opportunity ever did present itself, it might be too late, for I am steadily becoming what I can only describe as 'institutionalised' in this artificial environment and would, I have to admit to myself, be of little or no use outside of these four, confining walls.

Sadly, as the years advance, even that use and value will ultimately begin to devalue: age is a harsh mistress, harsher maybe even than the mistress who currently controls my fate and rules my existence with such stern and generally unsympathetic delight.

Making this tape is a risk in itself, for if she ever realises that I have recovered even the power to whisper again, then I think she would have my voice box removed completely, to ensure that I went back to being the dumb dolly into which I was originally made . . .

I say 'originally', but that of course is not true. Originally I was a boy, a young man, eighteen years old, fit and healthy, if not quite socially acceptable. That latter state of affairs existed because I suffered from a strange and overwhelming compulsion to steal, from shops, from cars, cars themselves and even – and I am ashamed to admit it now – from houses.

My big mistake was not so much that I tried to break into Farnley Grange, but that I was caught doing it, and by Mrs Olivia Farnley herself. I tried to struggle free, but I was, and am still, a small person and Mrs Farnley was a large and powerful woman. She overpowered me easily and tied me to a solid-looking chair with a length of cord she cut from the heavy drawing-room curtains.

'I know you,' she said, staring down at me. 'You're Peggy Watling's boy, aren't you? You're the one who ran away from home when he was fifteen and stayed missing for a year. Hmm, very interesting. Very interesting indeed.' There was a peculiar light in her eyes that sent a shiver up and down my spine and I had a sudden thought that maybe she intended to kill me.

Oh, how much kinder that would have been!

I had seen Dorothea in the village, usually accompanied by her weird-looking governess. She was about fifteen or sixteen, I'd guessed, though her style of dress would have been more appropriate for a ten or twelve year old. She was also very arrogant, snobbish, and terribly rude to the shop assistants. Village gossip had it that she was not only as spoiled as she behaved, but also a bit 'odd', due, it was rumoured, to some mystery childhood illness.

'He's no good, Mummy!' she exclaimed, when Mrs Farnley brought her in to show me off to her. 'I wanted a girl dolly. You said I could have a little girl dolly. You promised!' The terrible, overgrown infant actually stamped her foot and, as her pale features reddened, I thought she was even going to burst into tears.

'I know I did, darling, and you shall have a girl dolly,' her mother shushed her. 'But this will be a girl dolly soon, but a girl dolly with a big difference. Mummy will see to everything, as usual.' I looked from one to the other of them in mute amazement. What on earth were they on about?

'Off you go and play then, darling,' Mrs Farnley told Dorothea. 'Mummy has to make a phone call.'

Two white-coated men arrived for me an hour or so later. I had spent the intervening time snivelling and apologising, pleading with Mrs Farnley to let me go, but my whinging fell upon deaf ears until she decided to silence me by placing a broad strip of sticking plaster over my mouth.

I have little or no recollection of where I was taken. From the moment of that first injection, given whilst I was still bound helplessly to the chair, until my return to the Grange, everything was a vague dream. Even time had no meaning during that period and, when I finally regained consciousness to a great enough degree to take stock of my surroundings, I was stretched out flat under a soft quilt upon a double bed on the top floor of what I soon found out was Farnley Grange.

I tried to sit up, but, to my horror, found I could not move and seemed to have no feeling at all in either my arms or my legs. I wondered if this paralysis was some after-effect of whatever drugs I had been receiving. It was not, as Mrs Farnley herself delighted in explaining to me a few hours later.

'A very clever neurosurgeon has gone to a lot of trouble on my behalf,' she said, smiling down at me, smugly. 'You no longer have any connections between your brain and the nerves that control your arm and leg movement.' I opened my mouth to cry out at this, but no sound emerged, just a rush of air.

'Oh, and your vocal cords have been surgically immobilised,' Mrs Farnley added, seeing my futile attempt at speech, 'so I'm afraid you are now dumb as well.'

My brain was reeling at the horror of her revelations, but she was far from finished. Reaching down, she drew back the cover from my body, revealing a pair of perfectly formed, if slightly flattened out due to my prone position, breasts, complete with large, dark pink nipples.

'Before you worry overmuch,' she went on, 'your male parts are still intact and for very good reasons. Children learn about a lot from their dollies and my daughter is going to learn from you and will be more fortunate than most of her contemporaries in that she will have a life-sized working dolly to play with.

'There are so many dangerous influences on children these days and I do not intend for my daughter to be subjected to them. Therefore, I prefer to give her everything she needs for her life in her own environment here.

'Of course, I have had your actual reproductive system sterilised, so we won't have any unwanted accidents and the doctors have checked you thoroughly for any nasty little infections and pronounced you all clear, so you are quite safe for Dorothea to play with.'

Dumbly, I stared up at the woman, realising now that she had to be completely mad. If people thought Dorothea slightly odd, it was plain to me where she had inherited that trait. I kept trying to convince myself that this was only some sort of nightmare and that I would shortly wake up back in the real world, but I knew it was only too real.

As I was later to discover, my veins were awash with some sort of tranquilliser at this time, otherwise Mrs Farnley's words must surely have sent me insane. As it was, for a while my mind went almost as numb as my arms and legs, her words swirling around inside my aching head. Eventually, though, I began to understand.

Macabre and unbelievable as the suggestion might seem, I was to be a Victorian dolly, and Mrs Farnley had gone to a lot of trouble to make sure that Dorothea had plenty of choice in the outfits she could dress me in. There were also several different wigs and my own hair had been removed in order to make it simpler for the strange girl to interchange these on my head.

However, before I was turned over to her daughter, Mrs Farnley undertook my first outfitting personally.

She began with a black and red satin corset which looked outwardly to be a flounce of fripperies and extravagance, but which was so cunningly and heavily boned as to become an instrument of torture when completely laced.

There was nothing I could do but lie there as this mad woman handled me as if I were indeed a doll, rolling me over on to my face in order to tighten the laces, making me gasp and wince as the fiendish garment increased its awful grip about me. When she was finished, she heaved me up into a sitting position, propped up by a bank of pillows, and examined the effect of the corset on my breasts. The support cups supported all right, but they concealed little, leaving the upper half of each globe lifted and exposed, the nipples peeking over the lace frills. Mrs Farnley nodded with evident satisfaction.

'Very pretty, Dolly,' she said and I could hear that capital letter in the tone of her voice. I was not even to be allowed the dignity of a name, it seemed. No, I was merely Dolly, a limp, useless thing to be picked up and played with, or discarded at will.

'Perhaps I should show you your face, Dolly,' Mrs Farnley said. She took up a mirror from the nearby chest of drawers and held it up for me to see. I let out a noiseless gasp of disbelief, for, apart from the fact I was now completely bald, the face staring back at me was unrecognisable as my own. My eyes looked bigger and wider, my mouth fuller and pouting and I was made up in a parody of a Victorian burlesque performer, every feature exaggerated completely.

'The make-up is permanent,' she told me, 'tattooed into the skin to save my sweet girl having to keep redoing it every day. Don't you just look a sweet, pretty sight, Dolly?' I managed to shake my head in horror, about the only part of my body over which I retained any vestige of control.

'You should try to look more grateful, Dolly,' Mrs Farnley rebuked me. 'I paid those plastic surgeons a small fortune for you to be able to look so lovely.' They had certainly earned their money, I thought, for my features had been completely resculpted and even I did not recognise myself. The only blemish I could detect was a purplish scar where my Adam's apple had once been.

Satisfied that I was in no doubt as to what I now looked like, Mrs Farnley discarded the mirror and returned to the task of dressing me. She began with long, black silk stockings, which reached to the very top of my thighs, where, in addition to being anchored by broad frilly garters, they were also attached to the lower hem of the corset by means of four taut suspender straps fastened to each.

A fiercely elasticated gusset was then clipped in place and a thick absorbent pad placed between it and my genitalia and anus. Mrs Farnley took fiendish pleasure in explaining its purpose.

'You no longer have much control over your bowels and bladder,' she said, 'and we don't want your drawers getting soiled all the time. They are such a chore to wash and the fabric is on the delicate side.'

The drawers in question were long, Victorian things that reached to just below the knees and were secured there, as well as about my waist, by wide satin ribbon drawstrings. The crotch could be laid wide by untying a row of thinner ribbons, allowing access without the tedium of removing the garment completely. Mrs Farnley obviously did not want to tax her daughter's energies overly, I thought grimly.

Why she had taken so much trouble with my footwear, I could barely understand, as I was never going to walk in the delicate, high-heeled ankle boots which she buttoned on to my feet. I supposed it was to complete the overall effect, but I was in no position to ask.

My dress, which was mostly bright red with black piping and lace trimmings, came complete with several layers of frilled lacy petticoats which caused the below-the-knee-length skirt to billow out. It had long, close-fitting sleeves and a low, frothy neckline that left my full breasts barely decently covered. Soft gloves were then drawn over my hands and a satin and lace choker fitted about my throat, concealing the scar from view.

'Nearly done, Dolly,' Mrs Farnley said. She picked up a pair of diamanté earrings, shaped like daisy flowers and inserted them through the waiting holes in my ear lobes. 'There,' she said, patting my cheek, 'just your hair to do now.'

She selected a long wig of black curls and carefully stretched it over my naked pate, brushing it out and adding a broad velvet ribbon of vivid red to achieve the finished picture.

'Perfect,' she said, standing back. 'Now let's see what my sweet Dorothea thinks.'

'Sweet' Dorothea was beside herself with joy and enthusiasm.

'Oh, she's gorgeous now, Mummy!' she trilled. 'Are you really sure this is the same horrid creature you showed me that time?'

Mrs Farnley nodded and assured her it was. Her daughter stepped forward and gingerly prodded the exposed part of my bust.

'Oooh!' she squealed. 'They feel so real!'

'Yes, don't they,' her mother agreed. 'And there's something else, too. Reach behind her neck. Go on, she won't bite you, not unless she wants me to send her to have her teeth removed and replaced by rubber dentures. There, feel it? A sort of button embedded in the skin. Open your mouth a little, Dolly,' she said, addressing herself to me. Unthinkingly, I did so.

'Press the little button, my sweetheart,' Mrs Farnley urged. I felt Dorothea's fingers pressing against something in the nape of my neck and suddenly a metallic voice emerged from my parted lips.

'*Mama, mama,*' the automaton forced from my throat. Dorothea almost fell over as she dissolved into a fit of giggles and could not resist trying the button again. Before I could close my mouth again I was bleating: '*Mama, mama, mama, mama.*'

I forced my lips shut, but Mrs Farnley wagged a warning finger at me.

'You keep that sweet mouth open at all times, Dolly,' she snapped. 'Otherwise I'll keep it open for you.' Resolutely, I refused, determined to show that I was not completely beaten, but I should have heeded her warning.

Ten minutes later, two chrome clamps had been fitted at either side, inside my mouth and screwed on to the molars to keep my jaw from closing. Try as I might, there was now no way I could make my lips touch and I was then forced to endure a prolonged session of Dorothea playing with the control of the voice module.

'I'll leave you to play with Dolly, dearest,' Mrs Farnley said at last, evidently tiring of her offspring's obsession with the artificial voice unit. 'I'll just pop down and see that cook is preparing dinner and later I'll come back up and show you some of Dolly's other outfits.'

'I know you've still got a willy inside your knickers,' Dorothea whispered, as soon as the door had closed behind her mother. 'I'm supposed to learn all about thingy from it – and you, but Mummy really is a bit slow at times. She thinks I'm a complete baby over some things, but I made Miss Fenn – that's the lady who used to be my governess – get me some books from a shop in town.

'She didn't want to, but I'd found some horrid magazines in her stuff. There were pictures of ladies kissing each other and sucking their titties. Would you like me to suck your titties, Dolly? Oh, of course, you can't speak, can you, Dolly? All you can do is cry for Mama. Poor Dolly. Well, never mind, maybe I *will* suck your titties. Maybe I'll make you suck mine, as well. You can still move your mouth, after all.'

She clambered on to the bed alongside me, her freckled face beneath its ginger curtain of ringlets flushed with excitement.

'Yes,' she whispered, conspiratorially, 'Mummy still thinks I'm a little girl, but I was seventeen last month, you know.' She slipped a cool hand under my skirt and petticoats and stroked my silk-sheathed thigh. 'Would you like me to take your willy out and play with it, Dolly dearest?' she crooned, her hand moving further upwards. Despite the situation, I felt my trapped penis trying to respond.

'I know what "wank" means, Dolly,' Dorothea sniggered, leaning close to my face. 'Would Dolly like me to wank her?' I doubted it would matter whether Dolly wanted it or not, for there was a madly committed gleam in her eyes.

For a supposedly fairly uninformed and inexperienced girl, Dorothea certainly knew how to tease. She inched her way upwards, rustling the loose fabric of my knickers as she went, her fingers crawling spider-like towards the ribbons that held the crotch closed. I felt my pulse rate steadily quickening, despite the horror I felt at being so hopelessly at her mercy, and the ache in my groin bore testimony to my rebellious organ's attempts to respond to her advances.

'I'm going to wank you, Dolly,' she breathed, 'and then I'm going to feed you on your own sticky come juices. That's what they call them in my books, you know,' she added, sounding proud of her knowledge. 'You'll enjoy that, Dolly – not!' She laughed maniacally, as her fingers began tugging on the first ribbon. Then she began singing softly, to the sound of *Bobby Shaftoe*, but her words were far different from the version I remembered singing at school.

'Dolly dearest wants a wank,
'Naughty Dolly needs a spank,
'Wank first, Dolly, then I'll spank,
'Naughty Dolly dearest.'

She broke off into further giggles and then repeated her hideous song as she completed the task of untying the ribbons, but then had to concentrate all her attentions to the task of unfastening the front of the gusset.

Eventually, she managed it and pulled the pad clear, exposing my hairless genitalia to her ministrations. I tried to fight against it, but it was no good. Within seconds, my cock stood ramrod stiff in her grasp and she began slowly to masturbate me, her free hand cupped over the narrow slit from which my semen would ultimately spout. She did not have long to wait. I erupted, filling her cupped hand and she withdrew it triumphantly, forcing my head back and slowly trickling the milky fluid between my helpless, still parted lips.

'Dolly have a drink,' she taunted me as the salty liquid ran down to my throat. 'Sissy old Dolly drinks her own come. Tastes nice, doesn't it, you dirty Dolly you?' I choked and spluttered, but, as she kept her palm cupped over my mouth, there was no option but to swallow every last drop. Beneath the pale make-up my cheeks burned with indignation and shame.

'Good Dolly,' she urged, wiping her hand across my lips. 'Lick your mouth clean, there's a good girl.' When I had finished, Dorothea produced a large handkerchief and wiped away the last vestiges of semen from my now deflated cock, replaced the pad and gusset and began retying the ribbons on my drawers.

'Soppy old Dolly needs a nappy,' she chanted. 'Stupid Dolly can't stop herself from piddling and shitting herself, just like a big baby. I think Dolly deserves a good spanking with my hairbrush, then maybe I should go down to the garden and get some nice nettles to put inside Dolly's nappy afterwards. Ha-ha, silly Dolly. You're all mine to do whatever I want with, 'cause Mummy said so. You're a late birthday present for her own dear daughter.'

She stopped and stared fiercely at me, her flushed cheeks adding to the image of intensity. 'I'm never going to let you go, Dolly. I might even grow to love your silly face, who knows? Would you like me to love you, Dolly, or shall I go and get those nice nettles?'

Desperately, I tried to nod my head and shake it at the same time. The thought of having to endure a bunch of nettles against my most tender regions was enough to convince me that I must try to co-operate at all costs. The mother was mad, I already knew, but Dorothea was well on her way to being a match in that department.

Dorothea smiled. 'Perhaps I'll fuck you instead, Dolly,' she said. 'That's a naughty word, isn't it, Dolly? Mummy would be angry if she knew I used that word, but it'll be our secret, won't it, because you can't tell on me, can you, Dolly?' She stroked my face in an unexpected gesture of affection.

'I think I will love you, Dolly,' she said, quietly. 'After all, you're supposed to be my friend, aren't you? And you can't help yourself, after all. It's hardly your fault that you're now a stupid dolly girl and you do have something nice in your knickers as well as something nasty.' She turned about and nestled down next to me.

'Mummy doesn't know it, Dolly,' she confided, 'but I've seen some of the outfits she's bought for you. There's a lovely disco-dancing outfit, just like Barbie has on television. Mummy doesn't like me watching television, but sometimes, if she's away, I sneak out and go over to Gloria's house. She's our cleaner, but she won't be allowed in the nursery where you're to be kept. Mummy says I have to keep that room clean myself, now.

'And I'm not allowed to tell Gloria about you, Dolly. Mummy says she wouldn't understand and I think she's right. You're a special secret friend, Dolly, and I'm going to have a bed of my own in the nursery so that I can keep you with me all night when I want to.'

Dorothea's plans for me were delayed for a little while by the reappearance of her mother with something that was a cross between a large push chair and a wheelchair. Between them, the two females had little trouble in lifting me into it and I was taken out and down a passageway to be installed in the nursery that was to become my new, permanent home.

Mrs Farnley sent her daughter off to get bathed and changed for dinner once I had been safely unloaded on to a sort of chaise longue. I looked about me, taking in the details of the room. There was, as Dorothea had said, a large bed against one wall and a heavy old chest of drawers beneath the window, beyond which I could just make out a screen of elm trees about a hundred yards from the house. Beyond these again were the distant hills that I knew marked the county border.

The rest of the room's contents comprised a large, antique wooden rocking horse, a couple of small armchairs and what looked like a battered ancient toy box. Mrs Farnley finished arranging my skirts and straightened up.

'My daughter thinks I'm completely clueless,' she said. 'I know she's nowhere near as innocent as she tries to make out, which is why I have given her you, Dolly. A young girl has urges which are difficult to ignore and all the time she can satisfy those urges here, I know she'll remain safe.

'I expect she's already explored a few possibilities with you, hasn't she? Well, that's good. I'll not interfere with what she does in any way. You're her dolly now, so it's up to her.'

It certainly wasn't up to me, I reflected grimly. I wanted to scream out in frustration at what they had done to me, but of course I could do no such thing. My only option was to lie there, like a good little rag dolly and await the return of my new young owner.

Dorothea eventually returned in the early evening, having first dined with her mother downstairs. My eyes followed her into the room and I saw that she had tied her hair back and pinned it up in a slightly more mature manner, which was somewhat ruined by the childishly simple pinafore style dress she now wore. Even her stockings were plain and thick and I found myself wondering what she might look like if her mother ever permitted her to dress more like the young adult she really was.

In truth, I had to admit, she was quite a good-looking girl, her bright red hair and splattering of freckles adding to her attraction, rather than the opposite. From what I could see of it, her figure had matured nicely and her long legs, despite their bland hosiery and unflatteringly flat-heeled shoes, were well made. She was not as tall as her imposing mother, but she was still above average height for a female.

'I hope you haven't been naughty whilst I've been gone, Dolly,' she smiled. To my surprise, she then immediately drew the dress up over her head and tossed it atop the chest of drawers, revealing a surprisingly raunchy set of underwear beneath. Bra, panties and suspender belt were all bright pink and gauzy, against which the stockings made an incongruous contrast – though not for long.

Unclipping them, Dorothea swiftly rolled them down her legs and kicked them aside, replacing them with a sheer pair of black nylons which she took from one of the drawers. The final touch was a pair of pink patent court shoes with high heels, that added at least another three inches to her height. The transformation in her was staggering. She swayed across to my couch and stood over me.

'Mummy says she won't be coming in here until morning,' she told me. 'I think she's guessed, or else you've told her, Dolly. Have you told her, you bad Dolly?' I wanted to shout out to her that I'd be bloody grateful to be able to tell anybody anything, but then her expression softened and I realised that this stupidity act was just another refinement in her demonstration of her control over me.

'No, of course you haven't,' she said, quietly. 'You can't talk at all, can you, Dolly, not unless I make you.' Her hand snaked out and found the cursed button in my neck.

'*Mama, mama, mama, mama,*' I intoned helplessly. Dorothea grinned.

'Poor Dolly wants her Mama,' she chuckled. 'Well, Dolly, Mama is here and Mama is going to fuck her dirty dolly. Legs apart, Dolly.' She reached down and moved my inert limbs wider, throwing up my skirts and petticoats and scrabbling to open the front of my drawers. Within a minute, she had me hard again.

She bent and kissed the tip of my organ and then released it to wriggle herself out of the panties, revealing a neatly trimmed triangle of auburn pubic hair and a pinkly gaping gash from which tiny little silver rivulets were already oozing.

'I've been thinking about you all through dinner, Dolly,' she sighed, easing herself on to the chaise and straddling my thighs. 'And I've decided I'm going to fuck you all night long. You'd like that, wouldn't you, Dolly?' Without further ceremony, she seized my shaft and, with a low moan, lowered herself on to it, closing her eyes as my length slid into her.

'Ooohhh, Dolly,' she groaned, shivering ecstatically, 'that feels wonderful.' She opened her eyes again and her hands went to the bodice of my dress, fingers reaching inside to draw out my breasts and then slowly tracing the outlines of my nipples. I felt my heart beginning to pound harder and harder, for despite everything, I could not prevent myself from responding physically to her ministrations.

She smiled sweetly down at me. 'Oh, Dolly dearest,' she breathed, 'you are such a lovely, sweet, sissy little dolly, but I just know I'm going to love you best of everybody in the world.' And with that, she began to shake and quiver into the first stages of an orgasm that was to last well beyond the moment when I exploded my barren seed deep into her womb.

That was five years ago now, or maybe six, and I am still here, on the same chaise longue, looking out at those trees and the faraway hills beyond them. Dorothea has not tired of me in all that time, though she has long since regulated the time she spends here, as she has other duties since her mother's stroke three years since. I actually feel sorry for Mrs Farnley, lying helpless as she now does in a bedroom not fifty feet from where I, of all people, know how she must feel.

Her daughter runs the household now. She has brought in several new staff, Maudie being only the latest. Maudie is a pretty maid, but she is no more female than I am, for beneath that ludicrously brief uniform, safely strapped up out of harm's way, lies exactly the same panty content as hides within my more voluminous drawers. The difference is that her male equipment remains out of sight, if perhaps never quite out of her mind, for Dorothea remains as loyal to her Dolly as I am forced to be to her.

256

Maudie has befriended me out of a sort of horrified pity and she is the only person who knows that I have recovered at least this much power of speech. I dare not let Dorothea know my secret, for I am convinced she would simply send me back for the operation to be done again and this time she might well instruct the surgeon to remove my vocal cords completely. I have to suffer in a silence broken only by the stupid voice box, which has now been adapted so that I can be made to cry aloud.

Apparently I am soon to be fitted with a newer version, which will enable Dorothea to make me 'say' several different things to order. I don't yet know all of them, but Dorothea took great delight in telling me that one variation will be '*Dolly wants a fuck*'. Sadly, and to my great shame, that statement is often all too true, for at least it relieves the boredom of my days as a helpless toy.

Apart from my all-too-brief interludes with my mistress, the only highlights of my day are during those hours at the beginning and end of each day when Maudie is sent to wash and change me, rotating my ever-growing wardrobe of outfits at Dorothea's behest, so that I am always kept ready should she suddenly decide she has time to visit me.

Unfortunately, although I suspect Maudie would be as eager as I for things to be different, intimate contact on these occasions is restricted to that necessary for the completion of my ablutions, for should Dorothea suddenly appear unexpectedly, either to catch us in an act of flagrant defiance, or to suddenly find that I was not immediately able to perform for her, the consequences, especially for Maudie, would be too awful to contemplate and it is unlikely that the intricate strapping that maintains her feminine appearance down below would ever be required again!

Dear Maudie has done her best for me in other ways: there is now a radio in the nursery, tuned in to a music station, though sometimes, when Dorothea is away from the house for a few hours, Maudie sneaks in and re-tunes it so that I can listen to the odd play or story. She has also asked, on my behalf, whether I might not have a television set to while away my afternoons and my mistress has promised to consider this.

Meantime, I can only hope that she never becomes completely bored with me, for, as I am now, I am good for only one thing. Without the use of my arms, I cannot even hope to relieve my frustrations myself and so can do nothing except simply endure. I am beginning to believe, more and more, that I would truly be better off dead.

There are two other maids exactly like Maudie, though I see very little of them, and all three are kept here by a mixture of discipline and threats. Dorothea has some hold over each of them and they dare not go against her. There is also a new housekeeper, who is certainly not here against her will. Whether it is the generous salary Dorothea pays her, or the fact that she can exercise total authority and control over the sad little trio of submissive maids, I could not say, but I do know that she punishes them frequently and severely and she has even done so in front of me, caning their bare behinds savagely, whilst I look on in embarrassed silence.

Of course, I don't think she would ever risk that when Dorothea was about. It is just her way of showing how much she despises me, for I am the one person, apart from Mrs Farnley, who is safe against her vicious nature. I am, after all, Dorothea's Dolly and only she is ever permitted to punish me. Luckily, she loves her Dolly Dearest too much for that to be a frequent occurrence and then she uses nothing more severe than a hairbrush.

I pray that this situation, at least, never changes, nor that my mistress should ever decide to give me, likewise, into the care of this witch, for the thought of that long cane ever lashing across my poor defenceless buttocks is enough to bring tears to my eyes . . .

I see by the clock that tea time draws near and this tape is nearly finished. Maudie will be here shortly to hide the machine away until the next time Dorothea is away for the day. That may be in a few days' time, it may be another month and there is no guarantee that Maudie will be able to get another cassette for me.

258

If she does, I will go on with my sorry tale, though there is, in truth, little more I can add to what I have said here. But at least it prevents me from becoming totally bored with my helpless, useless life during those long periods when my mistress is too busy with her adult responsibilities to visit this nursery and play with her poor, devoted Dolly Dearest.

The End . . . or is it?